FRACTURED

LUCIAN & LIA

SYDNEY LANDON

Cover Design and Interior format by The Killion Group
http://thekilliongroupinc.com

ACKNOWLEDGEMENTS

A special note of thanks to my wonderful PA Amanda Lanclos. She makes my life so much easier!

A thank you to Kim Killion with Hot Damn Designs for your wonderful cover. And to my editors: Jenny Sims with Editing 4 Indies, Hot Tree Editing & The Formatting Fairies.

Also thank you to my beta readers: Amanda Lanclos, Heather Waterman, Lorie Gullian, Catherine Crook, Marion Archer, Shelly Lazar and Lisa Salvary. You are all awesome in more ways than I could possibly count!

And to my blogger friends, Catherine Crook with A Reader Lives a Thousand Lives, Jennifer Harried with Book Bitches Blog, Jenn with SMI Book Club, Chloe with Smart Mouth Smut, Shelly with Sexy Bibliophiles, Amanda and Heather with Crazy Cajun Book Addicts, Stacia with Three Girls & A Book Obsession, Lisa Salvary and Confessions of a Book Lovin Junkie.

ALSO BY SYDNEY LANDON

The Danvers Novels

Weekends Required

Not Planning on You

Fall For Me

Fighting For You

Betting on You (A Danvers Novella)

No Denying You

Always Loving You (Coming 2/15/15)

The Pierced Series

Pierced

Fractured

Mended (Spring 2015)

Rose (Late 2015)

Aidan (Spring 2016)

CHAPTER ONE

Lucian

My beautiful girl is almost completely nude and lifeless. Her pants are around her ankles, and her panties are lying to the side, visibly torn. Her shirt and bra look like they've literally been cut from her body. There are marks, which resemble handprints all over her small body. Her face is noticeably swollen and streaked with either dirt or mascara. Her nostrils are rimmed in red and were bleeding at some point. Gashes on her stomach and thighs steadily drip blood. I hear a gasp from behind me and feel a hand on my shoulder. "Oh, Christ, Luc," Sam says as he steps slowly forward. I am shaken from the trance I had fallen into when he drapes his jacket over her. I hear sirens wailing in the distance as I sit next to her.

I cup her head in my hand, saying, "Baby, it's Luc. Can you hear me? Lia, please open your eyes, sweetheart. I've got you; I'm right here."

Sam holds her wrist. "Luc, her pulse is slow, but it's there." I am stroking her hair, afraid to touch her anywhere else. I whisper repeatedly that I'm here, that I have her. I have no idea if she can hear me; she's so still. Sam has to pull me away when the EMTs arrive. "Let them work on her. She needs them now." He has Rose tucked against his side, trying to calm her down while they work on Lia.

As they are loading Lia onto the stretcher, she moans low in her throat and I leap forward. "Baby, can you hear me?"

Tears leak from the corners of her eyes as a cry like that of a wounded animal escapes from her throat. She struggles to move and seems to panic when she feels the straps from the gurney around her. I speak soothingly against her ear, trying to calm her before she hurts herself further. "Luc." She gasps before collapsing back as if that little bit of effort was too much.

They rush her into the waiting ambulance. We follow closely behind, and

I am momentarily surprised at the crowd of people who have gathered outside the apartment building. Word has spread quickly, and I want to push them all away; I don't want strangers gawking at her.

I try to accompany her into the ambulance but they refuse, saying they need the space to work on her. Instead, Sam pushes me toward the Mercedes and both Rose and I get in the back. Sam takes off at a fast clip, following the ambulance through the city and to the emergency entrance of Memorial Hospital. Rose sobs quietly beside me, but I am incapable of offering her comfort. I can't get past the image of Lia's broken body. Guilt reaches out to choke me. I should have taken better care of her. How could I have let her out of my sight? Jim Dawson is a fucking dead man. It's too coincidental to me that he was released earlier today.

When my phone buzzes, I pick it up with the intention of hitting the ignore button. When I see Max's name on the ID, I decide to take it instead; I need him on this, now. With no preliminaries, I say, "Max, he fucking got her."

He doesn't need to ask whom I'm talking about; he knows. "Goddammit to fucking Hell! What happened?"

"He pulled her into a damn storage room in her apartment building. He beat the hell out of her and I think...shit, I think he raped her." I choke on the last words, feeling them burn like bile in my throat. I take a deep breath as Max curses, sounding as shaken as I feel. "Her clothes had been cut off in places, and Jesus, she was bleeding and bruised all over. She was unconscious but came to for a moment as they were wheeling her out."

"Which hospital, Luc?" When I answer, he says, "I'm sure the police will be waiting when you arrive, but I'm going to call my friend, Carly, and have her meet us there. She's an investigator in the violent crimes division, and she'll do what she can to get things moving. Luc...I'm so sorry." I end the call without replying. There's no shortage of sorrow and guilt right now. In such a short amount of time, Lia has gained the admiration of my friends. Everyone in my inner circle cares about her, and this will hit them hard. Even now, in the rearview mirror, I see Sam wiping away tears.

I want nothing more than to disconnect, but I force myself to reach for Rose's hand and offer her what comfort I can. She is Lia's best friend, and she's falling apart. As if reading my mind, Sam says, "Miss Rose, Jake is meeting you at the hospital." Rose nods gratefully, mumbling her thanks. I don't even bother to ask how Sam knew to contact Rose's boyfriend. He is used to working behind the scenes and handling the details others don't think of; of course, he would do what he could for the distraught young woman sitting next to me.

I continue to stroke Rose's hand soothingly but lay my head back on the headrest to regroup. I am equal parts shattered and furious. I want to fucking kill the bastard who hurt her. The only thing that gives me any peace is knowing I'll find him. He will never touch a hair on her head again as long as I'm alive.

The ambulance doors are open and Lia is being unloaded when we arrive. Sam drops Rose and me at the curb so he can park the car. Lia has an oxygen mask over her mouth and an IV line in her wrist as they wheel her quickly past us. Her eyes are closed and her body still. We follow them into the hospital and only make it as far as the double doors, which lead into the emergency department before we are stopped. A nurse in blue scrubs blocks our path, shaking her head. "I'm sorry, but only patients and staff are allowed past this point."

I want to ignore her and follow Lia, but I know she's just trying to do her job. "Is Fae Quinn on duty?"

She looks surprised but recovers quickly. "Yes, I believe she's still here."

Relieved, I say, "Could you please tell her that her nephew is here?" The nurse relaxes; probably relieved I'm not going to give her any trouble. I'm sure they have their hands full here most days.

"Sure, just a minute." She walks through the double doors, and within a few moments, a worried-looking Aunt Fae comes rushing out.

"Luc, what're you doing here? What's going on?"

Running an agitated hand through my hair, I say, "It's Lia. She was assaulted at her apartment. She...fuck, I don't know what's happening. Other than one brief moment, she was unconscious when we found her." Before I can ask, she's running back through the doors. My chest lightens just a tiny bit for the first time since seeing Lia. I trust Aunt Fae with my life; if anyone can help Lia, she can.

Jake, Max, and the police arrive within seconds of each other. I realize Rose is still clutching my hand. I unwrap her fingers gently and hand her over to the arms of her boyfriend, who pulls her to a sofa in the corner.

Max walks up, clasping my shoulder. "Do we know anything yet, Luc?"

"No, but my aunt is checking on her now. We should have news soon." I turn to the attractive woman standing at his side. I assume she's the detective he spoke of, but her attire gives me pause. She's wearing an above-the-knee fitted dress with high heels, and her long, brown hair is curly and hangs loose on her shoulders. Maybe there's a reason Max is on a first-name basis with her.

"Luc, this is Carly Michaels. She's the lead investigator in the violent crimes division."

"Mr. Quinn, I'm sorry to meet under these circumstances. I know it's tough, but I need to take a statement from you and also from the young woman who was with you. Also, just to let you know where things stand, I have a couple of detectives at Miss Adams' apartment now overseeing the evidence collection." She motions for Max and me to follow her to a quiet area of the waiting room. Max gives me a hard look, which I can't interpret before she pulls an iPad from her purse and motions for us to sit. The nervous energy and my anxiety make this difficult for me, but I manage to lower myself to the edge of a chair, my feet moving restlessly. She had my complete attention with her next sentence. "Mr. Quinn, I understand you're Miss Adams' fiancé, is that correct?" She is busy typing, allowing Max a brief moment to nod just once. I have no idea what's going on but know there must be a reason for this deception.

"Yes, that's correct," I answer easily. It surprises me that I feel no panic at the thought. I answer her questions, giving her as much information as I have. After about ten minutes, she moves across the room to speak with Rose. I look to Max who exhales wearily.

"I told her you were engaged to Lia because otherwise they would have to limit the information given to you. I'd advise you to carry that forward with the hospital if your aunt will go along with it. Not one of my greatest moments as a lawyer, but Lia needs you." Lowering his voice, he looks at me with concern while asking, "How are you holding up?" I wonder if he has noticed the slight tremor in my hands. I have the fleeting urge to admit that I'm fucking falling apart, but showing weakness is something I rarely do.

Instead, I ignore the question. "I want that fucker found. I don't care how many people you need to put on it; I want to know every step he has taken since the moment he left prison."

"I've already made the calls, and we should have something soon. Is there anyone I should contact for Lia?" Max looks pained as he asks the question. Our minds both go to her mother knowing that's not even remotely an option. One person does come to mind, though.

"She has a friend she's close to. Her name is Debra. I don't recall the last name, though."

Max nods. "That's not a problem. I remember her from Lia's background report. I'll pull the information and contact her. Is there anything else I can do for either of you?" Before I can answer, the sound of a loud slap fills the room. Both of our heads twist around to see an angry Rose and a swiftly retreating Jake. I grit my teeth, not wanting to deal with any drama.

"Yeah, how about seeing what in the hell's going on with her and handling it." Without complaint, Max stands and walks toward Rose. He raises his hand in a wave to Carly who is standing outside the hospital doors now on her phone. She looks curious, having obviously witnessed some of the scene through the clear-glass walls.

Unable to sit still any longer, I start to pace again. I see Sam sitting in the narrow hallway with his eyes closed and his head bowed. I think he's praying, and for the first time in so long, I have the urge to drop to my knees next to him. A life filled with loss and tragedy had long ago turned me away from asking for miracles. Now I wonder if maybe having Lia come so suddenly into my life was indeed some act of divine intervention. If so, it would be a dagger to the heart to have her pulled from me in such a brutal and sudden fashion. Surely, God wouldn't be that cruel.

As I make another lap, there's a hand on my arm. Jerking around, I encounter the worried eyes of my aunt. She leads me past Sam until we have relative privacy. "I shouldn't be talking to you since you aren't her family," she says while looking back over her shoulder.

"I'm her fiancé," I say quietly. She simply looks at me for a long moment without comment.

"Lia is stable and sedated right now. The trauma team is working on her. It's going to be a while before the extent of her injuries is known. I..."

Before she can finish, I interrupt her. "Why is she sedated? She's been unconscious except for a brief time. Was she awake?"

She rubs her temple, as if debating her answer. Finally, she says, "She awoke right after she was brought back. She...asked for you, and then in the next instant became almost hysterical trying to move from the gurney. She had to be sedated before..."

That's all I hear. I'm down the hallway in an instant pounding on the locked double doors of the emergency entrance. "Open the fucking door," I snap to the startled receptionist gaping at me from the desk nearby. She hurriedly picks up her phone, just as my shoulders are grasped from behind. I shrug the hold off as my aunt steps between the doors and me.

She shakes her head at the receptionist, possibly trying to reassure her I'm not a lunatic, which is exactly what I am right now. Lia is lying somewhere beyond those metal doors, scared and needing me. All rational thought has left my body and I'm focused only on getting to her. "Luc!" she snaps. "Stop this right now! If you keep this up, you'll be banned from the hospital and you won't be able to see Lia. If you cannot think of yourself, then think of that girl who is going to need you."

As her words hit me like arrows, I allow the hands, which are once again on my shoulders to pull me away. As if expecting me to bolt, Sam and Max take up positions on either side and steer me down the hall and into an empty restroom. My frustration boils over as I brace my hands on the porcelain sink before throwing a fist through the mirror above it. Both Sam and Max are utterly still as I pull my hand back and send it through the now-shattered glass. Shards fly all around me as I prepare to do it again. Strangely enough, the pain searing through my knuckles grounds me, helping me to find an outlet for the torment, which is suffocating me.

Max grabs my fist before it can make contact this time. "Enough, Luc. Fucking get it together before they have you locked up." When I make no effort to fight his hold, he slowly releases me and slumps against a wall. "What in the hell happened to bring this on?"

My aunt walks into the restroom, followed closely by Sam. I hadn't even noticed him leave. She curses under her breath as she takes in the mess I've made. I'm shocked when she holds my hand up, shaking her head at the steady stream of blood staining the white sink scarlet. With little sympathy for my self-inflicted injuries, she takes a bottle out of a plastic caddy that she brought in with her and liberally douses my shredded skin in something akin to liquid fire. As I flinch and try to pull away, she holds me firmly until she's satisfied the area is clean.

Next, she brings out some tweezers and begins pulling out the pieces of glass, which had embedded themselves in my skin, and fuck, once again the pain is severe but almost welcome. This I can handle. Physical pain is a pleasure compared to the emotional pain, which has gripped me since finding Lia. That type of pain is sheer torment. My soul feels like it's been ripped from my body when I think of her. Without looking up, she says, "You'll be making a donation to this hospital because in a few moments, I'm going to report that this bathroom was damaged by someone unknown and have it cleaned up. I'm doing this for Lia because she's going to need you when she awakes again." When she finishes bandaging my hand, she finally looks up. "Promise me you have yourself together now? If you don't, I'll have Sam take you home."

I stare into her concerned eyes before nodding my head. "I've got it."

"Okay then." She starts repacking her supplies. "I'm going to go check in on Lia. I'll keep you updated as long as you can handle it."

Her meaning is clear: one more outburst from me and the information flow stops. Regardless of whether we are family or not, she can't have me wrecking the hospital every time I hear something I can't deal with. I don't bother to reply because we both understand each other. She leaves the restroom followed by Max. As I start toward the door, Sam stops me.

"Luc, do you need to take the edge off?" I open my mouth, wanting to say yes more than I want my next breath, but a sense of shame washes over me. It seems pathetic and cowardly that I need something to help me cope with Lia's attack while she is the one really suffering. What kind of pussy does that make me?

"No," I say as I pull the door open. A part of me knows this is probably the worst time to go cold turkey, but I refuse to attempt to alleviate my pain when Lia cannot. I walk back to the waiting room in a much calmer manner than I left it. My aunt is right: Lia needs and deserves someone strong, and I'll be that person…I'll be anything for her.

CHAPTER TWO

Lucian

I've long since given up pacing the floor, and I'm slumped in a chair in the corner. Nighttime in a hospital emergency department is bustling. I've moved away from crying babies and loud-talking people too many times to count. On her last visit, my aunt pulled a chair into the hallway for me, knowing I had no desire to be in a group of strangers.

"Lia is bruised and banged up pretty badly. She has fractures to her wrist, fingers, and her nose. What we're watching closely right now though is the small amount of swelling she has on her brain." At the look of panic on my face, she takes my hand reassuringly. "The doctor believes we can treat her with medication as long as the swelling doesn't continue to increase further. At this point, we are monitoring that." I notice vaguely that my aunt looks tired; I know she's working a double shift so she can be near Lia. I sent Sam, Max, and Rose home hours ago. I was in no mood for company, but I know they would be back in a moment's notice if I said the word. I've lived for years, though, as mostly a loner...until Lia, and it's something I've fallen back on for comfort today. "Luc...the old scar on her back...did he do that, as well?" I nod but don't bother to elaborate. In her years at the hospital, she has probably seen more women like Lia than I can imagine. Very little shocks her anymore.

I try to stand up from my chair, knowing my aunt needs to get off her feet for a few minutes, but she motions me back down before squatting next to me. "We're going to be moving Lia to a room in the ICU soon. One person can stay with her tonight. Have you reached any of her friends or family?"

I think briefly of Max's revelation that Lee Jacks is quite possibly Lia's biological father. That's a bridge to be crossed another day, though. "She doesn't really have any family." Max has called her close friend Debra. She was out of town but is on her way back now. I don't expect her until sometime tomorrow, though. If Debra was as upset as Max said she was, I figure she's burning the road up trying to get to Lia.

"There is one piece of news I think you'll be relieved to hear," my aunt says softly. I just look at her, not knowing if anything other than seeing Lia will give me relief. "Luc, it doesn't appear she was raped. There is no evidence to support it. If that was her attacker's intent, then possibly he was interrupted before he could do it."

I drop my head into my hands, feeling the urge once again to cry. My aunt was right; the feeling of relief is overwhelming. To know that Lia hadn't been violated in that way is enough to bring me to my knees. The bastard hadn't been able to take that from her. I have no doubt that she fought him with everything she had. The skin they removed from under Lia's nails gave validity to that fact. When her stepfather is found, Lia will have collected the evidence during her struggle to lock him away. "Thank God," I finally say. "Can I go to her now?"

When I feel a hand on my head, I look up in surprise. My aunt continues to run her hand through my hair. I stiffen at first because it's been many years since she comforted me as she did when I was a child. Except for the rare occasion, I've always preferred to find my comfort in solitude, which was hard for her to accept for many years. "You're in love with her, aren't you?"

I pull back sharply, causing her hand to return to her side. "What're you talking about?" I cringe when the question leaves my mouth. I've played right into her hands. I should have walked away without comment, but I've opened the door now.

"I have never seen you this way over a woman. To be honest, you're a complete wreck, which we both know isn't you."

I love my aunt, but I hate to be psychoanalyzed. I bite back my anger because I would have been barred from the hospital by now if not for her interceding today. She has also been my eyes and ears to Lia, breaking rules I know she normally wouldn't for anyone but me. "We both know I've been here before. In this very hospital, actually, and I think it accurate to say I was off my rocker then, as well."

My aunt is unable to contain her quick flinch at the reminder of my past. "That wasn't the same thing, Luc," she says quietly. "I'm not saying you didn't love

Cassie, because you did. You just were not *in* love with her. Lia, though—"

"Fae," I interrupt her. "Please stop. I don't have anything left in me for this conversation today. I'm hanging on to a fucking tightrope by one hand. If you want me to admit I care about Lia, then fine, yes I do. Leave it at that."

She looks quickly at her phone when a text sounds. "That's Sara. I told her to let me know when Lia was in her room." As I jump to my feet, my aunt halts me before I get further. "Lia's heavily sedated, Luc. Don't expect her to wake at any point tonight and maybe not tomorrow, either. Right now, her body needs the respite to heal. After you've seen her, you should go home for the night and get some rest. She'll need you more in a few days."

"That's not going to happen," I say flatly. My aunt purses her lips in frustration but doesn't comment. The thought of leaving Lia alone was enough to make my gut clench in agony. She had needed me earlier, and I'd been unable to go to her; that wouldn't happen again. I can no more admit to myself how I feel about Lia than I could to my aunt. Truthfully, I have no clue. Love? Maybe obsessed is a more accurate word. From the moment we met, the driving need to have her, to possess her, has ruled my every action where she is concerned.

The double doors to the inner sanctum of the emergency department open for me this time with a simple swipe of my aunt's ID badge. The irony that here she is more powerful than I am is not lost on me. I'm a rich, well-connected man, but that means little here. I am nothing compared to the heroes hurrying in these hallways, desperately trying to help those like Lia.

We reach a doorway to a room at the end of the hall, giving it a bit more privacy than the ones closer to the nurses' station. My heart pounds loudly in my chest as I follow my aunt into the small, dimly lit space. My aunt walks straight to the monitors next to the bed, checking each of them before stepping aside and motioning me forward.

Then I see her...My chest feels tight, and my feet so unbelievably heavy as I take small steps until I'm next to her. "Oh, baby," I whisper as I stand helpless at Lia's bedside. I reach down and take her small hand into mine, careful of the IV line attached to it.

My aunt steps up, rubbing my arm reassuringly. "Most of what you see is just to monitor her. You can touch her, just be careful you don't knock anything loose." At my nod, she says, "I'm going to head home for the night. Call me if you need me for anything...no matter the time, and I'll be here."

I give her my thanks, and she tells me she'll be back in the morning to check on Lia. I am strangely relieved when I hear the door close behind her; I need time to process what I'm seeing and feeling without her curious eyes on me. I turn on the bedside light and wince as Lia is almost fully illuminated. She is pale...almost translucent, making the dark bruises and red scratches marring her skin eerily visible. Her arm, which seemed at such an odd angle earlier now looks normal with the exception of another brace around the wrist area and bandages on her fingers. There are also bandages over her nose, which my aunt had already told me was broken.

The sheet is pulled up to just under her chest, making further examination difficult. At this point, I'm better off not seeing the full extent of her injuries. I pull a chair closer to her bed and drop into it wearily. Lowering the guardrail, I lay my head next to her side while holding her uninjured hand in mine. I just need to feel her body against some part of mine. After being terrified earlier that I'd never touch her again, I'm desperate to feel the proof that she hasn't been taken from me. "I'm so sorry," I murmur against her cold skin. "I'll never let anyone hurt you again, baby." I kiss her hand and am surprised when I feel myself growing sleepy. My adrenaline is crashing fast, and the stress of the day has depleted me both mentally and physically. Even injured as she is, being this close to Lia brings me temporary peace, and I allow myself to drift off while I hold her hand securely within mine.

CHAPTER THREE

Lucian

Lia has been in the hospital now for three days. Yesterday, they started decreasing her sedating medications, planning to slowly bring her back to consciousness; they need her awake soon so they can assess her condition. So far, other than more movement during her sleep and twitching of her eyes, she hasn't shown any signs of waking. She has had a CT scan daily, and thankfully, the swelling in her brain has been responding to the medication, but they still need to monitor her closely.

When a knock sounds at the door, I look up to see a tired-looking Aidan standing there. He and I haven't discussed the possible change in Cassie that happened before Lia's attack. When

Aidan found out about Lia, he came back right away, taking over the operations of the company until I return. I haven't left the hospital grounds since Lia was brought in. Cindy makes sure I have clean clothes daily, and Sam runs any errands that are needed. This is the first time Aidan has been here, so I'm momentarily surprised to see him.

He stands uncertainly in the doorway, and I motion him further into the room, walking over to greet him with a one-armed hug. When we step back, he looks at Lia and blurts out, "Holy fucking shit, I just..."

"I know," I say. "All of the bruising makes it look even worse than it is." It still astounds me when I see the black marks marring her face and arms, so I know well how it must be for Aidan, who is seeing her for the first time. Her nurse comes in at that moment, asking us to step out while she examines Lia. This happens multiple times per day, and I generally use the time to walk outside and smoke. When Sam saw how agitated I was on my second day without my drug of choice, he slapped a pack of cigarettes in my hand and told me to exchange one evil for another until I could get it out of my system. It's no miracle cure, and I actually find the whole smoking thing disgusting, but it does help to take the edge off. Right now, I need that any way I can get it short of using again.

Aidan trails after me until we reach the small courtyard at the back of the property. This is the one and only area where smoking is allowed. Aidan's mouth drops in surprise as I quickly light up, inhaling deeply before exhaling. "Damn, when did you start smoking?"

After another puff, I say, "Yesterday, before lunch, and yes, I know it's fucked. I just...need something to get me by while Lia's here."

Understanding dawns on Aidan and he steps closer, saying under his breath, "Luc, I can get you something. Fuck, you must be about to come apart at the seams."

In truth, I've gone far longer than three days without cocaine. I'm normally not a daily user; I could go weeks if I needed to. It is, however, my go-to answer for major stress, and Aidan is correct: three days under the type of pressure I've been dealing with has been hell, but I'm fighting it. "No, I'm trying to come off it. I'll just keep smoking these nasty things and eating a pack of gum afterwards to combat the taste. I think I brushed my teeth fifty times yesterday."

"Yeah, okay, man. Let me know if you change your mind." I wonder idly why all of my friends are always so quick to offer to supply me. Maybe they should have staged an intervention long ago instead of enabling me. I offer him a cigarette, knowing he smokes on occasion—usually promoted by stress, as well—but he shakes his head, dropping to one of the cement benches. "What are you doing?" He asks so quietly I almost miss it.

I turn to face him, raising a brow. "I thought we already established that."

Rubbing his face, he shakes his head. "No, what are you doing in this situation with this girl? Luc, you're the strongest person I've ever known, but you can't be here again. Lia reminded both of us of Cassie almost from the start, and now you're back at the exact place where you almost lost it all before."

Anger races through my veins, pissed he would dare to approach this subject right now. Feeling the need to hit back, I say, "You forgot one big difference. I'm not here because my fucking throat has been slit by my crazy girlfriend."

Aidan blanches, looking as if he's taken a blow to the face. "Luc...that's not fair..."

"What the fuck *was* fair about the whole thing, Aidan?" I snap, still angry over this whole conversation. "Was it fair that Cassie killed my child, almost killed me, and damn near killed herself? Was it fair to you that you were there to witness most of it? And it sure as hell isn't fair to Lia to compare her to Cassie! That woman lying in there beaten all to hell by her fucking stepfather has never done anything to deserve what's happened to her. I have no idea why everyone suddenly feels the need to warn me, put a label on my relationship with her, or compare her to Cassie, but I'm sick of it. I'm not leaving her here alone, and I'll destroy anyone who attempts to harm her. As my employee, I need you to run my company while I'm here, but as my friend, I need you to support my decisions. Even if they don't make sense to you."

Aidan looks at the ground for a moment before raising his head and grinning. "Damn, man, when did you become such a drama queen? Yeah, I'll run your company, probably better than you, but when this is over, I better get fucking Employee of the Month or shit's going to hit the fan."

I barely miss a beat at Aidan's quick-fire change of subject and mood. Sometimes when things get the better of him, he starts talking about the past, but just as quickly, he pushes it away. In truth, he can't deal with it any better than I can. The difference in us, though, is that Aidan is still very much tied to the past through his love for Cassie. He cannot walk away from her; therefore, he has never been able to move on. Sometimes, I think that out of everything that happened between Cassie and me, Aidan might actually be the one who has suffered the most for it. He'll never leave Cassie, though, so trying to convince him to move on is useless. We all have our crosses to bear in life, and his is tied solidly to the girl who was once one of us. I'm not even sure he loves her in the way he thinks he does anymore. His need to save her colors everything he does.

We talk for another few moments before I start to get restless. I don't like leaving Lia for long, and I want to be there when she awakes. Aidan and I continue to discuss the most pressing business matters as we walk back through the hallways of the hospital and toward Lia's room. When we are halfway there, I hear a commotion coming from that direction and take off running to the partially open doorway. When I step inside, I'm met by utter pandemonium. Lia is not only awake but also standing in the middle of the room, wires hanging off her body as she fights against a nurse who is holding her arms down. Another nurse circles her with a syringe, trying to talk to Lia soothingly. "What is going on here?" I say, but my words are lost as Lia screams, sounding weak and terrified.

"Fuck," Aidan breathes from behind me.

As I really look at what's going on, I immediately understand part of what is upsetting Lia. She's being restrained. To someone so recently overpowered by another, this is the worst form of torture to her right now. Moving in front of Lia, I say, "Release her; you're scaring her."

The nurse holding Lia ignores me while the one attempting to sedate her says, "Sir, please step out of the room. We'll handle this."

As if the sound of my voice finally reaches her, Lia lurches forward, trying to extend an arm toward me. "Luc, I need to get it off! Please, help me!" I have no idea what she's talking about, but I know she needs me and that they're hurting her more than they are helping. I ask them to release her a few more times before I've finally had enough.

"Take your fucking hands off her right now!" I roar. "If you hurt her, I'll own you and this hospital!" Both nurses freeze, seeming too shocked to move for a moment. The one holding Lia drops her arms, stepping back uncertainly. Lia takes a few halting steps toward me before I quickly cover the rest of the distance, scooping her into my arms as gently as I can. There is blood dripping from her hand caused by the IV, which she dislodged during her struggle. I know she needs medical attention immediately, but I also know she needs to feel safe before that happens. She curls into my arms as if knowing I'll protect her from the world. I perch on her bed, juggling her on my lap before finally getting us both settled. "I've got you, baby," I whisper against the crown of her head. "I won't let anyone hurt you. Shhh," I continue to soothe her until her body relaxes against mine.

By this time, two security guards stand in the doorway, along with Aidan and my aunt. The two nurses seem to have calmed down somewhat, and I motion to the one with the syringe. It kills me to have to do it, but I understand that unless Lia is sedated, they'll probably be unable to reattach her IV lines without hurting or subduing her. I continue to speak softly to Lia, trying to reassure her with my presence. When the needle goes into her arm, she flinches but doesn't try to pull away. I can feel her breathing grow heavier, and just as I believe she is asleep, her eyes pop open and she grips my arm. "Don't leave me, Luc," she pleads in a voice that slays me.

"Never," I vow, which seems to give her enough peace to close her eyes and drift off. I hear my aunt dismissing the security guards. She walks over to me, looking down at Lia with concerned eyes.

"She's out now, Luc. Lay her down so we can work on getting her lines reattached." Grudgingly, I stand with her in my arms. Dropping a kiss on her forehead, I slowly lower her to the bed and step back to let my aunt and the other nurses do their work. Aidan walks up beside me looking unnerved.

"Is she going to be okay?" he asks doubtfully. I know this is torture for him, and he'd rather be most anywhere else. Nevertheless, he is loyal to a fault and doesn't want to leave until he knows I no longer need him.

"She'll be fine," I say with more confidence than I feel right now. "I know you must have a million things to take care of today, so why don't you take off. I've got everything handled here for now." I see the relief that flashes across his face for just a split second before he disguises it. It's a testament to the strength of our friendship that he would stay here for as long as needed even though this hospital is filled with painful memories for both of us.

"All right." He briefly clasps my shoulder. "Keep me updated, and let me know if you need anything." With those words, he is gone and relax slightly. Having my friends and family study Lia and myself so intently is exhausting. I'm tired of trying to explain our relationship when even I have no clue as to what it is. All I do know is that she is mine and I am hers. The particulars of that statement are too complex to ponder, so I don't even attempt to try.

I walk back toward my aunt who is talking with her co-workers. "Do you have any idea what caused her to get so upset?" I ask, needing to know what happened in the short time I was gone.

The nurse who had been holding Lia spoke up, looking at me warily. "We were taking her vitals when she started to thrash around in her bed. Her eyes were closed, so I assumed she was having a bad dream. We tried to calm her, but it only seemed to upset her more. She had gotten out of the bed before she opened her eyes. I knew she was hurting herself by trying to walk with her injuries, but the more I tried to reason with her, the more upset she became." Pointing to the other nurse, she said, "So, Lettie ran to the nurses' station to get a sedative, and we were attempting to give it to her when you walked in."

His aunt stepped forward after checking Lia's IV line one last time. "It's not unusual for someone who was the victim of a violent attack to cycle between dreams and reality. More than likely, she was still asleep when she jumped from the bed but woke up at some point. She recognized you, Luc, and responded to your reassurances. Moving around in the manner she was would have caused her pain which is likely what finally woke her." His aunt dismissed the other nurses and took a seat next to the one I had pulled up at Lia's bedside. "Even though she wasn't raped, Luc, she's still going to need therapy when she is stronger. Lia has been traumatized in ways we probably can't even imagine."

"I'll get her all the help she needs," I say, feeling sick at the reminder of what was done to her. Her stepfather has gone completely off the grid, and no one has been able to find a trace of the bastard. The police have questioned her mother several times, but if she knows anything, she isn't talking. What a freaking waste of space it is for those two to even exist. Something I'd love to remedy. There are too many people looking for Jim Dawson for him to stay hidden forever. Before I can finish my conversation with my aunt, the door opens again and a woman and man who I've never seen before stand there staring across the room at Lia in horror. I know instantly that this is Lia's friend Debra and her boyfriend Martin. I had expected them a few days ago, but their car had broken down on their way home, delaying their arrival. Debra had kept me updated over the phone several times a day as she called to check on Lia.

My aunt's pager goes off, and with a smile of apology, she hurries from the room. Debra rushes forward, stopping when she reaches Lia's bedside. Martin trails slowly behind her. "Oh, my poor baby," Debra whispers brokenly, looking as if she's trying desperately to keep from breaking down. Martin puts a supporting arm around her shoulders, looking just as unsteady. It's readily apparent that they both care deeply for the woman lying so still and pale in the bed. Debra turns, surprising me when she pulls me into a firm hug. "You must be Lucian." When she finally pulls back, Martin and I shake hands and then we all turn back to Lia. "How is she today?" Debra asks as she gently strokes Lia's hand.

"She was awake earlier but had to be sedated again," I answer honestly. At

Debra's questioning look, I add, "She was upset and trying to leave the room. She pulled her IVs out. I was finally able to calm her enough for them to sedate her."

"What a fucking mess," Debra sighs, echoing my thoughts exactly. "I don't guess the police have found Jim yet, have they?" When I shake my head no, she grits her teeth, looking angry. "My little girl has been nothing but a punching bag for both of those animals all her life. I'd love to go pull Maria out of her house by her hair and show her how it feels."

"Calm down, honey." Martin rubs Debra's back, trying to settle her down. "We just need to be here for Lia in any way we can. Jim and Maria will get theirs in the end."

I resist the urge to comment on how soon I hope that end is. Instead, I lean back against the wall and let Debra and Martin spend a few moments with her until they turn their attention back to me. After being grilled for twenty minutes, I'm more than happy to see them leave. The love they feel for Lia is obvious, but they are also very protective and spent quite a bit of time questioning my place in her life. In the end, though, I think it was clear that I'm not going anywhere, regardless of whether they are comfortable with it or not. I have little doubt that I'll be under a microscope from them for a while, and instead of being annoyed, it comforts me to know that Lia has people in her life who care that deeply for her.

The rest of the day passes uneventfully. The nurses and doctors make periodic checks, and I see no one else until Cindy and Sam arrive with a surprise dinner for me. A greasy cheeseburger isn't something I indulge in often, but it's sheer Heaven after a few days of hospital food. Cindy sniffs me as she steps closer, causing me to cock a brow in question. "Have you been smoking?" she asks while wrinkling her nose.

Sam chuckles then turns it into a cough when she shoots him a glare. His ass would really be in trouble if I told her it was his idea. Of course, she has no idea that smoking is a lesser evil than what I'm trying to avoid using. I feel like a guilty child as I say, "Yeah, but it's just temporary."

She puts her hands on her hips in a move I know heralds a lecture. "Lucian Quinn, are you crazy? Why in the world would you pick now to start smoking...temporarily?"

I have to give Cindy credit for managing to inject an amazing amount of

sarcasm and disgust into just two
sentences. I can only imagine what she
would have to say to me if she knew of my
real vice. I can almost picture her putting
me over her knee, and not in a kinky way,
either. It makes me that much more
determined to quit and to make sure she
never finds out. I don't think I could
handle being such a disappointment in
her eyes. "I've just been a bit...unsettled
since Lia's attack. This helps to take the
edge off. I promise I'll stop soon."
Grimacing, I say truthfully, "I can't stand
it any more than you can."

She gives me a look of sympathy before
shaking her head. "I'm sure this has been
hard on you, Luc, but puffing on those
vile things won't change anything. I
swear I don't know what I'm going to do
with you and Aidan. To be such
intelligent men, neither of you have the
sense God gave a piss-ant sometimes."

I can't help it; I burst out laughing, not
used to being scolded and called an idiot.
There are few people who I'd let get away
with talking to me like that, but I know
she does it out of love and since that is in
short supply in my life, I choose to just
enjoy the fact that she cares enough to
lecture me. "I'm sorry to disappoint you;
I'll try to correct it as soon as possible."

They stay for a bit longer, while Cindy and I go over some messages she brought and I give her instructions for returning calls. Unfortunately, even with Aidan at the helm, there are things I must handle personally, and tomorrow I will need to find a quiet corner to do it. Sam has brought me more clothes, and Cindy not-so-nicely lets me know I should take care of that as soon as they leave. Hopefully, that's just a dig at the smoke smell and not my hygiene. I've managed to use the tiny shower in Lia's attached bathroom each day, but it's a far cry from what I'm used to and even I'll admit to feeling much less than my usual, well-groomed self.

Sam clasps my arm as they are leaving, saying, "All good?" I know the question holds a wealth of meaning, but I simply incline my head. With Cindy near, that is all the communication he will risk. She is far too perceptive and would ask a million questions at the first hint of trouble.

I am so tired by the time I'm alone again that I find myself drifting off as I return to my chair next to Lia's bedside. I finally stop fighting sleep and let it take me, knowing it won't be for long. Rest in a hospital is proving almost impossible, and

I've learned quickly to take it where I can get it.

Lia

The light in the room seems unusually bright as I open and close my eyes, trying to adjust. My mouth is dry, causing my tongue to stick to the roof of it. I shift restlessly and catch my breath. "Ow," I moan, trying to figure out why I feel as if I've been hit by a car. Again, my eyes flutter and this time, I'm able to keep them open long enough to look at my surroundings. My vision is blurry and I blink rapidly, trying to clear it. My body seems to be throbbing all over, making it impossible to pinpoint the source of the pain.

As I look around the unfamiliar room, I panic until I see him. Luc is sitting next to me with his arms crossed and his head lolling backwards in what looks like an extremely uncomfortable position. He is fully dressed and wearing what appears to be jeans and a polo shirt. Again, I look around the room, thinking we must be at his apartment, but nothing looks as it should. I close my eyes as my head begins to pound. 'You thought you had me, didn't you? You stupid little whore, who do you think you are?' my stepfather taunted. I gasp as the words ring in my head. I open my eyes, looking frantically around the room, but nothing has changed. Lucian is still asleep next to me and no one else appears to be in the room.

"Just a dream," I whisper. "It's not real."

Suddenly, the words are coming again and this time, I'm wide-awake. 'Not so tough now, are you, without your rich boyfriend? I'm going to show him and the rest of the world what you really are, and this time there will be no mistaking my mark on you, whore!'

As the memories come flooding back, I realize with dawning horror that I'm not dreaming. Pushing the covers back, I start fighting against the tubes attached to my hands and frantically attempt to pull up my shirt. "Oh, God, please no. Please, don't let it be there," I cry as I fight to reach my stomach. "Luc, Luc!" I sob. "Lucian, please wake up." As I struggle against the fabric covering me, Lucian suddenly sits up straight in the chair, looking around the room in confusion. My cries for help seem to finally register, and he jerks to his feet.

"Lia? Baby, what's wrong?" he asks as he reaches for me. His eyes are wild as he grasps my hands.

"I need to see, Luc; please, I have to see if it's there." I struggle against his hold, trying to look under the gown I'm wearing.

"Lia, what? What do you need to see?"

"I need to see my stomach! Did he mark me? He said he was marking me!" The fight is starting to leave me as my body weakens. Lucian seems to finally understand what I'm asking as he pulls the sheet covering the lower part of my body aside and gently lifts my gown. There are bandages on my stomach and I start to gasp for breath, feeling like I'm in the throes of agony as the white coverings mock me. I lower my hands, starting to pluck at the bandages frantically before Lucian stills them.

"Baby, stop! You're going to hurt yourself. The IV line is beginning to pull out of your hand again." I ignore him, continuing to dig against the gauze until he catches my hands, trying to subdue me. "Lia, STOP! Christ, I'll remove them, just please stop hurting yourself!"

My hands fall limp, and the sound of my breath wheezing through my lungs fills the room as I wait for him to do as he promised. I know with a certainty that I'll lose it completely if he has lied to me. "Luc," I say once, imploringly, and his hands move to my stomach without further words. Both our eyes are trained on his movements as slowly, piece by piece, he removes the tape holding the bandages in place. I look down as the last section falls away. I see long, angry lines and scratches and I think I can make out a W, but nothing else is readily clear. With a huge lump in my throat, I ask, "Does it...say anything? Can you see the word...whore?"

Lucian jerks as if I've struck him, and then his eyes scan the area, gently touching the exposed skin before looking up. "I...can't make out anything, baby. It just looks like a bunch of cuts and scratches to me. What—why do you think there is something there?"

Tears fill my eyes and slide down my cheeks as I whisper, "He said he was going to mark me so you and the rest of the world would know what I really am— a whore. He was going to cut the word into my stomach. I...remember him holding me down and feeling the pain of something digging into me. That's the last thing I recall, though."

Lucian looks completely devastated as if my words hit him hard. I see his eyes fill with rage before quickly turning to anguish as I sob in earnest. "Oh, fuck, baby," he rasps as he drops the rail all the way down on the bed so he can climb up next to me, gingerly taking me in his arms. "I'm so sorry," he whispers against my head as I cry into the soft skin of his neck. Within moments, he is soaked from my tears. He murmurs low words of comfort as he strokes my hair like a child.

"Please don't leave me, Luc," I plead, not caring if I sound desperate because I am. In this moment, as the memories come crashing down on me and my body aches from all the damage inflicted upon it, he is all that is keeping me from insanity. Without him, I would fall to pieces and it's unlikely I'd ever return to myself.

"Oh, Lia, I'm not going anywhere. The only way I'll leave this hospital is if you're with me. You're mine; I'll never let anyone hurt you again." His words are spoken softly, but the steel behind them is easily discernable and immediately comforts me. We lay that way until my sobs have faded into sniffles and then just the occasional shudder. I have started to doze when the door opens and I hear a snort.

"Lucian Quinn, what are you doing in bed with my patient?" I stiffen in his arms until he chuckles lightly against me.

"Sorry, Aunt Fae, I couldn't resist. I'm lying on top of the covers, though, so don't get too excited."

At his words, I look closer, recognizing his aunt. I'm immediately filled with embarrassment and shame at having her know what has happened to me. No doubt, she thinks Lucian is crazy for getting involved with someone so messed up. I can't even bring myself to meet her eyes when she stops at my bedside. "Honey, it's great to see you awake. We've been so worried about you." The concern and lack of judgment in her voice brings my head up, and I see only something that looks like affection on her face. How could she possibly feel that way toward me after what has happened? Shouldn't she be warning Lucian to run as fast and as far as he can?

"I...thank you," I answer shyly, fighting the urge to cry once again. I'm not used to kindness, and I find I want to soak it up like a sponge. This woman raised Lucian after he lost his parents, and it's obvious she loves him. My own mother never loved me a day in my life nor has she ever been concerned for my welfare. She's actually been the driving force behind every threat I've faced.

She walks over and looks at the monitors, which display my vitals. "Now that you're awake, I have to let the police know. They'll want to come take your statement." When I tremble, Lucian pulls me closer and his aunt pats my hand comfortingly. "There is nothing to be afraid of, Lia. They just need as much information as possible so they can find the person who did this to you. Remember, you're the victim here. You didn't do anything wrong."

With those words, I start crying again, wondering if I'll ever stop being the pathetic person I've turned into. Lucian and his aunt talk softly as he continues to hold and comfort me. I want nothing more than to go home with him and forget everything. I don't want to admit to anyone what my stepfather did to me. Feeling dirty, I'm consumed with the urge to be clean, to wash away his scent, which suddenly seems to be everywhere. I struggle against Lucian's hold, focused on nothing but scrubbing myself clean. "Shower," I say to him desperately. "I have to shower, now, please." I'm sobbing the words as he and his aunt try to calm me. I hear her say, 'sedate' and freeze. I vaguely remember that happening another time as Lucian held me. If I can just make them understand that I just need to make myself clean again... "Luc." I turn my head until our eyes are locked. He looks so upset; I almost end my quest, but God, I need it so badly. "I just need to wash him off me. Please, I can still smell him on my skin. Just...I have to be clean."

Lucian drops his forehead against mine, and we are communicating without words. He realizes what I need, and I know that nothing, even his aunt, will stop him from giving it to me. "Unhook her, Fae."

"Luc, we need to wait until tomorrow. Lia, it's really not a good idea to rush..." Fae's words trail off as Lucian gets off the bed and calmly starts pulling the covers from my body. I hear her bite off a curse, which would have probably been highly frowned upon by the hospital administrators. "She's taking a shower right now no matter what I say, isn't she?"

"Yes," Lucian answers firmly, giving no room for arguments. "I could really use your help, though, because I don't want to mess anything up."

His aunt brushes his hands aside as she pushes the call button on the side of the bed for the nurses' station. When they answer, she requests immediate assistance and in less than a minute, another nurse is standing at my bedside. "Wendy, Miss Adams is going to take a shower so we need to start unhooking her. Lucian, please step out into the hall until I call you." As both Lucian and I protest, she looks meaningfully at the catheter hanging at my bedside, silencing our protests immediately. He all but runs from the room, prompting his aunt to laugh. "Something about the threat of seeing that gets to them every time."

I feel my face heating. It might be comforting to know my nurse, but in this instance, I'd have rather have a stranger than Lucian's aunt touching my private areas, even if it *is* with complete clinical detachment. "Thank you," I murmur shyly as I'm finally free from everything that had me tethered to the bed. My body is throbbing like a toothache, but I'm determined to see this through. I have to. When Lucian's aunt asks me if I'm in pain, I say no. She looks at me as if she knows it's a lie but doesn't call me on it.

"All right, I think we're ready to try this. Lia, I'll change your bandages when you're finished with your shower. Wendy, I've got it from here. You can tell Luc to step back in on your way out."

Lucian comes back and walks to my side. "All ready?" he asks as he rubs my arm reassuringly.

"Luc, if you'll help Lia into the bathroom, I'll get the shower chair ready for her to sit in. Then you can wait for us in the room."

"No!" I cringe as my voice echoes throughout the room. They both look at me with concern. "I mean, I want Lucian to help me…bathe." His aunt is looking at me in surprise, but I see nothing but understanding in Lucian's eyes. "I…he knows me," I attempt to explain. In truth, I can't stand the thoughts of anyone else but him being with me as I try to wash the filth from my body.

Without a word, his aunt steps into the bathroom and turns the shower on. She then motions for Lucian and me to go in. Instead of allowing me to walk, he scoops me into his arms and carries me into the bathroom, pulling the door closed behind us. He places me gently onto the shower chair, which his aunt has situated close to the stream of water. He opens the ties on the back of my hospital gown and slowly lowers it from my shoulders before removing it completely. When I nod for him to continue, he picks up the detachable showerhead and brings it to my back, letting the warm waterfall against my skin. He uses his other hand to pump out soap from the wall dispenser into his palm and begins to alternate between soaping and rinsing my body.

I look down at his hand against my breast and silent tears fall as he gently washes the ugly, bruised and bitten areas surrounding my nipples. He sees evidence of every moment of violence I endured, and I know with certainty that it's tearing him apart. Instead of turning away, though, he looks for and cleans every bruise, scratch, and bite he possibly can. He understands that I need this, and in some ways, I know he needs it just as badly. This is no longer just about a bath for either of us; it's an attempt to cleanse our minds from the horror of my attack.

When he reaches the juncture of my thighs, he pauses for the first time, waiting silently for me to give him permission. I open my legs and we both see the mass of black and purple marks marring my inner thighs. As I open to him further, I hear him inhale raggedly as one area of my thigh shows a visible handprint etched into the skin along with jagged bite marks. I feel him tremble against me, and I hold my breath. If he isn't able to touch me there and replace the ugliness, which threatens to consume me, I'll snap. The thread holding me together is completely in his hands, and it will kill me if he turns away from me now.

As if sensing my focus on his hand, he moves it slowly and begins washing me. Even though I know it's hurting him, he continues to touch every inch of my skin with tender, almost loving strokes. I flinch and try to close my legs on reflex when he reaches my sex. I wasn't penetrated by my stepfather...he tried, but his failure to achieve a sufficient erection to violate me drove him into a rage which led to his complete loss of control. From that moment forward, his only aim was to punish me for his inability to perform. I said a word of thanks for every blow, that rained down upon me, because even if he killed me, he would never have that part of me. His beating, in a way, was my triumph over him and he knew it, he sensed it. That was what drove him to try to carve the word 'whore' into my stomach. When he told me he was going to do that, he finally saw and felt what he wanted to from me: desperation, despair, and anger. God, he had been thrilled to finally strike that chord of fear.

Lucian finishes with my body and begins washing my hair. A moan escapes my lips as his fingers gently massage my

sore scalp. The headache I had awoken
with begins to abate slightly as the
warmth of the water releases some of the
tension there. I close my eyes and give
myself up to the pleasure of his hands.

I am shaken from the trance I've fallen
into by the feel of Lucian's hand
encircling my neck and bringing my face
to his. "He's gone, baby. There is nothing
left of him on you. My hands and my
scent are all you'll feel and smell now.
Your bed was changed while we were in
here, as well, so we are beginning anew.
Okay?"

I nod in reply as the never-ending
tears, which seem to leak of their own
accord from my eyes continue. He rubs
them away with his fingertips, and then
as if it has just occurred to him, he grabs
a fresh cloth and wets it before washing
my entire face as if I were a child. My
love for him in this instant knows no
equal. He is here when most would have
walked away. He looks at my marked
body and it's as if he sees only beauty. No
matter what happens in the future, I
know with unerring certainty that I will
never love another as I love him. I touch
the scar at his throat, telling him without
words that his pain is mine just as mine
is his. We've both been hurt by someone
in our lives, but against all odds, we have

found each other. He is the answer to my prayers, and I can only hope that I'm not his worst Hell. Going forward, our fates are intertwined because the fragile bond that had been forming between us, has been solidified and only a deep tragedy could tear it apart. I wrap my hand around his and simply stare up at him. I know he must see my feelings for him in my eyes and I do nothing to hide them. "Thank you," I whisper into his palm before placing a kiss there, and we both know I'm thanking him for more than the bath.

He swallows audibly before brushing his lips against mine. His only answer is, "Always, baby."

I cling to those words, feeling a neediness I've never felt before. I understand it's normal considering the trauma I've endured, but I wonder if I'll ever be able to return to a time that I could exist without him. I lower my eyes, hoping he doesn't see the panic I feel at the mere thought of a life without Lucian Quinn in it.

He dries me as best he can before wrapping another towel around my body and carrying me back into the room. His aunt is waiting by the bed with fresh bandages. She points to the bed, and he places me gently on the fresh sheets as she approaches. Without looking at me, she begins to separate the tape and gauze. "Lia, I need to change the wet bandages. I know you would rather Luc do it, but I need to assess your injuries. He can stay next to you while I work."

"Okay," I whisper, knowing I don't have a choice. She has no doubt already seen the full extent of my injuries, but I'm still embarrassed at the thought of her opening my towel. Lucian takes my hand in his, rubbing circles on the top of it as he wills me to relax. When the towel opens, I look at him, letting her work. My skin crawls at the touch of her cool fingers against it, but I don't pull away. As long as he is here, no one will hurt me.

I am unable to control the wince when she goes to the other side of the bed and picks up my hand. I'm wearing a brace on it along with some tape on three of my fingers. It feels stiff and swollen and it hurts as she peels back the tape. "I know this doesn't feel too good, but this needs to be changed. I should have thought to put a bag over it before you showered."

"Wh...What's wrong with it?" I ask, wondering what could possibly be causing so much pain.

She grimaces before saying, "Your wrist and three of your fingers are broken. We'll put a cast on when some more of the swelling goes down."

Suddenly, the sound and feel of those fingers breaking comes back to me in a sickening wave. "I passed out when he broke the first finger, but he managed to rouse me enough to make sure I was aware of what was happening when he broke the next two." I fight the urge to roll into a fetal position and hope the memories of that day will stop coming to me.

Lucian abruptly drops my other hand and steps back. "I—just need some water. I'll be back," he throws over his shoulder as he leaves so quickly I'm left reeling from his departure. I blink back tears again, afraid he's leaving me now.

"Honey," his aunt says gently. "This is hard on him. I've never seen him this way with a woman before, and it's hurting him that he couldn't save you."

I have no idea where it even comes from, but I find myself blurting out, "What about Cassie? He loved her, didn't he?"

His aunt freezes, seeming just as shocked by my question as I am. Finally, she says, "Has he talked to you about her?"

Shaking my head, I say, "Not really. He has said that he will when the time is right. She's the one who hurt him, isn't she?"

She doesn't answer until she's finished with the last bandage. Then she looks at me for another long moment before finally speaking. "It's a long, complicated, and tragic story, Lia. It's up to Luc to tell you about it himself when he's ready. I will tell you, though, that he went through a very rough time afterwards. The fact that he's let himself get so involved with you is something I never thought would happen again. You have the power to hurt him, more so than Cassie ever did. Please don't abuse the trust he has given you."

I place my hand over hers and say honestly, "He holds the power in our relationship because he has my heart."

She pulls the sheets back over me, tucking them around my body carefully before reattaching the IV lines. "I'm going to get you something for your pain; I know you probably need it by now." I nod, feeling every ache and pain in my body jump to life. As she reaches the door, she adds, "You hold his heart, as well, even if he isn't ready to admit it." The door closes quietly behind her, and I find myself waiting for him to return to me. Could she be right? Does Lucian love me? Is he even capable of it after Cassie? I so want to know what happened between them. I am certain that it's the key to unlocking the remaining mystery of who Lucian is. The one question I desperately need answered is where *is* Cassie?

CHAPTER FOUR

Lucian

I pace the smoking area as I inhale and exhale, hoping it'll calm me. I've barely been keeping it together since seeing the damage to Lia's body. She is so tiny I can't even imagine how she survived the type of beating that would leave those types of bruises behind. When I saw the handprint on her thigh, I had to swallow down the bile threatening to come up my throat. Just thinking of that evil fucker touching her there is enough to make me want to tear this city apart until I find him. Aunt Fae says there is no evidence that she was raped, but God, I need to know from Lia that it's true. I can't stand the thought of him inside her. I'll fucking kill him somehow if he did. I'd gladly rot in jail just for that pleasure.

I just lost it when she told us how he had broken her fingers. I guess I thought maybe that had happened in the struggle— which would have been bad enough, but knowing he deliberately snapped them one at a time, makes me crazy. She hasn't said his name, always referring to 'him.' I had little doubt from the beginning; now there is none. How will either of us ever be able to live our lives knowing *he's* still alive?

I'm on my second cigarette when I hear, "Luc, when did you start smoking?"

I turn around to see Max behind me, waving the cloud of smoke floating by him away. I hold up a finger, signaling for him to give me a minute while I take a few more puffs before putting it out in the can provided by the hospital. No doubt, they are trying to avoid having butts lying all over the ground. "Max, sorry about that. I figured they'd frown on me sitting in Lia's room drinking scotch, so I'm giving smoking a try."

Max wrinkles his nose. "How's that working out for you?"

"It sucks," I deadpan, not even bothering to deny it. I'm going to need another toothbrush tomorrow because I've all but worn out the one I have.

Curious, I ask, "So, what brings you here this late?"

He shifts uncomfortably before saying, "I...was having dinner with Carly when the hospital called letting her know Lia was awake. She wanted to talk to her right away so I came along, as well. Thought I'd see if you needed anything."

I can't help raising a brow at his admission. It seems that my suspicions were right, and he has more going on than friendship with his police contact. Not that I'm surprised, really. Max isn't one to flaunt his relationships, but I know he has never had a shortage of female company. Instead of commenting on it, I ask, "Do you have any news for me yet?"

"Depends on what kind of news you are looking for. There's nothing on Jim Dawson. He's disappeared, and Lia's mother isn't talking. It's quite possible that she doesn't know anything this time. Carly said she seemed surprised to find out about Lia; actually she said she seemed shocked. Of course knowing what we do about the type of woman she is, I doubt she's been too torn up over it." With a pained grimace, he adds, "Makes me want to call my mom and thank her for not being a psycho."

I agree, thinking I'm better off without parents than having the type Lia's had to deal with. "Do the police have any leads?"

"I don't think so," Max answers in disgust. "It just boggles the mind that someone like Dawson with few resources can evade everyone so easily."

"You'd be amazed at the people who'll help someone like that," I add, knowing that evil people tend to help each other no matter what the cost to themselves. Rather like a code of honor among thieves.

"So, anyway," Max adds, seeming to come to the point of his visit. "If I were a betting man, I would say that Lee Jacks knows all about Lia by now."

His statement does not even vaguely surprise me. It's something I've expected from the moment Max told me what he'd found out about Lia's past. Asking questions about a man like Jacks was sure to be noticed. "Anything in particular which leads you to that conclusion?"

"I received a call earlier from Mark Wilks, who is one of several attorneys on retainer to Falco Enterprises. He and I play golf on a regular basis, and he wanted to let me know that my interest in Mr. Jacks' personal life had not gone unnoticed."

"Was he fishing?" I ask, curious as to why Jacks would choose such an indirect route to me.

"No, not at all. He didn't ask me any questions. It was just a courtesy call to give me a heads-up. I don't think Jacks is the type to use his lawyer for something like that."

I grin, catching his double meaning. "I think we both know you're more than my lawyer. Besides, I don't employ people to keep their ears to the ground like Jacks does, as I don't have as much to hide."

Max shakes his head. "We've all got skeletons in the closet, Luc. Some of them just rattle more than others."

"True," I acknowledge his statement before asking, "So, you think it's only a matter of time before he shows up?"

"You better believe it. If we're right, then Lia is his only child, at least that I know of. There's no way he'll be able to resist seeing her in person."

"We both knew it was inevitable from the moment we found out. I know his dealings are sometimes questionable, but really, could he be any worse than her mother?"

"I don't know, Luc," Max answers honestly. "He does maintain close ties with his brother, so obviously family means something to him. I don't think

he'll approach Lia without coming to you
first. You two are acquaintances. I figure
he will want to feel you out before going
to Lia. I have to believe he's as fucking
blown away by this turn of events as we
are."

"What makes you think he hasn't
known about her all along?" I ask, hoping
to Hell I'm wrong. The last thing Lia
needs is another parent who has failed
her.

"It's possible," Max admits. "But from
what I know about him, it's not probable.
No matter what he is, I don't see him
leaving a daughter in the situation Lia
was in. Lee isn't the type of man to let
someone else mess with his possessions."

I'm inclined to agree with Max's
assessment. Regardless of whether his
dealings are legal, not legal, or strictly in
the grey, Jacks is an accepted and sought-
after member of Asheville society. He'd
never leave a scandal like that to come
back to haunt him later. If Lia is his
daughter and he knew about her, either
she'd have lived with him or he would
have sent her somewhere far away. He
would have never left her here right
under everyone's nose for someone to
stumble across at an inconvenient time.
He's not a stupid man. Although, the
argument could be made that he must

have had a severe lapse in judgment at least once in his life. A relationship with Maria Adams is enough to make me shudder. It's hard to imagine that the bitch could have been that much different then.

"We'll see what comes of it," I finally say. I fight the urge to light another cigarette while I process his news. I've been gone a while, and I need to get back to Lia. I can't imagine what she must think at the abrupt way I left. I feel like it will be easier for her to talk to the police about what happened to her without me present, but I need to be close in case she needs me. If I'm truthful with myself, I'll admit that I'm afraid I'll have a hard time dealing with it, as well. The thoughts of anyone touching her makes me violent. I've never been this possessive of a woman before, certainly not of Cassie, and it's more than a little disconcerting. "Let's go back in." I wave Max forward.

I don't miss the look of relief that crosses Lia's expressive face when I walk into the room. I cross to her immediately, blocking the view of everyone in the room as I stop next to her bed. "Okay?" I ask, probing her tense expression. She nods just once, but looks so grateful to see me that I immediately feel guilty for leaving her. "I'm here, baby," I assure her before settling into the chair on the other side of her bed and rubbing her leg soothingly.

The police detective is obviously still dressed for an evening out.. If I were a little more juvenile, I would give Max a thumbs-up because Carly Michaels is a very attractive woman, and if the form-fitting black dress she's wearing is any indication, she looks just as good under her clothing. Who in the hell am I kidding; I'll comment on it to him for sure the next time we're alone.

"Miss Adams...Lia, I know this is hard, but let's go over it one more time from the top. If you don't have any objections, I'll record your statement this time. I'm sorry to put you through this again, but I've found that sometimes things are clearer after you've had time to reflect on your initial memories of the event."

When Lia's eyes fly to me as if concerned by my presence, I say, "Honey, I can step out in the hallway if it'll be easier for you?"

She looks conflicted for a moment before saying, "Please, don't leave. I want you here, just..."

I know what she is trying to say. She's afraid that what I hear will change how I feel about her. It's likely to tear me apart and infuriate me all to Hell, but it won't make me walk away. She doesn't realize the hold she has over me; even I don't understand it. I never intended to be in this kind of position again, especially with someone just as damaged as I am. Nevertheless, Lia became a part of me before I even knew what was happening. I can no more cut her from my life and survive than I can stop breathing. "It won't change anything," I reassure her while bracing myself for her story. Max excuses himself from the room, not wanting to make Lia more uncomfortable.

"All right, Lia, I'm ready," Carly says as she lays a recorder on the bedside table. "Just take your time and go from the top, please."

Lia takes a couple of breaths before beginning haltingly. "I...finished my last class at school early and had some time to kill before Sam was to pick me up. I had been staying with Lucian and needed some clothing from my apartment, which was just down the block from school. I thought I could pick up my things and be back in plenty of time to catch my ride. I was checking the mail in the lobby of my apartment building when suddenly someone grabbed me from behind. I was so surprised I didn't even try to fight until after I was pulled into the storage room. I was turned until I was facing my stepfather, Jim Dawson. When I started to struggle, he punched me in the stomach with his fist, driving the breath from me. While I was trying to recover, he took his belt off and used it to tie my hands. Then he stuffed some type of cloth into my mouth and put tape over it. The taste was so bad I started to gag, but he told me if I vomited, he would leave the tape on so I choked to death on my own puke."

When Lia stops to take a drink of water, her eyes dart to mine and I do my best to give her an easy smile. I hate that she's going through something so traumatic and appears to be more worried about me than herself. I vow, as I look into her apprehensive eyes, that I'll keep it together. All of my feelings of anger, despair, and helplessness are solely because I let the bastard get to her. In her vulnerable state, though, I realize it would be entirely too easy for her to assume I don't want her anymore, which is fucking far from the truth. Uncaring of our audience, I lean over and press a kiss to her lips. "Doesn't change a thing, baby." She blinks back tears before turning back to Detective Michaels. The other woman looks intrigued by the interaction between us but quickly drops her professional mask back into place.

"Do you need to rest for a bit before continuing, Lia?" she asks, seeming to understand how difficult this is for her. I wonder if Lia would be afforded this courtesy if not for Max's relationship with the police detective.

"I'm okay," Lia says quietly before continuing. "He was so angry, almost hyper with it. I thought that maybe he might be taking something because he seemed almost manic. I remember he kept laughing, as if the whole thing was hysterical. Then, in the blink of an eye, he would be raging. The first thing I remember him saying after he had me subdued was, 'You thought you had me, didn't you? You stupid little whore, who do you think you are?' Then he bent over, laughing as if he had said something so funny. He chanted, 'I'll show you...I'll show you,' repeatedly as he...started trying to remove my clothes. He got mad when he couldn't get my shirt over my hands since he had them tied together. He started yanking them as if somehow it would help. Finally, he pulled a knife from his pocket and cut them, both my bra and shirt. When I tried to turn away so he couldn't look at me...he slapped me before throwing me to the floor. My head hit the corner of one of the lockers, and I was disoriented for a few minutes. Just enough time for him to take off my pants and underwear." Instead of looking at Detective Michaels, she turns to me, almost pleading as she continues. "I tried to fight—I really did, but he was so much stronger than me. He straddled my legs and...started touching me."

When she pauses, Detective Michaels asks, "Where did he touch you, Lia?"

Lia closes her eyes for a moment as if gathering strength before opening them again. I know she is watching me to gauge my reaction, which lets me know that what she has to say next is going to be painful for both of us. I hold her gaze without looking away, trying to convey without words that no matter what she says, I will still be right here next to her. "First, he grabbed my breasts," she begins quietly but resolutely. "He pinched them until I cried out and then squeezed them repeatedly. Then he...lowered his hand between my legs and stuck several fingers into my...vagina. He seemed to want me to cry, and he continued doing it until I did."

"Fucking bastard," I snap, unable to hold the words at bay. Even though I had guessed at what happened to her, hearing the words from her lips is sheer torture. Knowing he had his hands on her—in her—was enough to wreck me. When Lia stops talking, I squeeze her leg, nodding for her to continue despite my outburst.

In a husky voice, she picks up where she left off. "He then lowered his pants enough to release his penis. I...I bucked and twisted, trying to throw him off." Pointing to her nose, she adds, "That's when he hit me with his fist. Before I knew what was happening, he was trying to push inside me, and even as I cried, waiting for it to happen, it never did. He...he couldn't get it to go in. He wasn't hard enough. That's when he really lost it and started hitting, kicking, and biting me." She wipes at the tears trailing down her face as she says, "It hurt, but I didn't care because it was better than the alternative. He kept calling me a filthy whore and saying it was my fault he couldn't perform because I was too disgusting to him. I began getting really dizzy and fading in and out. When he picked up his knife and said he was going to show Lucian and the rest of the world what I really was, and this time there would be no mistaking his mark on me, I went crazy. He was going to carve the word 'whore' into my stomach with his knife. He punched me again when I kept fighting, and that's the last thing I remember. I must have passed out."

Detective Michaels stops her recorder before walking over to look down at Lia. "I know this may sound trite, but you are lucky to have survived something like that intact. I've seen so many who didn't make it out. I realize you have a long road ahead of you, but please remember in the end that he wasn't able to take what he wanted from you. You won because you're here."

"I know," Lia agrees softly. "I had already accepted the fact that I wasn't going to leave that room alive. So when I woke up here in the hospital, I thought I was still there...with him. I just...wanted to die rather than let him have me. I don't know if I would have wanted to live if he had been able to do what he wanted to."

"You'd be surprised at what you can overcome, Lia," the other woman says before changing the subject. "I think that's all I need for now. We're doing everything we can to locate him, and I'll keep you updated if anything new develops." After she leaves, Lia studies her hands, as if afraid to look at me.

I get to my feet and ask if she needs to go to the restroom before we settle in for the evening. "No, your aunt helped me earlier before Ms. Michaels arrived. I think I'm good for a while." I nod before removing my shoes and lowering the rail on her bed before climbing in. I pull her gently into my arms and attempt to relax.

"I'm so sorry, baby, about everything you went through. I'd give anything if I could go back and keep that from happening to you."

The sound of big, gulping sobs fills the room as she cries against my chest. "Do you think I'm ugly now?" she asks between racking sobs. My heart breaks at her question, and I wonder how to convince her that she'll never be anything but beautiful to me, both inside and outside. No matter how much ugliness has tried to touch her.

"No, baby; God no. I will never see anything but beauty when I look at you. I am in awe of your strength. Few people could survive what you have and worry only about the feelings of others. You make me and everyone around you want to be a better version of ourselves just to be worthy of you. There is nothing in the world that your stepfather could have done to make you ugly. I hurt when I look at you because I know you are suffering. But when you are healed and ready, I'll worship you, every inch of you, and I will only ever see you, Lia...only you."

She relaxes into my arms and raises her head to kiss my neck. As I lay holding her, lost in my own thoughts, I hear her say the words that almost stop my heart. "I love you, Luc." Her rhythmic breathing lets me know she's asleep or close, and I wonder if she's even aware of what she just said. I cycle between wanting to pull her closer and wanting to run away. Even though I know that deep feelings exist between us, I'm nowhere near ready to put a name to them. I don't know if I'm even capable of entertaining it. Her emotions are all over the place right now, and it's understandable that she would say things she might normally not. I swore I'd never give that kind of power to a woman again, and no matter how strongly I feel for Lia, I can't break that oath, at least not right now when my world seems to be on the brink once again of descending into chaos. I decide not to mention it and hope it won't become an issue between us. I can't bear the thought of losing her, but right now, I feel we both have enough to deal with in our lives without adding the extra complications that love could bring with it.

CHAPTER FIVE

Lia

I'm being released from the hospital today, five days after my attack. Detective Michaels, as well as the nurses, have told me how lucky I am to have survived. When I look at myself, seeing my once-clear skin now riddled with black and blue marks along with the teeth impressions of a monster, I don't feel lucky. I'm tainted with the type of dirty no amount of bathing can remove. My body, which was so familiar to me only days before now, seems foreign. The cuts and bruises will heal, I'm told; soon, there will be nothing but possibly a few scars left. I can put it all behind me and get on with my life as if it never happened. I hear some version of that almost every day. Do they really believe it to be that easy, or are they that fucking delusional? Would they be speaking these same patronizing words if they had been brutally attacked by someone who should have only protected them? Can anyone other than another victim truly understand the sense of betrayal and shame which comes from being sexually assaulted by a parent or stepparent? I have learned to live my life despite the fact that those feelings rise at times to suffocate me, the burn on my back a constant reminder of the atrocities that someone can commit against another.

The fact that my mother knows, has always known, is an even greater cross to bear. In my lifetime, I've never known what it was like to be loved unconditionally until I met Debra. She is a loud, brash, business owner, but she's a fierce protector of those she loves. The day I walked into her restaurant, desperately needing a job, was one of the best days ever for me. Debra and her boyfriend, Martin, took me under their wing, and I wouldn't have made it as far as I have without them. She visited me yesterday, and thankfully, she was one of the few people not to tell me how lucky I am to have made it. I don't think I could have handled her sugarcoating things for me, because that's just not who she is.

Instead, she called my stepfather a 'fucking, evil prick' who needed to be taught a lesson. She was very detailed in what that lesson should entail, too. I loved her for understanding that I can't sit around and just be thankful that my lot in life wasn't as bad as it could be. She understood that I needed to vent even if I could only do it with insults.

And Lucian...I've alternated between wanting to hide myself away from him so he can't see all the ugliness, which now seems such a dominant part of me and wanting to stay wrapped in his arms so he can protect me from the world as he's promised to do. When he makes that vow, I know he genuinely believes he can keep me from harm's way. He is loyal to those he cares about and gives more than he ever realizes to protect them. I don't know the details, but I feel certain that he almost gave his life to save his friend, and possibly lover, Cassie. What I wouldn't give to know what transpired between them. Is her story similar to mine? Is he drawn to me because I represent someone he couldn't save in his past? I've spent a lot of time the last few days obsessing on what I don't know about him. Maybe it's easier to focus on his problems and avoid my own, or maybe I just need to understand the man who hasn't left the hospital since I was admitted.

I've allowed myself to fall in love with Lucian Quinn, and at a particularly weak point during my hospital stay, I admitted as much to him. I pretended to be asleep afterwards, not wanting to face what was sure to be an awkward moment between us. I know he cares about me; no one would do all he has for me unless they felt something. Sexually, we catch fire when we're together, never seeming to be able to get enough of each other. Even now, as broken as I am in both body and spirit, I long for his possession. He makes me feel beautiful and desired when we are together, something I've never had before. He is a brilliant, intense man and everything he touches flourishes under his hand, just as I do.

He has held me, comforted me, teased me, and took great care of me while I've lain in the hospital bed, with what has seemed like an endless stream of tears. I've wallowed in self-pity, something I've never given into before, no matter how bad my life was. His aunt talked to me yesterday about possibly taking some medication in the short-term until I have a better handle on my emotions. When I mentioned it to Lucian, he seemed upset. It was almost as if he took it as a personal challenge to help me take back control without medicating. He asked that I try to hold off and give myself time before taking any medications. It made me curious as to what his aversion to antidepressants was. Had he used them in the past and had a bad experience? From the way he had been fidgeting and pacing at times during the last five days, I had to wonder if maybe he wouldn't benefit from something for anxiety himself. I was sure that he had been smoking, as well, though he had yet to admit it when I'd asked him about the smell. At first, I thought it was secondhand from Aidan, or even Max, but inevitably, when he walked outside, he came back smelling like tobacco. For all I knew, it was something he had randomly done for years. I'd never noticed the smell before, though, nor seen any hints of it in his apartment. Lucian was a man with many layers, and just when I thought I knew most of them, he showed me another.

He walks back into the hospital room, holding the door open for his aunt who pushes a wheelchair in. I cringe, knowing there is no way I can get out of riding in it out to the car. She has already told me not to even bother to try; hospital policy is gospel. I put up a token argument, but I am still so sore and weak from lying in a bed for a week, that I'm more than happy to accept a ride to the parking lot.

"Ready to roll, Lia?" She smiles when she brings the chair to a stop in front of me. She and I have bonded during my stay here, and I will miss seeing her each day. She has assured me that she will visit soon. She made me feel very much like a part of their small family for which I am touched and grateful.

"God, yes," I sigh, mostly meaning it. I'm tired of staring at the small walls of the room but am a little nervous about leaving somewhere that has felt safe to me. The hospital is so busy, but there was always someone in and out of my room. I know Lucian has to return to work. He might own the company, but eventually he'll need to get back to his life. I am amazed that, true to his word, he never left the hospital during my stay. Other than what I suspect was his smoking time, he stayed in the room with me. Sam dropped off food for us so we weren't completely dependent upon hospital food. I found I had very little appetite yet, so mine was mostly wasted.

"Come on, baby, let's go home," Lucian says as he holds my arm to help me into the wheelchair. I know he would rather just carry me to the car, but he's playing by the rules to make his aunt happy. He drops a kiss on my forehead. "Sam's waiting on us at the curb so we don't have far to go."

His aunt wheels me through the hallways, and I wave shyly to a few of my regular nurses who I have come to know. I suspect I received more visits from the nursing staff than most patients do for two reasons. One, because of Fae, and two, because of the 'wow factor' that is Lucian. They literally melted at his feet when he showed them any attention. I just rolled my eyes as they swooned. I secretly wondered, though, if I act in a similar fashion. He is so effortlessly sexy and charismatic that it's almost impossible to be immune to him. I would have thought their behavior around me would have been awkward, due to the nature and cause of my injuries, but instead, after the initial shock had worn off, I was more like a visiting celebrity. I knew this was solely due to Luc's presence and his gentle care of me.

Sam is standing on the sidewalk beaming when we come through the doorway. He walks forward, dropping on a knee to take my hands in his. "Miss Lia, I'm thrilled to be taking you home today. We've been so worried about you."

I tear up at the sincerity in his voice. In such a short time, I have grown so fond of the man in front of me. "Thank you, Sam," I whisper. "I've missed your smile." Even though I argue against using Lucian's car when he insists, I always enjoy being around Sam. Spending time with him somehow makes me feel closer to Lucian. Just knowing that he knows most everything about the man I have become so attached to is nothing short of intriguing. I try not to pick him for information, but he says things in passing about Lucian as a child or teenager and I find myself hanging on his every word.

As Lucian helps me to my feet, his aunt walks up to me, taking me into her arms. "Call me if you need anything, even just to talk," she says low enough that only she and I hear. She hadn't been happy with Lucian for asking me to hold off on the medication she had talked with me about. I understand that she's trying to tell me without saying the words to let her know if I can't cope on my own. I nod my agreement before thanking her for everything she has done.

Lucian settles me in one side of the Mercedes, closing the door carefully behind me before walking around to the other door and getting in. He surprises me by pulling me onto his lap and belting us both in together. "Okay?" he asks, looking at me searchingly.

"Yes," I answer honestly, glad to be in his arms where the rest of the world always seems to fall away.

He releases a breath before easing me closer, until my head is tucked under his chin. "I'm so happy to be taking you home."

I rub his arm, attempting to comfort him. "I know it was hard for you to be at the hospital for so long. Thank you for staying."

He pulls back, taking my chin in his hand to stare into my eyes. "That's not what I meant. I...fuck, baby, when I found you, I was afraid I'd lost you. The fact that you're here now..." He doesn't seem to know how to finish his sentence, but he's said enough to give me some measure of peace. I understand what he was trying to say, because when I had been completely at the mercy of my stepfather, I had felt anguish that I'd never see Lucian again, never feel his arms around me, and never get the chance to see if someday we could have been more. I had mourned the loss of him as my body was pummeled. The fact that he now cradles me gently in his arms as if I am precious to him seems surreal.

We don't speak for the rest of the drive, both seemingly lost in our own thoughts. One thing I both love and hate at times about him is that he never feels the need to fill the silence. I know he has a mind that is seldom at rest, and I long to hear his thoughts, but sometimes, like today, relaxing into a peaceful silence is its own kind of comfort.

Lucian insists on carrying me from the car and into his apartment. I do not bother to protest when he walks through the living area and straight to the bedroom, sitting me down on the bed; my body is still weak from both the trauma and the battering it sustained. I am more than happy to let him take off my shoes and tuck me under the covers. "This feels so good," I murmur drowsily as I snuggle deeper into the soft bedding.

He drops a kiss on my temple before standing. "I'm going to go through some emails for a bit if you're okay alone?"

"I'm fine," I mumble in reply, already starting to doze.

"I'm just down the hall in my office. Call out if you need me. Lia?"

Apparently, my nod wasn't sufficient, and he needs my verbal agreement before he will leave. "K...in your office," I repeat to appease him. When he walks out of the room, I have to fight the sudden urge to call him back. Knowing Lucian watched over me was the only way I was able to rest easy in the hospital. I knew that, true to his word, he would kill anyone who tried to hurt me again. I'm home now, though; Lucian has become that for me. If I know nothing else, I know I'm safe within these walls with him standing guard. As I start to drift away, I wonder how I'll ever make myself leave the security of this apartment again.

Lucian

I drop into my leather office chair, running my hand through my hair. It feels so fucking good to be home again, and the fact that Lia's back in my bed is enough to bring me to my knees. For agonizing hours after I found her, I was afraid we'd never be here together again. Truthfully, I don't know if I would have ever walked back through the door to this place if she had died. This might be my home on paper, but Lia now owns every square inch of it. There isn't a room, nook, or corner I don't feel her presence in. Maybe it stems from the fact that I've never had another woman here romantically. It scares the hell out of me to even try to analyze why I can't imagine wanting her to leave...ever. Whatever the reason, I finally feel as if I can breathe again.

Even though I want nothing more than to go crawl into bed with Lia and feel her against me, I have business that needs to be dealt with. Aidan and Cindy have done a good job at handling the day-to-day operations at Quinn Software, but I cannot be away from the helm forever. There are always decisions to be made that are solely my responsibility.

I have been returning emails for an hour when the doorbell rings. "Fuck," I hiss, hoping the sound doesn't wake Lia. I can't imagine who it could be since everyone I know would call before they dropped by. When I look through the peephole, I squint in surprise. I recognize the face; after all, I purchased this apartment from his company. It also explains why he made it to my apartment without my okay; I guess his employees don't say no to the boss. Opening the door, I stand with my arms crossed, saying simply, "Jacks."

"Quinn," he answers back in kind, appearing amused by my resigned expression. I know it is obvious to him that his visit is no surprise to me. I'd known from the moment Max and I talked that he'd make an appearance at some point; I'm only surprised it has taken him this long. We hold a bit of a stare-off/male-pissing contest before I finally move aside and motion him into my apartment. There is no way he's going to go away easily, and I'd rather get this over with while Lia is asleep.

He stands in the foyer, waiting until I close the door and motion him to follow me to my office. When he sits in the chair I've indicated in front of my desk, I take a moment to study him. Maybe I'm prejudiced by the information I have, but damn, he does look like Lia. Their hair and coloring are almost the same, but it's the eyes that really give me pause. His eyes are the same brilliant blue as Lia's. I realize that half of the people in the world probably have blue eyes, but there is just something about Lia and Lee's eyes, which look almost identical. I scrub a hand over my forehead thinking that maybe I'm just seeing things that aren't even there. I have a feeling Lee knows for sure one way or the other, so my curiosity has me asking, "So, what can I do for you?"

His lips turn up in a slight smirk as if to say, 'so you're going that route.' I don't intend to make this easy for him, though, so I wait. "When I was told you were asking questions about me, it didn't cause much of a blip on my radar. After all, we have some similar business interests, and I figured you had some future venture in mind." He pauses, crossing his legs before continuing. "What *did* surprise me was that the questions had nothing to do with business and everything to do with my personal life, or more accurately, my past. I'm not saying it doesn't happen, because it does...often. However, it's usually by the same nosy crowd that wants to dissect me for personal gain. Your sudden interest in a period of my life twenty-some-odd years ago was enough to get my attention. So, I did a little digging of my own into your life."

After delivering his last statement, he waits as if curious to what my reaction will be. I lean back in my chair, wishing for one of the nasty cigarettes that are in my desk drawer. I refuse to give him the satisfaction of acting like a pussy. Men like Lee Jacks only respect one thing: strength. Something tells me that how I react to him today will set the tone for our future relationship. If he *is* Lia's father, and he deems me as weak, he'll end up being a problem—a big one. Therefore, with a carefully blank face, I say, "I would have done the same. I'm only curious as to why it's taken you this long to make an appearance."

I think I must be imagining things when he looks almost guilty for a split second before wiping his expression clean. "I was out of town when I first heard of your unusual...interest in me. I just returned late last night. After I found out that you were at home instead of your office, I came straight here."

Deciding to cut through the rest of the small talk, I ask bluntly, "Is she your daughter?"

He doesn't bother to act ignorant; he simply says, "Yes."

I have little doubt that he knows exactly what he's talking about; this isn't a man who would answer that type of question without facts to back it up. I feel rage rising to choke me as I snap, "Have you always known about her?"

"Fuck no!" He almost shouts the words, losing his composure for a moment before taking a breath. "The things you were asking made me dig. When I couldn't find a connection between my past and yours, I had my men look at her. I knew when I saw her picture, but the first line of her background report confirmed it for me."

"You don't look that much alike," I argue, not even sure why I'm protesting. Maybe because I think Lia deserves a

parent who isn't just as bad as her
mother is. Without replying, he pulls his
wallet from his suit pocket and takes a
picture from it. When he tosses it in front
of me, I gape at him. In the picture stands
Lee Jacks with his arm around...Lia?

"What the hell?" I ask, staring at the
picture in shock. Lia knows who he is.

"Pretty uncanny, isn't it?" he asks as
he hands me another picture. The same
woman stands next to a man who closely
resembles Lee, but clearly is not. "That's
my brother Peter and his daughter Kara."

I take a closer look at both
photographs, finally noticing a difference
in the other woman's hair color and
height. At first glance, she could pass for
Lia's twin. However, upon closer
inspection, knowing what I now do, I can
see it is not her. It does seem to lend
support to his statement of being Lia's
father. I hand the pictures back, saying,
"This doesn't really prove anything. Don't
they say everyone has a twin somewhere
in the world?"

"Let's not waste our time doing the
denial dance, Quinn. Both you and I know
I have more proof than this."

"So, what now?" I ask, knowing he
speaks the truth. There is no way Lee
would be here right now if he had any
question about whether Lia was his

daughter. "I'm not sure of what kind of reaction you are expecting from her."

"That's why I sought you out first instead of Lia. I thought maybe you would have some suggestions as to how to approach her." The surprise I feel must be written all over my face. He gives me a wry smile, saying, "You're involved with her, so it stands to reason that you know her much better than I do."

Before I can formulate a reply, a voice sounds from the doorway. "Luc, I'm sorry. I didn't know you had company. I was just going to sit with you for a while."

I jump to my feet, noting the break in her voice and the redness of her eyes. She's been crying again. I cross the room in a couple strides, pulling her into my arms. "Are you okay, baby?" I ask, feeling her shudder against me.

"Just a bad dream," she whispers against my neck. Looking toward the man who sits staring at us, she pulls out of my arms. "I'm...um...just going to take a shower. Sorry to interrupt your meeting." Lowering her head, she quickly turns away, seeming embarrassed as she pulls nervously at the loose clothing she is wearing.

"It's fine," I assure her. "I'll be in to check on you in just a minute. Why don't you wait for me before you shower?" I don't like the thought of her possibly falling while I'm not close enough to hear her. She nods before walking back down the hallway. When I can no longer see her, I close the door quietly and turn to find Lee in my face. "What the..." I choke off as his hand comes around my neck, pinning me against the door I had just shut.

"How dare you lay hands on her!" he hisses as he draws his fist back. I am momentarily confused, thinking he is pissed off about me hugging her before it hits me. He had seen her face. He thought I...

"Fuck," I bite off as I reach out to hold his fist. "I'd never hurt her." I jerk out of his hold, shaking my head. "You don't know, do you? Apparently your employees aren't as thorough as you thought." My neck throbs from the crushing hold he'd had on my windpipe. Lee might wear a thousand-dollar suit, but he packs some serious muscle underneath. His calm demeanor makes more sense to me now I know he had no clue as to where Lia had been for the last five days. I can't understand how his people had missed something so recent, though.

"You need to stop talking shit, Quinn, and tell me what happened to her. If you did that to her, I'll find out, and I'll visit the same on you, only much worse." Rage radiates from every pore of the other man's body, leaving me in little doubt that he means every word. I don't want to have this conversation with Lia awake, but I know there is no way Lee is leaving without some answers. Maybe a part of me even hopes the truth will cause him even a piece of the pain Lia has felt all of these years.

Rubbing my neck to ease some of the tension, I say, "Lia has been in the hospital for the last five days. I just brought her home today. Her stepfather tried to rape her and would have probably killed her had something not interrupted him."

"WHAT?" Lee roars, clenching his fists.

"Keep your voice down," I demand, looking toward the door. "I don't want her to know we're talking about this. If you would like to hear this, then you're going to have to refrain from yelling." Giving me an incredulous look, he motions for me to continue. "If you didn't know that, then you probably don't know that she was abused for years by her mother and her stepfather. She—"

"Maria hurt her?" he interrupts, looking pale as a ghost. I am surprised a man like Lee Jacks would be shocked by anything, especially violence. He doesn't appear to be acting, though. He genuinely looks like he might pass out.

"Yes, she did," I answer truthfully. "Then she married Jim Dawson, and he did everything short of raping her for years after that." When the other man sinks down into the chair he had vacated earlier, I go back to my own before telling him all that I know, including the courtroom drama we'd had recently. A part of me even feels a tiny bit sorry for him, as he looks sick to his stomach.

"I...I didn't know any of this," he says quietly before rubbing his temples. Looking down at his hands, he adds, "She's had a horrible life, hasn't she? Goddammit, I can't believe this!"

I sigh, feeling my anger at him drain away. There is no denying the fact that he is devastated at the news I've delivered. I hadn't doubted he would be angry over what Lia has endured if for no other reason than someone had dared to touch a Jacks. What I hadn't expected was what appeared to be a father's anguish over his daughter's pain. It doesn't really seem to fit with the detached person I've known him to be. "Her life hasn't been easy," I agree. "But she's an amazing woman. She's the most intelligent, determined and strong person I've ever known. She's taken everything that has been done to her and turned it into a stepping stone to survive."

He raises his head, and his eyes blaze. His words, when they come, are spoken so softly I almost don't hear them. "Anyone who has ever hurt her will pay; I can promise you that." He stands, walking toward the door. "I'll be in touch," he adds before walking out.

I slump back into my seat, feeling drained from the encounter. Strangely, I also feel myself relax more than I have since Lia's attack. I have no idea what his intentions are where she is concerned, but there is one thing I'm certain of: he'll rain Hell down onto anyone who even thinks of hurting her again. I'm also certain that there is no corner of the world big enough for Jim Dawson to hide in now. I'm under no delusions that he plans to suddenly turn into father-of-the-year, but his loss of control where his emotions were concerned seemed very real. The only thing that makes me uneasy is how this revelation will affect my relationship with Lia. I'd love nothing better than for her to finally have a family who cares for her as she deserves, but I don't know if Jacks will ever offer that. I don't want this to be another source of pain for her. He is a powerful man, but I'm not without contacts and

allies of my own. If I have to protect Lia
from her own father, then I will... without
hesitation.

Standing, I go in search of Lia only to
find her asleep once again on the bed. I
move her gently, trying to make her more
comfortable before pulling the comforter
back over her small frame. Just as I lean
down to brush a kiss over her lips, I hear
the doorbell. Our first day home and my
apartment has suddenly turned into
Grand Central Station. As I look through
the peephole, I'm surprised once again at
my unexpected visitor. Swinging the door
open, I motion for Max to come in.
"What's up?" I ask without preamble.
Silently, I wonder when people stopped
calling before just dropping in. Especially
knowing Lia has just come home hours
before. As I wait for his reply, I notice his
disheveled appearance. Max generally
looks like an ad for Brooks Brothers.
Even though he's wearing his usual suit,
he looks almost as if he slept in it before
coming over. "What in the hell happened
to you?"

"Rose Madden is what happened to
me!" he growls in response. "That woman
is fucking nuts."

I wonder vaguely if I look as confused
as I feel at his answer. "Lia's friend
Rose?"

"Oh, yes, one and the same."

After having to deal with Lee, I'm too burned out for obscure answers. I fight the urge to open the door and push him back out of it. Instead, I rub the bridge of my nose before asking, "What kind of problem could you possibly have with her? You've met her, what, once?"

Loosening his already-lopsided tie, he says, "Until last night, yes. Then at one this morning, when Rose called me from the police department as her one phone call."

"She did what?" I ask, thinking I must have heard him wrong. I just saw her at the hospital the day before Lia was released and she seemed fine.

"You heard me. Apparently, her boyfriend has been cheating on her, and she's flipped her lid or something. The police said she took a shovel and smashed out all the windows in his car before..."

"No fucking way," I gasp, unable to comprehend Rose doing something so crazy. And Jake? I'd only been around him at dinner one night, but they seemed like a solid couple.

"It gets better, believe me. She used her .357 Magnum to shoot his tires out. I guess the shovel wasn't working too well on those."

"Holy shit," I mutter, unable to believe what he is saying. Lia's best friend is a fucking whack job. Seriously, what else today?

"You know when she slapped the guy at the hospital and you asked me to go and see what was going on?" When I nod, he continues. "Well, she said something about smelling perfume on him. I talked to her for a few moments and gave her my card in case he caused her any problems. I never thought I'd hear anything else from her. After she called, I went to the police station as a favor to Lia since it's her friend and fuck, it was like the Twilight Zone or something. There she sits, in—I kid you not—a white blouse, a pink cardigan, and a black skirt. She was wearing pearls, and she didn't have a hair out of place. I swear she looked more like a Stepford Wife than the card-carrying, concealed-gun-toting NRA gold member she is."

My shock gives way to amusement as I start laughing. I knew Rose had some spunk, but I never suspected she had that much. "She's a member of the NRA, as in National Rifle Association?" Surely, there was another meaning for that.

"Not just a member, a gold member, meaning she's a big supporter of the cause. She's no dummy, though; she refused to tell them anything until I got there. I knew a couple of the cops handling her case, and they were so fucking cracked up over the whole thing that they were willing to take a plea from her and just let her off with paying for the damages."

Shrugging, I say, "Well, that's good, right? I'm sorry she called you, but thanks for helping her out. I know Lia will be grateful." When he looks uncomfortable, shifting from one foot to the other, I ask, "That *was* the end of it, wasn't it?"

"Not exactly," he mutters. "I...gave her a lift home and when we got there, she...came on to me."

"Pardon?" I ask, thinking I must have heard him wrong.

"She climbed into my lap and kissed me while grabbing my...dick."

I motion him toward the living room and sink down into the chair behind me, wondering how many more crazy things I am going to hear. Rose was now some kind of horny Annie Oakley. "Jesus. Was she on something?"

"Hell yeah," Max retorted. "My cock."

Dropping my head back, I can't contain the laughter at his dry response. It's so freaking crazy it's funny. My usually unflappable lawyer looks completely bewildered at what occurred, and I am damn blown away myself. Maybe there was a full moon last night or something. "Please tell me you didn't fuck her in the car?"

"No!" he snaps, looking indignant. "I mean, it went further than it should have because her hands were just everywhere before I knew it. And damn, she's kind of scary, but beautiful."

"She got to you," I say in disbelief.

"No." He shakes his head. "No way. It was just a surprise."

"Come on." I point to where he is pacing in a circle, clenching his fists. "You wouldn't be here otherwise."

He drops down on the couch across from me, releasing a breath. "Yeah, holy Hell, she's something else. I didn't know whether to run for my life or propose."

"Trust me," I wince, "I know exactly where you're coming from." As we both sit there in silence staring off into space, I say, "Lee Jacks just left."

He expels a loud breath. "This day is just one big fucking mess, isn't it?" I agree as I get up and walk to the bar in the corner to fix us each a glass of bourbon. He takes a big gulp, grimacing at the sting. "All right, let's hear it."

CHAPTER SIX

Lee Jacks

I stride from Lucian Quinn's building, pausing as my driver opens the back door of the Rolls Royce Phantom idling quietly at the curb. My temples throb as I settle onto the buttery-soft leather interior. "So?" a voice asks.

I turn to face my right-hand man in both business and personal matters. My brother Peter sits waiting for the results of my meeting. "First off, fire Sears, now." The fact that I was not informed about Lia's hospitalization as well as her court appearance against her stepfather is inexcusable. I do not tolerate sloppy work; I pay too fucking well to accept something like that. Without asking questions, he calls the office and hands the order down. One of the reasons Peter and I have always worked well together is that we are able to communicate without an overabundance of words. He knows I don't make decisions lightly, and he doesn't second-guess any work-related decision I make. Hell, he's one of the few people in my life who doesn't seem terrified of me.

In our lives, it's always been Peter and me against the world. We were raised for our first ten years by a junkie mother who finally overdosed after years of doing just enough to keep us out of foster care. We never knew our father, and I suspect our mother didn't either. Although my mother wasn't physically abusive, the similarities of my childhood to Lia's are not lost on me. It makes me sick to my stomach to think of a child of mine going through what Quinn said she had. I had always been so careful to ensure I had no children. To me, that was a weakness I didn't want to risk. Peter, on the other hand, went in the complete opposite direction and wanted the American dream. He has a sweet and loving wife, two children, and a house in an exclusive, gated community where he sits on the homeowners' board.

He and I have come a long way from surviving on the streets and fending for ourselves. After our mother died, we lived in foster homes until we were sixteen. No one puts much effort into looking for runaways with no family ties. The day Victor Falco caught me stealing scraps from his restaurant kitchen was the day our lives changed forever. The man became the father I'd never had and would go on to show me how successful I could be when the lines between right and wrong were no longer a factor. I would spend years after Victor's death trying to keep my promise to Peter to leave the shadows I'd been operating in for far too long and return to a life where death or jail weren't constant dangers.

"Well?" Peter prompts me, breaking through my walk down memory lane. I know he's impatient for news of Lia. He had been just as shocked as I to learn that I might possibly have a daughter. I was afraid he had even let himself dream of my redemption at the hands of the child I hadn't known existed.

Before I speak, I take a bottle of water from the mini-fridge and gulp half of it. I tell our driver to take us to the office before raising the privacy glass. "It's completely fucked, Pete," I admit, defeated. Whatever I had been expecting from today, it had been nothing like the reality.

"You don't think Lia is your daughter?" he asks in surprise. We had both seen

Lia's photo that Sears had attached to the report. There had been little doubt in either of our minds as to who her father was from them. Of course, I had confirmed it via DNA testing from a brush and a toothbrush of all things from Lia's apartment. Luckily, there were plenty of papers in her room with her name on them; otherwise, we would have been testing her roommate's items, as well. At least Sears had managed to secure what was needed without fucking it up.

"Oh, I'm more certain than ever that she is. What I wasn't expecting was to find out that her mother had beat the hell out of her all her life and her stepfather had been touching her." At Peter's indrawn breath, I pause before adding, "And that she was just released from the hospital after her stepfather attempted to rape and kill her." I fill him in on everything Lucian had told me, leaving nothing out. Peter and I don't keep secrets from each other.

When Peter remains silent, I look over to see him sitting stock still, his face ashen. "Oh, no," he finally chokes out. "Dear God, not her." He looks physically sick as he drops his head into his hands. Peter and I had seen enough in our lives to never want someone of our own flesh and blood to be subject to something like that. Attempting to get himself back under control, he asks quietly, "What now?" He and I both know I cannot and will not let this go unpunished. Lia might not have a clue that I'm her father, but I will serve justice on her behalf.

"I want Jim Dawson found immediately."

Peter doesn't bother to talk about *what ifs*; he simply asks, "And when we do?"

I know my answer will stun him and it does. "I want to speak to him first, and then I want him handed over to the police."

"You're just turning him in?" Peter gapes at me. Maybe I should be insulted that my own brother automatically assumes I'm more likely to end someone's life than take the legal route, but I know that if this were his daughter, there would be no question of the outcome. "Why would you want for Lia to live her life worrying about him being released at some point?"

"He needs to suffer just as she has, Pete. I don't want the bastard to be let off that easy. He will sit behind bars and endure the same things he has subjected her to, only worse." When Peter opens his mouth to speak, I add, "And he'll never leave there."

"Lee, even you can't keep him from being granted parole when they deem his time is up. That's a big risk to take."

"I didn't say he'll never get parole; I said he'll never leave there." He looks at me for a moment, finally seeming to understand what I'm saying. A man like me has friends in every walk of life. Even though I'm an upstanding citizen now, I'm still owed debts by people who won't think twice about paying them. When I told Quinn that Jim Dawson would never touch her again, I had meant every word.

I drop Peter off at the office before giving my driver another address. When the car stops before a white house with peeling paint and tall grass, I wrinkle my nose in distaste. This area is the old mill village, which is now mostly home to lower-income families and some minor gangs. My usually silent driver looks over his shoulder, clearly confused. "Are you sure this is the correct address, Mr. Jacks? Maybe I misunderstood you."

"No, this is it, James," I say resigned. The anger I feel at Maria comes back tenfold as I think of my daughter living here at the mercy of her mother and stepfather. "Go somewhere and have lunch or coffee. I'll call you when I'm ready to be picked up." He nods once but still looks nervous. The whole thing would be damn funny if I had it in me to be amused right now. My driver has dropped me off in far more dangerous places than this, but he didn't have a clue. The only person in the vicinity who needs to be afraid is Maria. Her fucking miserable excuse for a life is going to change forever.

When James drives away, I walk up the overgrown pathway and onto the porch. The boards are loose, and I think fleetingly that I'll probably kill someone if I finish this day off by falling through one of them. Opening a screen door that is louder than a gunshot, I rap loudly at the door. I am just at the point of knocking again when the door is opened a crack with a security chain in place. A hostile voice snaps, "I don't have anything else to say to you people. I already told you he isn't here. Now leave me the fuck alone!" When the door starts to close, I stick my foot in the crack, holding it open. Indignant curses fill the air.

"You either open the door, Maria, or I break it down. One way or another, I'm coming in...now." There is dead silence for what seems like minutes but is probably only seconds.

"Who are you?" she rasps out, sounding shaken.

Letting out a laugh completely devoid of humor, I say, "I think you know. Now, open the door. It seems you and I have some unfinished business." I don't know who is more surprised when she actually does as I ask. She looks like she's on autopilot when the door swings open and she steps stiffly back. "Lee?"

I'm only mildly surprised she still recognizes me. Other than a few more lines, I still look much the same as I did when I first met her. Unfortunately for her, she barely resembles the girl I once knew; I doubt I would have recognized her on the street had I walked past her. She is thin, pale, and frail looking. Her beautiful blonde hair, which had easily been her best feature, is gone, and now dark hair hangs limply down her back. She looks like someone who has long used and abused drugs. If I didn't know what I do, I would pity her. Once she had been a beauty. I had been completely taken with her for months before Victor had wanted me to oversee one of his business ventures in South Carolina. I had even pondered taking her with me, but where I was going was no place for a woman, and Victor wanted my head in the game. Therefore, I had broken things off and moved on. There had been no room in my life then for a long-term relationship, and it would have ended eventually. When she starts smoothing her hair self-consciously, I want to tell her not to fucking bother. If she were the most attractive woman on Earth, she would still be ugly to me now. I would look more kindly upon a whore than her. I now know her for the monster she truly is. In answer to her question, I simply say, "Maria."

"Wh-What are you doing here?" she stutters over the words. She looks around the room as if searching for an escape route. Maybe she isn't as stupid as I had thought. She looks scared of me, which gives me a perverse feeling of pleasure. Seeing anything close to the desire that used to fill her eyes when we were together, would make me physically ill. I reach back to close the door behind me, wondering if she also thinks the sound of it shutting seems unusually loud.

Turning back to face her, I put my hands in the pockets of my suit pants, rocking on my heels. "Ask yourself, Maria," I begin idly as if I'm discussing the weather, "what possible reason could I have for seeking you out after all these years?"

She knows; I can see it in the widening of her eyes and sudden paling of her face. Her back stiffens as if preparing to ward off a blow. "I...um, have no clue. We don't have anything to say to each other. Just...get out." Her voice wavers on her last words. To someone trained from an early age to detect deceit, she might as well be holding up a guilty sign. From the moment she looked me in the eyes, I could see the truth. If I had any doubt that I was Lia's father, Maria's actions in the last few minutes would have given me the answer I needed.

Still not raising my voice, I walk farther into the rundown house, masking the distaste I feel at the shabby, soiled furniture in what I assume is the living room right off the foyer. "It's a little late to play dumb, Maria. It will only serve to anger me further, if that is even possible."

After a moment of silence, she pleads, "Lee...I didn't know. I mean, I named her after you because I loved you so much, but I slept with other people after you left me. I never had her tested and—"

"Stop," I say quietly, barely holding onto my temper. When she ignores my demand, continuing to rattle off excuses, I snap. I reach her in two strides, wrapping my hand around her throat and lifting her off her feet. "You fucking cunt, don't you dare continue to lie to me! Even if you *did* screw others after me, which I certainly believe, you knew the moment she was born. Her face is the mirror image of mine! Admit it, that's why you named her Lia, because you fucking knew!" Her hands are clawing at mine, trying to loosen my grip on her windpipe. In that moment, I would love to be the type of man to crush a woman. For the pain she has caused my daughter, she doesn't deserve to draw another breath. I could end her right now, and she would never be found. I want to; God, I want to so bad. I tighten my hand in disgust one more time before dropping her to the floor where she crumbles. "You deserve to die for what you've done. You allowed and encouraged your twisted fuck of a husband to lay his hands on her, to touch her. You betrayed her as a mother and as a human being at every corner."

"No," she croaks out, trying to protest. She doesn't bother attempting to get to her feet. Instead, she cowers at mine as if seeking mercy.

"Lie to me again, and it'll be the last thing you ever do," I warn her, tired of her denial when we both know the truth.

She begins sobbing, curling into a ball. I look down at the woman I once cared for and feel nothing but hate and revulsion. How can I possibly still be shocked by the evil that lives within some people after seeing so much in my life? A woman who doesn't care for her child, though, is the dregs of society; my own mother had instilled that in me long ago. "I'm sorry," she cries repeatedly.

I walk away in disgust, looking out the dirty window that faces the street until I've regained control. "Quiet!" I snap, and her sobs stop as suddenly as they had started. No doubt another ploy to deceive me. "Someone will come back within the hour to pick you up and take you to the police station. You will have a chance for one tiny scrap of redemption by going to the police today and recanting your earlier testimony about Lia and your husband. You will corroborate every word Lia said in that courtroom and also add any relevant testimony of your own concerning your time with Jim Dawson."

"Bu...But, they'll lock me up for lying on the stand," she protests, shaking her head.

Kneeling, I take her chin in a grasp that is filled with barely restrained fury. "And I give a fuck about what happens to you about as much as you gave a fuck about my daughter. You'll give your statement, and you had better not miss a single fucking detail. I'll have someone privy to every word you say, so you can rest assured I'll know if you try to screw me over. When and *if* they release you,

you'll be relocated permanently. You will never return to North Carolina, or to any of the states surrounding it. If you do, I'll end you. Don't mistake my leniency for kindness. You're the mother of my child no matter how pathetic you have been at the job."

"Why can't I just leave now?" she pleads. "The police aren't going to believe me."

I shake my head in wonder. "Still the same selfish bitch to the bitter end, aren't you? Just when I think you can't possibly fall further in my eyes, you manage to prove me wrong. I've known the worst scum of the Earth, and yet somehow you make them look like pillars of the community. You really would not lift one hand willingly to help your daughter, would you?" For a moment, I think I see a small flicker of shame flit across her face, but it's gone so fast I'm not sure if it was ever there. Still holding her face, I carefully enunciate each word. "YOU WILL DO AS I SAY OR WHAT THE POLICE MAY DO TO YOU WILL PALE IN COMPARISION TO WHAT I'M CAPABLE OF." I give her a moment for my words to sink in before shaking her chin and asking, "Now, have I been completely clear with you?"

"Yes," she whispers as what looks like the first genuine tear she's shed since I've been here slips down her cheek. I drop my hold on her, feeling the need to wash my hands.

I take out my phone, calling Peter and arranging for him to come immediately. While we're waiting for him, I take a chair from the kitchen and sit next to where she is now lying on the floor, slumped with defeat. Looking at my watch, I'm irritated to realize that so much of my afternoon has been wasted here dealing with someone I've come to loathe almost overnight. "Now, Maria, I need to know one last thing. Where is your husband?" The smile I give her seems to chill her to her very bones.

CHAPTER SEVEN

Lia

I've been home from the hospital for a week now, and it's been chock-full of surprises. On my second day, we were notified my mother had turned herself in to the police for lying under oath, child abuse, and child endangerment. She could also be charged as an accessory in my attack if it's proven she had knowledge of it. I am still in shock over the whole thing. What could have possibly brought about this sudden change of heart? Actually, the heart has nothing to do with it, because she doesn't have one; she never has.

Detective Michaels had dropped by to tell us the news in person. After she was gone, Lucian had pulled me into his arms and held me as if I were made of spun glass. He's been so restless and edgy since we returned home from the hospital that I was hopeful the news of my mother's confession would bring him some relief. Lucian is a man almost constantly in motion, and I'm afraid this inactivity is starting to get to him. I've tried to talk him into returning to his office, at least for a half of a day. His new habit of pacing is beginning to drive me crazy.

He is in his office on a conference call when the doorbell sounds. Rose told me earlier that she was stopping by today, so I assume it's her. A quick look through the peephole confirms it. I unlock the door, swinging it open to smile at my best friend. "Oh, my God," she squeals as she pulls me into her arms. "You look so much better, chick! I mean, not that you looked bad before..." We both look at each other before bursting into laughter. "Yeah, you looked like Hell warmed over."

I pull the cardigan I'm wearing over my T-shirt and yoga pants closer around my body and motion her to the leather couch in the living room. The bruises on my face have started to fade some and now are more of a molten purple color than black. My face is freshly scrubbed and devoid of makeup and my hair is up and tied with one of the ponytail holders Lucian bought for me. I think he was secretly afraid I would use more of his designer underwear to make my own. After we're settled side-by-side with our feet tucked under us, I say, "It's so good to see you. I'm sorry I missed you the last time you were here. Lucian was determined that I sleep around the clock for the first few days after being released from the hospital." I don't add that I really haven't wanted to see anyone. Here in this apartment, staring at the walls, I don't have to pretend to be okay. Well...maybe when Lucian is with me, but even then, I don't put a lot of effort into it. I just need time to deal with what happened to me in my own way, away from prying eyes that see too much.

"That's okay; I got to stare at your hot boyfriend for a few minutes at least," she jokes. Then she adds, "At least he's not a complete cheating asshole like mine."

My mouth drops open at her statement. Is she talking about Jake? I look at her carefully, thinking maybe she's joking, but by the way she's twisting her hands together, I don't think she is. "Rose, what's going on?" She lays her head back wearily against the couch.

"I shouldn't have said that. The last thing you need is to hear about my problems. Just forget I mentioned it."

I'm already shaking my head before she finishes speaking. "Oh, no, you don't. You can't drop something like that on me and then clam up. And trust me; I'd rather focus on anything other than myself right now, so spill."

She groans loudly before turning to look at me. "Jake's been cheating on me. I started suspecting something a few weeks ago when things just didn't add up. Suddenly he would forget to call me or show up late for our dates. He was going off the grid for long stretches of time with no real explanation for where he'd been. Then there was the perfume I smelled on him, and when I asked him about it, he actually had the nerve to get angry with me for questioning him. So...I followed him one night when he said he was studying with the guys. He went to a house I didn't know and locked lips with some skank right in the doorway."

"NO!" I interrupt, unable to contain my amazement. Oh, my God, Jake cheating on Rose? They were like a super-couple. Together forever and sure to marry in the near future. They always seemed perfect for each other. They were one of the few things in my life I thought of as a constant. "Oh, Rose, surely there is some explanation. Maybe she's just a friend."

"Hmph, you don't stick your tongue all over a friend's tonsils while grabbing her ass."

"Wow," I say, still shocked. "I can't believe that. Did you confront him?"

Fidgeting in her seat, she smirked, "Well, kinda..."

"Uh-oh." I know that look well. Rose has done something evil; I can always tell.

"I might have waited until they went in her house and took out my heartache on his car...and possibly got arrested."

She tagged the last part on so fast I almost missed it. "Wait, what?" I ask as my mouth falls open. Rose, smut-mouthed but law-abiding Rose.

"Yeah," she says while shaking her head. "I guess the gunshots woke the neighborhood and my shouting match with Jake when he came flying out of the whore-bag's house probably didn't help much."

"Holy crap, gunshots?" I know my eyes are bugging out of my head, which no doubt makes my battered face look even more unsightly than it already does.

Rose shrugs her shoulders. "I got a little excited and took my emergency shovel out of the boot of my car and knocked his windows out, but I wasn't strong enough to puncture his tires with it, so I had to use my gun." She looks so matter-of-fact that I feel like I'm overreacting for a moment before I shake it off. Hell, no I'm not!

"Oh, my God! Are you crazy? And what are you doing with a gun and a shovel in your car?"

Sounding perfectly reasonable, she says, "You know how much it snows around here in the wintertime. Sometimes, you need a shovel to navigate sidewalks or parking lots. As for the gun, I've had one for years. My daddy is a firm believer in protecting yourself. I've been able to hit a bull's-eye in target practice every time since I was eight." Cocking her finger, she points at me, adding, "Honey, if you're ever in a gunfight, you are going to hope and pray I'm on your side."

"Who are you, and where is my Martha Stewart best friend?" I ask, still flabbergasted. *Do I know this girl at all?*

Rose starts giggling, clutching her sides as she rolls around on the couch. "I'm still your Martha, bitch, but I'm also your Dirty Harry. Thanks to Mama and Daddy demanding equal time, I can bake and shoot with the best of them."

I laugh with her for what seems like the first time in years. I've had nothing to laugh about lately, and my voice sounds rough as if it hasn't been used nearly

enough. Before I can catch my breath,
Lucian comes into the room at a fast clip,
looking startled by the scene in front of
him. The male fantasy of two girls lying
all over each other is probably a little
skewed for him as he takes in me
slumped over a reclining Rose as we both
hold our sides and howl with laughter. I
don't know what's so funny anymore, but
I can't seem to stop the flow. He pauses
next to my head and as I stare up at him,
I only laugh harder. He looks adorably
confused, but I also see the glimmer of a
smile at the corners of his mouth. He's
been so serious and uptight the last few
days that it pulls at something deep
inside me to see him relax if even for a
moment.

"What's so funny, ladies?" he asks
when our laughter finally dies down to
something more like hiccups.

"Just talking to my friend Martha
Harry here," I say with almost a straight
face. Beside me, Rose giggles while
Lucian looks between us as if trying to
solve a puzzle. In a move that surprises
me, he lowers a hand to my face, gently
tracing my smiling lips before cupping my
cheek.

"I'm almost afraid to know what that
means, but if it puts this smile on your
face, I don't care. I'm even going to brave

it and ask." He lifts a brow in inquiry to Rose.

She raises a brow right at him, saying, "I'm pretty sure you already know."

"You do?" I frown, wondering why I'm the last to know about my best friend's crazy antics.

Lucian looks confused for a moment before saying, "Ah, maybe I do, Annie Oakley." He gives me a look of apology. "Sorry, baby; Max asked me not to tell anyone. He didn't want to betray Rose's legal rights."

Completely puzzled by his statement, I ask, "What does Max have to do with it?"

Rose speaks up before Lucian can, looking a bit embarrassed. "I had to call him to get me out of jail. Although my daddy would have probably been proud to come get me, they were out of town and I would have been forced to stay in jail until they could get there."

I barely know Max, so I'm not sure when Rose could have become acquainted with him. "Oh, did you call Luc?"

"Er...no," she answers. "I kind of met him while you were in the hospital. Jake and I got into a small argument, and he came over to check on me. He gave me his card in case I had any other problems and I stuck it in my purse. When I was arrested, I remembered it and made him my one phone call. He's pretty hot, too, so I thought it was a good opportunity to get to know him better."

Lucian seems totally bemused by her explanation. He drops down onto the couch, tucking me under his arm almost absently before looking at her. "You thought having him bail you out of jail was a good way to take the next step with him? Did you ever stop to think that it might not make the best impression?"

"Nah," she winks, "when there's a spark between two people, the circumstances you meet under don't matter. I felt it that first day at the hospital, but I was too upset to act on it. When I saw him again at the police station, the spark was more like a raging inferno, and this time I didn't miss the opportunity to explore it further."

"So I heard," Lucian muttered under his breath, causing me to jerk around to stare at him.

Exasperated, I huff out, "All right, what else have I missed here?" I can't believe he has kept all this from me. Attorney-client privilege be damned—this is my best friend and frankly a freaking juicy tale, which no one has shared with me. I want to pitch a childish tantrum right here between them.

Lucian looks at Rose to fill me in. I cross my arms, giving her my best, 'you better start talking now' look. She takes what seems like an unusually long amount of time to get comfortable before finally answering my questions. "Well, after Max got me out of the whole mess with just a slap on the wrist and a minor dent in my bank account, I asked him to take me home. The police had impounded my car, and I couldn't get it until the lot opened later on. So, when we reached the apartment, I wanted to leave him with a little parting gift to think about." She wiggles her eyebrows suggestively. A quick glance at Lucian shows he looks both fascinated and leery. I'm surprised he hasn't bolted yet, but I guess it's hard for a guy to turn down a sex story.

"What kind of parting gift are we talking here?" I ask warily, not sure if I want to know. I just can't imagine the normally suave and composed Max Decker having car sex with someone he barely knows. It seems so...beneath him somehow.

"Oh, just a little slip of the tongue and hand here and there. I have to say, he sure hides a big..."

Lucian jumps to his feet, looking a bit harried. "I think I need to go now." He looks down at me as if he's not sure he wants me to stay, either. Hearing my best friend tell me about the size of his friend and lawyer's penis is probably not something he relishes. In the end, though, he decides to retreat after he says over his shoulder, "Call me if you need me, baby."

Rose starts laughing as he leaves just as quickly as he had arrived. I elbow her, hardly able to believe Lucian had been just a bit embarrassed when he left. That's something that doesn't happen to him often, I'm betting. "That man is just too fucking sexy, and the way he dotes on you is out-of-this-world adorable. If I didn't love you, girl, I'd hate your freaking guts for having a boyfriend that fine."

"Stop trying to change the subject." I secretly agree that Lucian is everything she says, but I'm beyond curious as to what has transpired between her and Max. "I'm still waiting to hear what happened."

"Well," she purrs as she licks her lips dramatically. "When he put the car in park, I climbed from my seat and into his lap."

"No, you didn't!" I hiss, unable to believe it. I mean, I know she talks about sex like a sailor sometimes, but she knits, for God's sake. That just seems like such a contradiction.

"Oh, yeah, I did. I crawled him like the tall tree he is and kissed him until neither of us could breathe."

"Did he…kiss you back?" I quickly look to where Lucian disappeared just to make sure he isn't somewhere listening. I want details, but I don't want to sound like a complete pervert.

"It took a few seconds, because I think he was in shock. But he caught on fast." Fanning herself, she continued. "That man knows how to use his tongue. I thought I was a good kisser, but he made me feel like a virgin. He was just everywhere. It was the hottest fucking kiss of my life. My panties were totally in danger of melting from the heat he generated."

"Shut up," I whisper, even though I don't mean it. I want to hear the rest, and if she stops, I'll pop her.

"Oh, no, it's all true. I know he felt the same way because he was so hard and I'm not just saying that. I felt him against me and then I slid my hand in his pants and wrapped it around him. At least I tried to. The man is huge. I shit you not; my fingers didn't come close to meeting." I think briefly of Lucian and how well-endowed he is. I can't imagine that Max could compete with him in that area, but I decide to keep that to myself. The last thing I want is for him to come back and find Rose and me discussing his penis size.

"So, did you?" I ask, unable to resist finding out if they went all the way in his car.

Rose rolls her lip out, pouting for a moment before grinning again. "Nope, he finally called a halt, but I wasn't going to let it go much farther. I wanted him to know what it would be like between us, and by that point, he got the big picture, believe me. I pulled my skirt back down, climbed off him, and walked away without a second glance. Max might not know it yet, but that was my way of saying 'game on.' Now, I'll just give him a couple of days before I make my next move."

"But...what about Jake? Aren't you in love with him?" I hate to be the voice of reason, but how can she move on so quickly? I would be lying in a sobbing ball somewhere if Lucian had done that to me. I almost panic at the very thought of it, which is more than a little unsettling. He has become my world in the months we've been together, and it scares me that I can't imagine my life without him.

For just a moment, I see a crack in her happy veneer before it's quickly gone. "I'm a realist, chick. I have to brush myself off and move on. I'll make him sorry and then I will forget him. I won't allow him to screw me over and ruin my life." When she straightens her demure outfit, I feel a touch of awe. How can she seem so calm and collected after what's happened to her? As always, she looks ready to attend a society gathering, but as I glance down at her purse lying on the table in front of us, I wonder if there is a gun inside. My friend is a badass in disguise; I still can't wrap my mind around it.

Suddenly, my brain rolls backwards to something she just said. "Whoa, wait. What do you mean you'll 'make him sorry'? Are you talking about what you did to him already?"

Oh, no, she's checking her nails and looking evasive. "Sure, of course…"

"Rose…" I say, trying to get her to look at me, but she jumps up from her place on the couch and grabs her purse.

"I've got to run, chick. Dinner with the parents. Daddy wants to hear all about my arrest."

"Oh, crap, are you in trouble?" I ask, concerned for my friend.

She rolls her eyes at my question, seeming to think it's absurd. "Hell, no. He's probably told everyone he knows by now. Daddy's a firm believer in jail yard justice. I mean, don't get me wrong; he wouldn't tolerate me being some random brawler, but he wants me to defend myself. If someone wrongs me then I should retaliate—within reason, of course."

"By 'within reason,' you mean?" I ask, needing some clarification. Her daddy sounds a little crazy to me, but it's not as if I have any room at all to throw stones.

She drapes her purse strap over her shoulder and starts walking toward the door. "No killing anyone," she answers over her shoulder before giving me a backwards wave. "Talk soon, muah!" With those words, she strolls out the door, looking as freshly put-together as usual. Just thinking of how...clean she looks makes my skin crawl. No matter how hard I try, I haven't been able to feel that way since my attack. I have showered so many times since I got home from the hospital that Lucian had started to ask questions. I try to do it while he's occupied in his office. I don't want him to think I'm crazy, but I need just the brief respite, which comes from scrubbing myself.

I walk down the hallway toward his office and hear his voice. *Good, he's on the phone.* I quickly make my way to the bedroom and straight into the bathroom. I wrap my hand in plastic to keep the cast on my wrist dry and turn the water on as hot as I can tolerate. I've stopped wearing most of the other bandages, as my cuts have healed enough to do without them. I quickly remove my clothes, turning to avoid seeing my reflection in the mirror, and take a fresh loofah from the bathroom cabinet. The rough texture gives me hope that eventually I'll be able to scrub away the feel of him on my skin. My stomach churns at the very thought, and I quickly jump under the scalding water.

Again and again, I add liquid soap to the loofah and scrub my body. I work the hardest on my stomach, breasts, and the area between my thighs. Those places never seem to be free of the filth I feel crawling back almost immediately. I have no idea how long I've been in the shower, but as I start to sway, weak from the hot water and exhaustion, I realize I'm sobbing almost hysterically. When I look down, I see blood on my hands and on the sponge. A scream rips from my throat as the door is thrown open and Lucian stands there looking terrified.

"Lia!" he yells frantically. "What's wrong?" He looks around the room, as if expecting to see someone else here with us. I'm still in a daze at the sight of the blood...the red against my hands is mesmerizing and it's hard for me to look away. His voice has lowered considerably when he says, "Baby, fuck, what have you done to yourself?"

I'm so confused by his question that I look to him in inquiry before following his eyes back to my body. I sway on my feet as I really see what he's looking at. The loofah has dug deep, breaking the skin in what looks like more than one place. My stomach seems to have gotten the worst of it with me possibly breaking open some of the healing cuts there. My thighs and breasts both look bright red and are starting to throb. The most alarming thing is that I don't remember rubbing hard enough to do that kind of damage, nor did I feel the pain I should have felt. I don't want him to see me like this. He's going to know now that I'm not as okay as I've been pretending to be. There is no way to explain away what I've done to myself. For some reason, all I can do is apologize. "I'm sorry, Luc. I'm sorry," I repeat again and again as he looks just as broken as I feel.

"Stop, baby," he whispers shakily as he reaches one hand out to brace me and uses the other to turn the water off. The bathroom is filled with so much steam it's hard to breathe. I drop the loofah from my hand, unable to bear the sight of my blood on it.

"I just wanted to get clean," I try to explain. "I don't know why I can never get it off me."

He flinches at my words, looking like he's taken a hit. Without commenting, he picks me up and lifts me from the shower. He manages to grab a towel from the closet and wrap it around me before walking into the bedroom. The air feels frigid after the heat of the bathroom making me shiver. With little regard for the expensive bedding, he lays me gently on the sheets before pulling the comforter over me. I want to protest because I know I'm not only getting water but blood, as well, all over the expensive linens. He drops a quick kiss on my forehead, looking just as shaky as I feel. "Hang tight, baby; I'm going to grab the first aid kit." For some reason, I have the insane urge to laugh. Where would I possibly go right now? I'm a wreck in more ways than one. Thankfully, I'm able to control myself, because he would probably think me completely insane after what he just

walked in on if I were to start laughing
hysterically.

He returns with a white box, setting it
on the nightstand before sitting next to
me. When he pulls the comforter back, I
freeze, not wanting him to see the
ugliness that has become so much a part
of me, both inside and out. Some of what
I'm feeling must show on my face because
he stops. "I hate for you to see me this
way," I whisper as I feel the tears rising
to choke me once again. When will they
ever stop? I don't understand my sudden
descent into this kind of despair. My
stepfather has abused and touched me
before. Yes, it was worse this time, but
still, why can't I get past it enough to
function? I have someone who cares about
me; someone who I know would kill to
protect me. I'm alive, I wasn't raped, and
I'm home with the man I love. Why can't I
crawl out of this horrible shell of self-pity
and take my life back?

Lucian drops the comforter back into
place, moving to take my head between
his hands. "Lia, you're beautiful to me, no
matter what. When I see the marks on
your body, all I think of is how strong you
are and how many battles you've fought
in your life. Most people would have given
in to their circumstances years ago, but
you've persevered. I hurt when you hurt,

baby, but I never, not for one moment, see anything but the woman who brings me to my knees with her courage." His lips settle on mine in something more than a brief peck for the first time since my attack. He possesses my mouth in a way that leaves little question as to whether he still wants me. As our tongues tangle, I feel a flicker of life which I was afraid was lost forever. Somewhere deep inside, I was terrified he would never want me again as he had before. If this kiss is any indication, though, those fears are unfounded. When he finally pulls back, his eyes are heavily-lidded with desire and his breathing is rough.

Words of love are on the tip of my tongue. I love this man so much it's a physical ache in my soul, but I can't bear to have him pull away from me today, so I leave the words hanging between us once again. It needs to continue to be enough right now that he cares for me. Doesn't he show me that every day? Never breaking eye contact, I pull the cover from my body, exposing my injuries to him. I see the distress he's unable to hide as he looks at what I've done to myself. As he takes an alcohol wipe and starts cleaning my new injuries, I say quietly, "I didn't mean to do it, Luc. Since...I haven't been able to wash it all away. I keep trying, but I still feel his hands on me."

Lucian inhales sharply, looking crushed at my admission. "Why haven't you talked to me, baby? You've every right to feel what you're feeling, but you keep saying you're okay. I knew…with all of the showers, that something was going on. I've been standing outside the door until I hear you get out, but this time, I heard you crying. You don't have to hide anything from me, Lia. I'm here. Let me help you deal with what you're going through."

"I want to," I admit huskily. "But…I'm afraid you won't want me anymore if you see how weak I am right now. You might think I'm strong, but I'm scared of my own shadow. I'm afraid that I'll never be me again and we'll never be us."

His hands still as he gapes at me. "Oh, baby, I can't believe the thought of me not wanting you would even enter your mind. I feel like a sick bastard because I want you so fucking much every time we're together that it keeps me tied up in knots." He takes my uninjured hand and puts it on his crotch. My eyes widen as I feel him hard and throbbing against my palm. With a rueful smile, he releases my hand. "Yeah, that's how much I don't want you. I know it's fucked, but my cock

wants you immediately when you're near.
As soon as you're healed and ready, I'll be
inside you again where I belong."

Lucian's words help to relax me a little
as he continues to tend to my old and new
wounds. I want nothing more than to
believe nothing has changed in that area
of our relationship. From the moment we
met, the air has literally crackled with
the desire we feel for each other. I was too
inexperienced to even realize and
understand a lot of it at first, but I knew
that I'd never felt anything even close to
what I felt when he was near. After we
had had sex, the feelings only
strengthened. When we weren't together,
I was in a constant state of slow burn for
him. Even with my thoughts and
emotions all over the place now, I still feel
the hum of electricity between us.

He has been so distracted and restless.
I think we both desperately need to
return to some semblance of our former
routine, but I don't know how. Thus far,
I've avoided leaving the apartment. The
few times Lucian has mentioned it, I've
felt myself shutting down. I've begun to
feel terribly guilty, though, over the last
few days. I've watched him seeming to
struggle with something, and I have to
believe it's my situation and his inability
to make things better overnight. Lucian

is a man of action and unfortunately for both of us, there doesn't seem to be a miracle cure for me mentally. Physically, my body is healing, and each day I see the evidence of my attack lessen. Well, at least it had been until my freak-out in the shower moments ago.

Rose had asked me earlier when I planned to register for my last quarter of school. I need to check on the test scores of my final exams and meet with my financial counselor. Now, though, I can't stand the thoughts of going back on campus at least until my stepfather is behind bars. Lucian seems to think that is imminent, but I don't have his confidence. Of course, I never would have imagined my mother turning herself in, either. Lucian didn't seem surprised at all, which is even more puzzling. Apparently, he has more faith in humankind than I do. When I feel my hand being shaken, I look up, realizing I've completely zoned out while he applied my new bandages. "Sorry, baby," I murmur absently, noting as I always do his pleasure when I use that word. Although Lucian addresses me in that manner often, I feel shy about doing the same. Maybe some part of me has never been able to believe I'm entitled to use words such as those with a man like Lucian Quinn.

"No worries," he assures me as he sits back to study my face. "Better now?"

I nod shyly, feeling the urge to drag the covers up over my head. I can't help but think that he's wondering when the woman from a few weeks prior will return. I only hope for my sake, as well as his, that it won't be long. With that in mind, I find myself saying something I wish instantly that I could take back. "Would you...like to walk to Leo's for dinner?" I feel even worse when Lucian lights up like a kid at Christmas. I may have underestimated how difficult it's been for him to stay cooped up in the apartment. I want to panic as the words are hanging between us, but the look of relief on his face keeps me silent. If he needs this, I'll do it no matter how hard it is for me.

His voice is carefully blank, as if he doesn't want to pressure me, when he asks, "Would *you* like to?"

No, no, no! I'm screaming inside as I say, "Sure, I think it would be nice. Unless you'd rather not?" Shit, I hope my voice doesn't sound hopeful at that question. I started this and now I need to see it through.

"No, I'd love to. I believe getting out for a bit would do us both some good. Do you need help getting ready?" I think of the yoga pants I've been wearing daily and guess this is his way of assuming—or hoping—that I plan to leave my present wardrobe mainstay behind, at least for dinner.

"No, I can manage." He drops a light kiss on the top of my head and leaves the room with more spring in his step than I've seen lately. I wait until he's completely out of view before pulling myself slowly from the bed. I ache from a combination of my injuries and my lack of recent activity. Lying around has caused my body and my mood both to be sluggish. Even though it scares the hell out of me, I need to get out of this apartment just as badly as Lucian apparently does.

I step into the walk-in closet which now contains all of my clothing, thanks to Lucian sending Sam to pick it up, and look through the hangers until I find a maxi-dress that flows to my ankles. I add a scarf and black cardigan to hide the worst of my remaining bruises and slip my feet into a pair of black ballet flats. In the bathroom, I take the ponytail holder from my hair, letting it fall around my shoulders. I quickly brush it and add some lip-gloss. There is no use in adding further makeup with the ugly bandage on my nose. Lucian's aunt has said I should be able to remove it soon. I have an appointment with Lucian's personal physician next week.

He walks into the bathroom, looking gorgeous in a pair of dark jeans and a black button-down shirt. "Ready?" he asks before pulling me into his arms and holding me against his muscular chest. He has no idea how much I need what he is giving me right now. He has treated me more like his sister since we've been home until today. Feeling his arms around me for more than just a brief hug is Heaven. I know he has been afraid of hurting me, but I've missed this between us. He has taken to holding my hand at night when we go to sleep, and I wake almost every morning to find him already gone from the bed. I am starting to realize now that maybe he has just been trying to follow my lead. I've given him little reason to believe I want more from him, that I need more from him than ever before. While I've been trying to deal with the mess in my head, I've pushed him away. I know in my very bones that I couldn't make it through all that has happened to me without him, and it's time I tried to let him see that. I know I can't bounce back to normal overnight, but he needs to know I need him.

I draw back slightly and he automatically loosens his hold, thinking I'm pulling away. Instead, I go up onto my tiptoes and press my lips to his. His arms tighten, and he groans. The kiss is gentle and I pour all the love I feel for him into it. When our lips finally part, he lays his forehead against mine. "I've missed you," I admit, trying to convey so much into so few words.

He looks into my eyes as if he can see directly into my soul before saying, "I'm here, baby. I never left. I'm right here waiting for you whenever you're ready to come back to me."

Then it happens. The words flow from my mouth and my heart before I can stop them. "Oh, Luc, I love you." His eyes widen and I feel him catch his breath. Even as the words hover in the air between us, I don't regret them. The need to tell him how I feel has been choking me. The thing that surprises me the most about the moment, though, is that he hasn't pulled away. He is still looking at me, as if trying to gauge the truth behind my words. I wordlessly cup the side of his face in my hand, letting him know it's okay that he can't say the words back. When I began to pull away, thinking it will be easier for him if I do, he tightens his hold on me before moving his hands from my back and curving them around my neck, holding me immobile.

"I want to give that to you, baby, I really do." Looking tormented, he says raggedly, "I lose the people I love, though, and I...God, I can't lose you, too."

"Luc," I whisper brokenly as I choke back a sob. "You won't lose me," I try to reassure him. It's obvious from the rigid set of his jaw and the shadows in his eyes that my attack has been harder on him than I imagined. Even though I was the one hurt physically, we both bear the scars of the last few weeks. I turn my head and kiss the side of his arm. "I'm not going anywhere. I'm right here."

He shudders, seeming as emotionally invested in our conversation as I am. "Just give me time, Lia, and know that when I can say the words again, it will be you and only you who will hear them. I'm not going anywhere, either. I'm committed to you." We kiss tenderly for a few moments before he finally releases my neck and takes my hand. My stomach growls loudly in the quiet room, making it impossible to miss. Lucian smirks at me, raising both of our hands to kiss my fingers. "Let's find my girl some food," he teases, looking so impossibly relaxed and handsome. I feel a twinge of desire inside which takes me by surprise. I was afraid I would never enjoy that simple pleasure again, but I should have known that no amount of ugliness could ever take away my body's reaction to him. I didn't truly start living until I met him, and my heart and body will always respond when he is near because he owns them both.

CHAPTER EIGHT

Lucian

I walk down the familiar streets of my neighborhood feeling lighter than I have since before Lia's attack. Just doing something so normal feels better than I could have imagined. Lia is tucked under my arm while I twirl a strand of her blonde hair around my finger. I could tell earlier when she suggested having dinner out tonight that she regretted it almost as soon as she spoke the words. She has shown no interest in leaving the apartment since we arrived home from the hospital. She's spent the majority of her time either in the bed, or curled up on the couch pretending to watch television while she actually stares off into space.

When I admitted as much to my aunt, she again suggested counseling and possibly medication. It's not that I'm opposed to either in principle, but I remember well that neither seemed to help Cassie through her erratic years of highs and lows.

When I found her in the shower earlier with blood on her hands and stomach, I was hit with a crippling sense of déjà vu. Spots danced before my eyes and I was damn close to a panic attack at the very least and having a fucking heart attack at the worst. Thank Heaven I had been able to get myself together and take care of her. For just a split second, I'd thought she had cut her wrists or something equally as bad.

I'd almost called my aunt then, feeling lost as to how to help the woman who had become my world. Losing her would shatter me, and this time, I don't think I could put myself back together again.

While I was quietly panicking and trying to keep my mind occupied with taking care of her, though, something happened which maybe we both had been needing. We talked to each other for the first time in days. She told me how she had been feeling since her attack, and I listened in shock as she gave voice to her fears that I no longer wanted her physically.

I wanted to slump over in relief because I had been experiencing the same fear—that Lia no longer wanted what we had had before her stepfather got his vile hands on her. Our talk had continued before we left for dinner when Lia had admitted she loves me. A part of me wanted to run when the words left her mouth. But the other part had needed to hear them again, since the first time she said them in the hospital and I hadn't been sure she even knew it because of the medication she was on. If I were honest with myself, my heart had soaked up her declaration like a flower seeing the sun for the first time in years. I was afraid, though, to give those three words back to her. I'm afraid to move forward and terrified of losing her if I don't.

The past and all of the secrets festering there are getting to be too much to bear. I cracked yesterday morning and snorted a line of my white powder of denial. I was coming apart at the seams over everything that had happened to Lia, my fear of losing her, and pressure from Lee Jacks wanting to talk to his daughter. The daughter who had no clue he existed. I had given up the smoking, as it didn't seem to help that much, and Lia had begun asking too many questions about why I reeked of smoke constantly.

Lee Jacks. Shit, the other man might be piling on the pressure to meet his daughter, but I can't fault his dedication to avenging her years of abuse. How he had managed to get her bitch of a mother to turn herself in and admit to everything under the sun was a mystery to me. Judging by the rumors that circulated about Jacks, maybe I was even a tad surprised that she hadn't just disappeared. Lee had also assured me that Jim Dawson would soon be in police custody to answer for his list of crimes, which was somewhat disappointing to me. No matter how much I enjoyed thinking of him rotting away in a cell with others hopefully torturing him just as he had Lia, I still would have preferred a world in which he didn't exist at all. I had to believe that Lee was thinking of some bigger picture here. I couldn't imagine that he would let Dawson off that easily if he had any say in the matter whatsoever. I was trusting him to have a plan that both he and I could live with.

Suddenly, I stumble, looking up in alarm when I realize I've almost plowed Lia down. At some point in my inner musings she had stopped as we reached Leo's, and I being in such deep thought had continued to walk forward. I catch her in my arms, trying to steady us both. "Damn, baby, are you okay? I'm sorry; I didn't notice you'd stopped."

She gives me a wry smile, saying, "Yeah, I sort of gathered that when you kept right on going even when I called your name a few times. You were a million miles away."

I hug her to me briefly before placing my hand in the small of her back and leading her to the doorway of Leo's. We are ushered to my favorite table in the back, giving us the privacy I know Lia needs for her first outing. I help her into the corner booth before sliding in next to her. I immediately drop my arm over her shoulders, pulling her into my side. I'm so proud of her for doing this tonight, even though I know she didn't really want to. I order us a bottle of wine and our waiter brings some fresh bread and olive oil. After a week of very little appetite on either of our parts, I find myself suddenly starving. Lia grins at me indulgently as I polish off the small loaf and ask for another. I point to it, saying, "You better get in here before it's gone."

After our first glass of wine, I feel her relax. We are in our own world, with only the waiter appearing briefly to refill our glasses and bring our next course. I'm trying to talk Lia into splitting dessert with me when someone clears their throat, bringing both of our heads up. I stiffen in anger when I see Lee Jacks standing before us; there is no way that him being here is a coincidence. I was sure he'd had someone watching Lia, but now I'm certain. It fucking pisses me off after telling him he needed to give her time to recover before trying to spring her long-lost father on her. I know I'll lose my shit if he tries to make any revelations to her tonight. I wasn't lying to him when I said she wasn't ready. After what happened earlier in the shower, I'm more certain than ever that she needs more time.

Lia looks at me apprehensively when I continue to sit woodenly, not acknowledging the other man. Finally, he steps forward with his hand extended and an amused expression on his face. Fucker. "Quinn, it's good to see you again."

Yeah, I just bet it is. I have little choice but to return his handshake, saying simply, "Jacks." He makes a point to turn to Lia next, and my good manners won't allow me to exclude her from the greeting. "Lia, this is Lee Jacks." I turn back to the other man, narrowing my eyes before I add, "Lee, this is my girlfriend, Lia Adams."

Two things happen when I finish the introduction. First, Lee takes Lia's hand gently, surprising me with the level of emotion that seems to flit across his usually impassive face. Second, I think of how absurd it sounds for someone my age to be addressing the woman who lives with him as his 'girlfriend.' It seems so high school to me, but I'm not sure what a more appropriate word would be. I guess, truthfully, I wasn't much older than a teenager the last time I had a woman in my life who qualified for a status other than one-night stand, or in Laurie's case, more like a high-class hooker. Lia had been a bit angry over my description of Laurie's former place in my life, but as I assured her, there was no comparison between the two. Lia might have had a tough time financially trying to put herself through school, but Laurie's need to spend more money than she had on frivolous items to keep up with her high-society friends made her as different from Lia as night and day in my mind. That left Lia being the only woman to occupy a close place in my life since Cassie. So, yeah, I was treading water every day balancing my need to protect what is left of my heart with my overwhelming desire for the woman sitting next to me. I'd been fucking lost the first moment I met her, and the days that pass only make my desire to keep her in my life impossible to resist.

Lee makes no mention of the bandages on Lia's nose as he says, "It's a pleasure to meet you, Lia. I believe we saw each other briefly at Lucian's apartment a few days ago." I wonder if she even remembers since she was still taking pain pills then, but she seems to recognize him.

"That's right," she answers shyly. "I remember seeing you in Luc's office. I'm sorry I didn't speak, but I wasn't feeling well then." I doubt that Lia notices, but I see Lee's mouth tighten briefly before he relaxes. It's obvious that Lia's injuries bother him a great deal. I recall Max saying something about not knowing if Lee would be more interested in a daughter because she was family or a possible social problem for him if the knowledge fell into the wrong hands. Seeing his reaction to her tonight, I almost think it's the first. Whatever the reason, he seems to feel something for her; trapping me into this informal meeting so he can be near her attests to that fact.

They both look at me when he continues to stand there, and I reluctantly indicate the other side of the table to him. "Would you like to join us for a moment?" I hope like hell that he'll turn the invitation down, but he wastes no time seating himself opposite from us. I dart a quick glance at Lia and find her self-consciously rubbing the bandages over her nose as if trying to hide them from our unwanted guest. I shoot a glare at Lee, hoping he'll get the message, but the bastard completely ignores me and turns his attention back to Lia...his daughter.

"So, Miss Adams, Lucian mentioned that you are in college. What is your major?" I feel the childish urge to kick Lee under the table. No doubt, he already knows the answer to the question he is asking.

We both turn to Lia and I have to give her credit; if she is surprised by his knowledge, she doesn't let on. "I'm majoring in Business Administration."

"And what type of position do you hope to obtain after graduation?" he continues to probe. I see Lia loosen up slightly because this is a comfort zone for her. She knows exactly what she wants to do and the passion comes through as she tells Lee about her desire to be a business analyst to help a company remain competitive by proposing ways to improve their structure, efficiency, and profits.

Dammit to Hell, if I wanted to lessen his growing obsession with her, then I should have steered this conversation another way, because Lia is glowing as she talks about her career goals and Lee looks like exactly what he is: a proud father. "That's very impressive," he praises when she's finished. I can tell they aren't just meaningless words to him, either. Hearing Lia detail her business knowledge to me the first time was the sexiest fucking thing I'd ever heard from a woman's lips. I know Lee is blown away by her intelligence and drive, which comes across so clearly when she speaks. Even if he wasn't her father, her little spiel would have wowed him, I have no doubt. He talks with her about his company and his real estate holdings. He also adds in the fact that I purchased my apartment from him. When he tells her, "I hope you'll keep my company in mind when you graduate," I decide I've had enough. When Lia finds out he's her father, it's going to be even worse that Lee and I sat here with her for an hour and didn't tell her the truth. This needs to end—now.

I begin sliding from the booth, surprising Lia with the abruptness of the movement. When I'm standing, I throw some money on the check the server had dropped sometime during Lee's visit and offer my hand to help her up. Lee stands before she reaches my side, raising a brow at my hasty departure. He knows he holds all of the cards here. When he's ready, he'll find a way to tell her, and there is damn little I'll be able to do to stop him; tonight has proven that to me. "It was good to see you again, Lee," I say as she slips under my arm.

"You, too, Lucian," he replies, but his eyes are only on his daughter. "Miss Adams, it was a pleasure talking to you. I'm sure we'll see each other again soon." She smiles in reply, seeming to think nothing strange of his words. If only she knew.

We walk back toward the apartment, both lost in our thoughts. When we arrive home, I'm shocked when she continues to hold onto my hand and pulls me toward the bedroom. She shifts on her feet nervously when we're standing in the middle of the room. "Luc...I need you. I want your hands to be the last ones that have touched my body. I need to know that I belong to you again, all of me."

My cock immediately jumps to attention at her words, fully willing to give her everything she is asking for. My heart, though, shatters just a little more at the way she has averted her eyes as if expecting me to refuse her. My God, doesn't she understand yet that she owns me? Pulling her body snugly to mine, I ask huskily, "Are you sure?" My body throbs in anticipation as I try to bank the fires building inside me.

"Yes," she whispers. "I want you to make love to me, Luc." With the insecurity she's feeling over her body, I know how hard this must be and how much courage it's taking for her to risk rejection. As if that was ever a possibility. I want to erase those bastard's hands from her body just as much as she does. After not being inside her for two weeks, I'm desperate to feel her again. No matter how hard it will be for me, though, I'll take it slow and look for any sign that she's in distress. Tonight is all about cherishing every inch of her body and alleviating any doubts she might have that I feel differently about her.

"You have no idea how much I want that, baby," I reply as my hands drop to her waist before releasing her. I turn the bedside lamp on, needing to see all of her but also knowing she would prefer the room to be dark. I leave the light on the lowest setting, giving us both some of what we need. I also don't want her to think for a moment that I need the darkness now to make love to her.

I stay fully dressed as I return to her, easing the sweater she is wearing from her shoulders and letting it fall to the floor. This isn't the time to worry about neatness; my only focus is her. Next, the scarf she has wound around her neck follows the path of the sweater and I pause to make sure she's still in the moment with me. She gives me a slight nod, letting me know she wants to continue, and I almost sag in relief.

Her dress is a little trickier and I find myself studying it as if trying to solve a puzzle. It's so long that I hate to pull it over her head, but at the same time, I'm afraid it will ruin the mood somewhat if I try to push it downwards and she gets stuck in it. When she lifts her arms, I give her a quick smile, thanking her silently for answering my question. Having a wrestling contest with her clothing right now isn't something I want to do. I ease the dress as gently as possible up her body and over her head before tossing it behind her. Then I step back and swallow as I take in her beautiful body in nothing but a pale blue bra and matching tiny lace panties. Most of her bruises have now faded to a purplish color, and her cuts, scratches, and bites are almost healed. The bandages I applied earlier look stark white against her creamy skin but do nothing to distract from her appeal. She looks achingly fragile but so damned gorgeous it's almost painful to look at her. "Baby, you are beautiful," I say and mean every word. In my eyes, there is no equal to her.

Next, she does something that takes me by surprise and shows me again how very strong she is regardless of how many blows life has landed upon her. She takes a couple of steps back, putting space between us. My heart plummets, thinking she is pulling away; instead, she raises her hands to unclip her bra, before dropping it on the pile of clothing already on the floor. The bruises and marks on her breasts have faded as well to just faint outlines. Her dusky nipples are erect and tipped to perfection, as if begging for my mouth. Instead of stepping forward as my body is urging me to do, I wait as her hands drop to the waistband of her panties, slipping inside the material and lowering it over her slim hips and down her long, slender legs before letting the slip of blue material pool around her feet.

I stand before her with all of the composure of a schoolboy as my erection strains at the fabric of my jeans. I am painfully hard, and the urge to pick her up and bury myself in her silken depths is almost unbearable. Again, I'm taken aback as she comes back to stand just inches from me and asks, "Can I undress you, Luc?"

"Fuck yes, baby," I rasp, dangerously close to losing what little control I have left. Feeling her hands begin working the buttons of my shirt has me gritting my teeth in a mix of pleasure and pain. After she has released the first few buttons, she starts dropping kisses on each inch of skin she exposes. Having her take control tonight was not what I was expecting at all, and I'm both taken aback and tremendously excited. Maybe her need to take charge isn't completely unexpected. Her choices have been taken from her far too often in her life, and if I can give just a piece of that back to her, then I'll gladly defer to whatever she needs tonight. I shrug my shirt from my shoulders as she trails her fingernails lightly over my chest. A hiss escapes my lips as I lower my arms to cup her ass. Kneading the firm flesh, I attempt to bring her against me, but she isn't done yet. She seems intent on finishing the job of undressing me, and I drop my hands once again to let her.

Her hands drop to the top of my jeans and her fingertips dip inside the waistband, teasing me for a moment before she grasps my belt and unbuckles it. She leaves it hanging open and moves to unbutton and then slowly lower the zipper of my jeans. With the confining material gone, my cock springs forward as far as possible against the silk of my boxers. I help her finish pushing my jeans and boxers to the floor before kicking my feet free of them. She moans low in her throat when my cock juts forward against her belly as if looking for a way inside her. "I want you, Luc," she says as she wraps her hand around my length, causing my body to shudder. I'm dangerously close to blowing my load in her hand when I pull back and swing her up into my arms. I need to cool down for a moment and put the focus back on her.

I lay her back on the bed, spreading her legs as I settle between them on my knees. I take one of her legs in my hand and slowly kiss up the length of it. When I reach the apex of her thighs, I pay special attention to the injuries still visible there, licking and stroking over every inch before moving to her other leg and repeating the same process.

When I again reach her center, I feel her stiffen slightly as I raise her hips and drape her legs over my shoulders. She is completely open to me and I'm drowning in the sight and smell of her. As I lick along the line of her slit, she digs her hands into my hair, seeming to both push me away and pull me closer at once. I raise my head, forcing her to open her eyes when I stop. "Okay?" I ask, needing confirmation before I continue.

She gives me a jerky nod, adding, "Don't stop," which is all I need to hear.

My tongue devours her sweet, spicy taste like a starving man. I suck her throbbing nub into my mouth, and she screams incoherently. I barely release it before I'm darting my tongue inside her wet heat, fucking her slick folds with everything I have. She is thrashing around on the bed, and I can vaguely make out my name among the garbled words she is moaning. When I replace my tongue with two fingers, I feel her body spasm. I nip her clit with my teeth and her legs lock around my head as she comes all over my tongue. Her juices seep down the crevice of her ass as they flow from her pussy faster than I can lick them up. When her legs loosen, I rise up over her. My cock is rigid and painfully hard as I lubricate it in her wet heat. With super-human strength, I start to push into her slowly, ignoring the urge to bury myself to the hilt in one thrust and fuck her hard. Since we haven't had sex in a few weeks, she is even tighter than usual, and I don't want to hurt her. I know I have a big cock, but she always manages to take everything I give her.

I lower my body onto hers, taking her lips in a hot, carnal kiss. I feed her my tongue at the same time I give her my cock...inch by inch. Making love to her mouth gives me just enough of a distraction that I can enter her slowly without losing my mind. "Oh, baby," I groan when I'm fully seated. "You feel so damn good."

Her hips move against mine, almost impatiently. "Ahhh, Luc, please." She bites my bottom lip and almost kills me when she says urgently, "Harder, I need it harder!"

The tenuous control I've been holding onto is shot to Hell with those words. My cock hears nothing but the word, 'harder,' and I'm helpless to do anything but obey. The sound of our skin slapping together fills the room as I go balls-deep with every thrust. She is chanting my name in a throaty, high-pitched way that drives me fucking crazy. I pull her hips closer, grinding against her core. This added stimulation sets her off and she's coming hard on my cock, milking me from the inside. I barely retain my control, letting her come down before I push into her in a couple of rapid-fire thrusts and explode, coming so hard I feel lightheaded for a moment. I hold my full weight from her, just coherent enough to remember her injuries. She strokes my damp hair, raising up enough to meet my descending mouth. We leisurely kiss now, having taken the edge off.

"That was insanely good," I whisper against her mouth before I drop a kiss on her chin. I move to lie beside her, pulling her into the curve of my body. "Are you okay?" I ask as I stroke her hip. I see the evidence of our love making glistening on her thigh, and know it's probably twisted, but I lower my hand and rub it against her pubis. Yeah, I'm a bit of a caveman, but I like marking her with my cum.

She remains quiet while I do this but doesn't seem to mind. Maybe we both need to know it's my scent and essence on her body. "I'm good," she answers, "the best I've been since..." I'm grateful she doesn't finish her sentence; I don't want that bastard here between us. I pull the cover over our rapidly cooling bodies and we drift off, both sated and relaxed.

I awake sometime later to Lia straddling my body. I moan in pleasure as she lifts up then impales herself onto my length. I run my hands over her hips then up her torso. I think it's odd for a moment that I don't feel the bandages I put there earlier. Something else feels strange, as well; her stomach feels huge and distended. My pace falters as I try to push her off me. Something is wrong. The voice saying my name sounds like hers but she doesn't feel like Lia. "Stop!" I shout, trying to move away from her. I can't understand how my cock is still hard and inside her when I'm so freaked out. She laughs in a way that makes my skin crawl; only it's not her this time...it's Cassie. The room, which had been so dark, is suddenly filled with light and Cassie is riding my body with Lia nowhere in sight. One moment she is laughing down at me and in the next, she is screaming as she raises her arm. Too late...again too late, I see the glint of metal before it plunges into me. Blood, so much blood everywhere, I think as I lay choking. *Aidan, where is he?* I wonder as the familiar scene plays out. Then it hits me. *Lia, oh my God, I can't leave her!* "Where is Lia? What have you done to her, Cassie?" I yell frantically as I try to free myself from the woman now slumped on top of me. "Lia...Lia," I slur, feeling it all slipping away from me once again.

Lia

I try to roll over and block out the sound, but it's relentless. *Who is crying at this hour*, I wonder before it hits me. I jerk upright in bed, looking around the darkened room. The mattress moves and I turn to find Lucian flailing around next to me. Oh, no, that sound, I know the choking sound from his nightmares, but he's crying? As I reach for the lamp on the nightstand, I hear him whimpering my name over and over. I learned the hard way to approach him cautiously when he's in the middle of a nightmare. The one time I didn't, I ended up flying through the air and striking my head on a nearby table. I try calling out to him, hoping he'll hear me. "Luc, wake up! Luc, you're dreaming, baby. Wake up!" I try a few more times but even though he calls my name, I'm almost positive he's still asleep.

"Cassie, what have you done?" he sobs, breaking my heart. I want so badly to know what she did to him all those years ago that still torments him to this level today. I get close enough to take his hand and try shaking it.

"Luc, it's me, Lia. Please, wake up...please," I call out to him as he begins to choke again. I drop his hand and quickly leave the bed to turn on his lamp. His face is pale and tears leak from the corners of his eyes. I want to launch myself into his arms and hold him to me until whatever haunts him releases its grip. "Lucian!" I call sharply. "Wake up!" His head turns toward me, and I see his eyes moving rapidly behind the still-closed lids. "Luc! Look at me!" I hold my breath as his eyes finally flicker open then blink against the glare of the light.

"Lia?" His voice is scratchy and strained, but I think he sees me. Before I can move to approach him, he springs from the bed and hurls toward the bathroom. I'm still trying to process his sudden movements when I hear the distinctive sounds of him being sick. I want to go and take care of him as he has done for me in the past, but I know how raw he is after one of these dreams, especially when I witness them. I force myself to stay where I am and take my cues from him.

After a few more minutes, I hear the toilet flush and then him brushing his teeth. There is dead silence afterwards until he finally walks back into the bedroom with his eyes carefully averted. I go to him, putting my hand on his arm. He has always worried about hurting me during one of his nightmares so I'm quick to reassure him. "Luc, I'm fine. I stayed back until you awoke. I'm worried about you, though. Do you...want to talk?" I see the shutters click tightly over his beautiful eyes as he moves restlessly on his feet. I'm surprised when he pulls me into his arms instead of walking away immediately.

"I'm sorry, baby," he murmurs against my temple. "I didn't mean to scare you."

"Luc, I'm fine," I attempt to comfort him. I kiss his throat and nestle into his embrace. "Please talk to me. Maybe it would stop if you told someone about it."

He's quiet for so long I think he's going to ignore my comment before he finally says, "I can't tonight. I'm too close to the edge. Just...give me some time, and I'll try—for you."

"I love you," I say softly, thinking that even if he can't give me the words back, he might need to hear them right now.

"Oh, Lia." He inhales loudly, shaking for just a moment before pulling away. "I'm going to work in my office for a few hours until I key down. Try to get some sleep and I'll be back later." I almost offer to go with him, but I know he doesn't want that. He needs time alone to sort through the ghosts raging in his head. I've been there before, and I understand the urge to run away from it all.

"Okay." I give him a smile of understanding and let him walk away to deal with his demons. Fighting the things you can't see or touch are sometimes the battles that wound you the most.

Lucian

I drop my head in my hands as I make it to the sanctuary of my office. My heart is still racing from the dream that seemed so horribly real. I've had nightmares for years... since the night Cassie tried to kill me. Tonight, though, it was different. Cassie and Lia had intertwined in the dream, taking even my subconscious by surprise. Before I awoke, Cassie had been stabbing Lia, yelling that I was hers. It had been so fucking real that I was choking on my own bile as I bolted from the bed.

Would I ever be able to get past what happened all those years ago? Just when I think there is a chance of moving on, I'm hit with this. I'm tired of the fucking dreams, and I'm even more tired of worrying about them happening. The stress of it all coupled with my fears for Lia are eating me alive. I don't even hesitate as I unlock my desk drawer and pull the small bag from inside. If not this, then I'd be walking the floors for hours, trying to get back to level ground. I need it and the sweet oblivion that only it will bring.

Lia thought that talking to her about what had happened could make it better. But how can you tell someone that your pregnant girlfriend had been so twisted that she had literally tried to slit your throat and let you bleed out, while you were inside her? That she had continued to move against you even as she stabbed herself while laughing. The sound of her crazy, fucking cackles would forever haunt me. Maybe even more so because I know deep down that she was paying me back for what I did.

With a shaking hand, I make a less-than-perfect line and take the rolled-up bill to snort it. I'm in the middle of doing the white line when I hear a noise and look up. I freeze in horror as Lia looks at me in shock. I know there is no mistaking what she's seeing. Maybe...just maybe, if there hadn't been any cocaine remaining on the mirror in front of me or if the damned rolled bill wasn't still hovering under my nose, I could explain it away. I wait for her to speak, though, just on the outside chance that she has a different take on what I'm doing.

She drops into a chair in the front of my desk, and I quickly put my drug paraphernalia back in my desk drawer. I have never felt like less of a man than I do right now. To be caught doing something like this because I can't cope, by the strongest woman I've ever known, is humiliating. For the first time since we met, I feel like a complete disappointment to her. The silence in the room is deafening as we both wait for the other to speak. Finally, she says, "I never knew. How long?"

Not bothering to lie, I tell her the truth. "On and off for years." I don't add 'since Cassie'. I know it's not an excuse. There is never an acceptable reason for using coke.

She looks more curious than anything else when she asks, "Do you even want to stop?"

"Not enough to really try...until you. I never wanted you to know." When she stands, I think she is walking away in disgust. I'm astonished when she walks toward me instead and pulls my chair back enough to crawl into it with me. She sits sideways in my lap as if seeking comfort. I automatically close my arms around her, breathing in her familiar scent.

"Am I doing this to you, Luc?"

"What?" I take her chin in my hand, bringing her eyes to mine. "No, baby, God no. I'm not proud of it, but as I said, I've been using for much longer than I've known you. Sometimes weeks pass in between...and sometimes they don't."

She puts her small hand over mine, continuing to study me as if she can see into my very soul; sometimes I believe she can. "The dreams seem like they are getting worse. You had stopped having them before my attack."

"They hadn't stopped. You knew I was taking something to help me sleep." When she nods, I continue. "It wasn't working that great, and I had a few that didn't wake you. Therefore, I did the only thing I knew would keep them at bay. I couldn't risk hurting you again, baby." I know it sounds like an excuse, even to my ears, but I would and will do everything I need to do to keep her safe, even if it's from me.

"We've been quietly falling apart," she says softly as she threads her fingers between mine. I panic for a moment, not understanding what she means.

"We're fine, Lia. Nothing is going to tear us apart. We are always going to be stronger together."

"That's not what I meant, Luc. I'm not talking about our relationship coming apart. We are unraveling inside. Our past is festering within each of us, eating away who we are, bit by bit. I've been wallowing in self-pity since my attack, and I can't seem to stop. Everyone tells me I'm so lucky. I'm alive and I wasn't raped. I'm a survivor. I lived to tell the tale. What they don't seem to understand, though, is that those words describe my life, not just one incident. I keep getting up, brushing myself off, and trying to move forward. I'm the fucking queen of making lemonade out of lemons, Luc. But each time, I keep wondering what's going to happen to me when I finally just don't get up. Was I doomed to be just a sad statistic from the moment I was born?"

Her gut-wrenching words hit me hard. In our time together and all of our conversations, this is the most defeated I've ever heard her sound. As strong as she is, she can't save me and I can't save her as the damaged man I am. If I wanted to continue on the self-destructive path I've been on, I should have walked away from her in the beginning. Now, it's too late. She is the very air I breathe, and even if I cannot say the words, I acknowledge to myself for the first time that I am hopelessly in love with her. Maybe if we had each lived normal lives with no past traumas, our draw toward each other wouldn't have been as strong. In an alternative life, she would have grown up as Lee Jacks' daughter with a wealth to match or exceed my own. Would any of that have made a difference to either of us the first time we looked into each other's eyes? I have to believe that my soul would have still recognized hers, no matter what our circumstances were at the time of our paths crossing.

I lower my mouth to hers, kissing her with all the pent-up emotion I feel when she is near. "You were born to be the beautiful, vibrant, intelligent, and courageous woman you are today," I say as I nuzzle against her soft cheek. "Every hardship you have endured has added another dimension to the person you are. There is nothing lucky in having to survive repeated attacks. Luck has had no place in your life, baby. You have made it this far because you refused to let them win. No matter how much they tried, you bested them. They never broke you, or you wouldn't be here now." Lowering my hand to her heart, I add, "You'll never be a sad statistic because this will never let you." I feel her crying softly against me, and I let her get it out as I stroke her hair. She needs the release. When her tears have quieted, I can literally feel the air charge as she gathers herself from the abyss she has been in. Her strength is beginning to return, and I wonder if she realizes that it never really left.

"I need to know about Cassie. Not tonight, because I don't think either of us can handle it, but soon. She is still ripping you apart and you can't move on, which means neither can I, until you face it. Can you do that? Can you promise to trust me with your past?"

"Yes," I answer without hesitation. She is right; the time for secrets is rapidly ending. Not only does she need to know about Cassie, but she also needs to know about Lee Jacks...her father. The cocoon we've built around ourselves during the last few months is imploding, and I can only hope with everything I am that she'll still be here in the end as the people from our pasts rise up to tear us apart. "Let's go back to bed," I say, knowing we are both exhausted enough to sleep through any night terrors that try to plague our dreams.

CHAPTER NINE

Lia

It's been three days since Lucian's last nightmare—that I know of—and my discovery of his addiction to cocaine. By unspoken agreement, we've both avoided talking about anything stressful and have just been content to spend some quiet, uninterrupted time together. We've watched movies, ordered in most of our meals, and mostly made love leisurely with the occasional round of hard fucking thrown in for good measure. I'm looking forward to starting my day with the hard variety of his loving when he walks out of the bathroom with a towel riding low on his hips, causing me to almost swallow my tongue. *Holy mother, will the sight of him, especially half-dressed, ever not affect me like this?* No matter how many thoughts or concerns are churning in my head, my body still tingles with awareness. I go to him, wrapping my arms around his still-damp body. He smells like soap, aftershave, and sexy male. God, I just want to lick his hard chest. His hands settle on my hips, pulling me snug against him, and I feel his cock stir. Obviously, I'm not the only one wishing we were still in bed this morning. "Good morning, baby," he says in his sexy, husky morning voice I love so much.

"Morning," I reply absently as my hands wander of their own accord up and down his back. As I reach the crease of his ass, I hear his breath hitch and smile. I'm tired, but I would love to feel his tongue between my legs this morning. It seems to be the magic cure for helping me keep the blues at bay.

He pushes his morning erection into me before pulling away. "You don't know how much I hate to say this, but you have your doctor's appointment in less than an hour, so don't start anything we can't finish."

My mouth drops open in disappointment as I sputter, "What? But, I want to—"

"Yeah, me, too," he interrupts as he smacks my ass. I follow his gaze down to the tent he's pitching in the front of his towel.

"Babies, kittens, and bunnies."

He looks at me as if I've lost my mind. "Just repeat babies, kittens, and bunnies over and over and it'll help you with that," I say, pointing downwards.

He chuckles before dropping his towel suddenly and palming his length. "Thanks for the suggestion, but I think I know a faster and much more pleasurable way to handle my problem." Wiggling his brows, he adds, "Emphasis on handle, of course." I stand rooted in place as he walks back into the bathroom, not bothering to shut the door. "Be right back."

"Er...um...okay," I manage to croak out. As I shift uncertainly, squeezing my legs together, I try to tell myself that he doesn't want me to watch, but the devil on my shoulder keeps shouting, 'he left the door open!' Finally, I can resist no longer, and I creep to the open door. He's sitting on the shower seat, leaning against the wall as he works his cock in his fisted hand. His moan fills the bathroom and I freeze. *Oh, shit, it wasn't him, it was me!* My face is bright red when he opens his eyes and sees me standing there gawking at him.

He gives me a sexy grin as if he'd been expecting me all along. Pumping his hips in my direction, he growls, "Screw the hand job. Come fuck me, baby." I'm so wet and horny that I don't need to be asked twice. I go to him, taking his hand as he helps me into the shower. I stand hesitantly before him until he takes me by the waist and lifts me over his hips and impaling me onto his shaft. We both shout as he penetrates me deeply before lifting and dropping me repeatedly. My body struggles to adjust to his girth, but the pleasure far outweighs the discomfort I feel from his size.

When he leaves me seated deeply on him to take my nipple in his mouth, I moan, "Luc! Oh, God, Luc, please..." Ignoring my pleas to move again, he insists on sucking and licking both nipples before moving on to my neck and earlobe. I never knew an ear could be an erogenous zone until Lucian's tongue and teeth first showed me it was a direct link to my clit. I begin bouncing my hips against his, needing the friction of his cock, prompting him to take command once again. Instead of lifting me, he pulls me down while grinding his hips upwards. He's so deep inside me that twinges of pain mingle with the pleasure, causing me to spiral quickly toward my release.

"More," I pant, so close to the edge. My nails are raking his back as I reach for the pinnacle that he is keeping just out of range with shallow thrusts of his hips. Taking handfuls of his hair, I tug it sharply, snapping, "Dammit, Luc, fuck me!" His growl of approval fills the shower as he surges upward, rubbing against my magic trigger spot, causing me to spasm around him without warning. "Ahhh, too much!" I cry as my orgasm seems to go on and on.

"Lia, fuck!" he shouts as I feel him release into me. "Fucking hell," he groans as we both collapse against each other. "I can never get enough of you," he murmurs absently as he rubs soothing circles against my sweaty skin.

"Me, either," I admit, not really knowing if he expected an answer, but helpless to deny it. We sit still joined for a while before he gently pulls my body off his. I groan, feeling my swollen tissue clinging to his semi-hard length. No part of me ever wants to be apart from him, it seems.

He turns the shower on, causing us both to gasp before the water turns from cold to hot. Shivering, he laughs. "I think we both needed that blast." I hold my arm with the cast to the side as he washes me quickly and helps me from the shower before turning to wash himself. I remove my soaked bandages and dry off. The tape holding the splint on my nose is wet as well, but I just pat it dry knowing the doctor will be removing it today. When he steps out, he makes quick work of reapplying fresh bandages before walking once again toward the closet. I wrap a towel around myself before following him.

"Luc," I call to him, knowing I'm going to have a battle on my hands. When he steps out holding jeans and a button-down shirt, I prepare to present my case. "I want you to go to the office today after my appointment."

He looks at me as if I'm speaking a foreign language. "Pardon?"

I walk past him to select a loose-fitting T-shirt and jeans from my side of the closet and then return to his side to select one of his expensive power suits. When I hand it to him, he takes it, still looking puzzled. "I want you to get back to your normal routine. You've been away from your office for weeks now."

He is already shaking his head before I finish my last sentence. "No, I've got things under control. Aidan is in the office, and we talk several times a day. I can handle things from here fine."

When he turns with the obvious intention of hanging the suit back up, I grab his arm. "I need for you to do this. I have to try to get my life back, and that's not going to happen as long as I cower in this apartment."

"Then we'll spend the day doing something. What would you like to do?" His handsome face is so eager and sincere that I feel horrible for trying to push him away for a few hours. Not only do I need to attempt to stand on my own two feet again, but Lucian needs it, as well. If I continue to stay behind the safety of these walls with him every day, then I'll never want to leave his side. He has already given me more security than I've ever had before, and I can't continue to depend on him for my wellbeing. I need to return to a few weeks ago, when he was one of the best parts of my life but not my entire world. We both need to have our own independence again.

I take the jeans and shirt from his hand, leaving him only the suit. Looking up at him, I implore him to understand. "I love you, Luc, but I have to try to shake off the fear and self-pity that have taken over since my attack. If I can't be alone for a few hours, then how will I ever be able to leave this apartment again by myself? My last semester of school starts soon, and I have to be able to return to my life by then." He looks so torn by my words. He's no more ready to leave me than I am for him to go, but I can also see that he understands what I'm trying to say. I know I've won, and he'll leave me for the first time this afternoon. I also know it'll tear him apart to do so, which makes me love him even more—if that is possible. If I'm being completely honest with myself, I'll also admit that my bid for freedom today is about helping Lucian return to level ground, as well. Being trapped in this apartment can't be good for him mentally; he has too much time to think about the past.

He pulls me close, dropping his forehead onto mine. "I don't want to do this."

"I know, but thank you. I promise I'll be fine."

He curses once under his breath before sighing. "You promise to call me if you need anything at all? Even if you're just lonely." I nod, blinking back tears.

"Fuck, Lia, I mean it. I want to hear the words."

"I promise," I manage to say, even as I'm choking back the urge to beg him to stay with me. At this point, it seems to be a toss-up as to who will have a panic attack first when we part. I know one thing: if we're both this emotional already, I need to make our actual goodbye very quick or I'll break down and he won't consider leaving me again anytime soon. In an attempt at self-preservation, I pull away and dress before drying my hair and securing it in one of the ponytail holders Lucian has provided. I need to cut up another pair of his underwear and use the waistband as a holder again; I bet that would bring a smile to his face. Maybe tonight, if I'm still holding it together by the time he gets home.

Lucian

I stand next to Lia patiently waiting for her to finish the hug marathon she seems to have going with Sam. This is the first time they've seen each other since he drove us home from the hospital. Of course, he has called to check on her daily, as have Cindy, Aidan, and my aunt. "It's so good to see you, Miss Lia," he says, clearly doting on her. "You look just beautiful."

"Thank you, Sam," she says in that shy way she has. Lia always has a tough time accepting compliments, probably because her bitch of a mother never did anything but tear her down. She has finally gotten somewhat used to my compliments, even though I wonder sometimes if she believes them or just tries to humor me and accept them gracefully now. "I've really missed you," she adds, making Sam literally crumble at her feet. There is little doubt that my driver, and longtime family friend, is completely enamored with her. Her mixture of sweetness and innocence, especially considering what she has survived in her life, is hard to resist. She draws people like a moth to a flame, especially my friends, it seems. I am quite aware that some of them, or maybe all, like her more than me right now.

He opens the door, ushering her in before turning finally to me. "Good morning, Luc. It's good to see you, as well."

Giving him a sarcastic smile, I say, "Yeah, I'm sure." He grins in return, seeming completely unrepentant. He's been with me long enough to know when I'm kidding. Truthfully, I love the fact that my inner circle is so taken with her. I would never tolerate them being less than courteous to her, so it makes things easier for all concerned. He and I had discussed the agenda for the day earlier. I thought he was going to throw a fit when he found out that he would be dropping me at the office and returning Lia to the apartment...alone. I'm certain he thought I was an insensitive bastard before I assured him that I was only honoring her wishes and didn't like it any more than he did. I've also arranged for a couple of security guards from Quinn Software to screen any visitors to our home. I wouldn't be at all surprised if Sam sits on the street in front of our building until he picks me up later.

The drive passes quickly as we were lucky to miss the normal Asheville downtown rush-hour traffic. I help Lia from the car, settling my hand into the small of her back as we walk toward the modern structure that houses Dr. Patricia Kay's practice. She has been my physician since I was a child, although I rarely see her more than once per year at my physical. As we approach the reception desk, the bored-looking attendant hands Lia a stack of forms on a clipboard that looks like they will take hours to complete. She seems overwhelmed, but determined, as she takes a seat and squares her shoulders. I

see her pen pause when she reaches the
section on insurance. I calmly take the
pen from her fingers and cross the section
out, writing 'cash' below it. "Maybe I
should have gone somewhere...cheaper,"
she mumbles as she looks at the
expensive décor surrounding us.

I chuckle as I tweak her nose. "It's fine,
baby. Don't worry about it." She'll be
trying to clean the damned toilets in the
apartment again to pay for the
appointment. I'm going to have to hire a
housekeeper before she gets any ideas.
She is so fucking adorable sometimes that
I wonder how I ever lived before her. The
answer there is simple: I didn't; I existed.
Each day for the last ten years of my life
was a repeat of the day before. The only
thing that really changed on a regular
basis was the woman I was screwing. The
thought has no more than left my mind
when a perfectly-manicured hand lands
on my shoulder, causing both Lia and I to
look up.

"Luc! How wonderful to see you... at a
doctor's office of all places." I inwardly
wince as my past collides once again with
my present. I get politely to my feet and
kiss Laurie's proffered cheek before
quickly pulling away. Her blonde hair is
carefully styled in the usual sleek bob.
She is immaculately dressed in tailored

cream slacks and a silk top. Her jewelry is understated but expensive. I recognize the diamond bracelet encircling her wrist and am surprised she hasn't managed to solicit a new one from someone else by now.

"Laurie, you're looking well," I say as I attempt to block her view of Lia. Like most of the women I've dated or slept with in recent years, Laurie is a jealous and petty person, and I don't want her anywhere around Lia.

"Thank you, darling," she gushes as her nails curl into my arm. I'd love nothing better than to tell her to fuck off. I abhor small talk, especially when it's with someone who I'd be happy to never see again. She is doing her best to dart her eyes behind me at Lia. The office is almost empty, so it seems obvious that she and I are here together. "I hope everything is okay," she says in a voice full of false concern. I feel the crazy urge to tell her that I'm here about my genital herpes but figure instead of having a little fun at her expense, she'd go screaming it in the streets at the top of her lungs. Damn, it would be fun to see her go off the rails for a bit, though.

With a perfectly blank expression that doesn't encourage questions, I say, "I'm fine." The irony of that answer isn't lost

on me. Of course, she didn't specifically
ask me if I was messed up in the head or
snorting coke like fucking Pez lately, so
it's not technically a lie. She has now
given up all pretense of being discrete
and has moved to the side to look directly
at Lia, who I see as I turn around is also
looking at her with rapt curiosity. No
doubt, she remembers Laurie's name as
the person I last dated before I met her.
When Lia starts smoothing her hands
over her ponytail and looking down at the
stack of papers on her lap, I know I've
hurt her feelings by not making the
introductions. She thinks that I'm
ashamed of her, which couldn't be further
from the truth. The expensively coifed
woman on my other side could never hold
a candle to the beauty who owns me body
and soul. Therefore, I try to control my
protective instincts as I extend a hand to
Lia and pull her to her feet. I drop my
arm around her shoulders and pull her
possessively into my body, wanting
Laurie to have no question as to our
relationship.

"Laurie, this is my girlfriend, Lia." I
see the other woman's eyes bulge at the
title before she manages to get herself
under control. Again, I hate the fucking
juvenile word 'girlfriend,' but if nothing
else, it scores a direct hit to Laurie

because she knows she was never anything close to that, nor did I address her as such. "Lia, this is an old friend, Laurie." As Laurie draws up even further, I decide that I'm just an evil bastard today. Maybe Lia's right, and I have been in the apartment for too long, which is very unfortunate for Laurie.

Lia extends a polite hand to Laurie, who just looks at it as if it's a snake while sputtering, "Girlfriend? Since when?"

Ah, the fake veneer is off now, and she's insulted to have been replaced. As she takes in Lia's appearance, I know the fact that she is younger is the real kick in the ass here. Before I can answer, the door to our right opens and a voice calls out, "Lia Adams."

I turn my back on Laurie and grab Lia's purse for her. "I'll walk you back, baby," I say before turning back to Laurie briefly. "Take care." I don't bother telling her it was nice to see her because we both know it would be a lie. I do get a small bit of satisfaction from seeing her still standing where I left her, looking like someone who just found out her trust fund was empty. Wait...wasn't this almost a replay of our first date? And they say there is no justice in the world.

CHAPTER TEN

Lia

Shit, why didn't I dress better today? How could I have possibly known, though, that we would run into Lucian's ex-whatever at my doctor's appointment? The woman looks like she belongs on a runway, and I look just a touch above a homeless person. I almost dropped my pen when he said her name. After seeing both Monique, who he had admitted to having sex with, and now Laurie, I see a definite trend in the type of women Lucian prefers—or used to prefer. Looking down at my jeans and flip-flops, I wonder how he can't help but find me lacking compared to the woman fawning all over him. Dammit, even my toenail polish is chipped! I haven't exactly been thinking of stuff like that since...

She is doing her best to check me out over his shoulder. I waver between wanting to slide down a few seats and hope that she'll think we aren't together and kicking him in the shin for not bothering to introduce me. I'm leaning toward being pissed off at him when I feel eyes burning into me. Looking up, I find her staring at me in puzzlement. I decide I'm skipping the shins and going straight for a kick to his balls if he doesn't speak up. Before I can finish with my plan to maim him, he takes my hand and pulls me gently to my feet before wrapping his arm tightly around me. When he introduces me as his girlfriend, I feel the childish urge to stick my tongue out at the now shocked other woman. *That's right, sister; Lucian is now slumming. Stick that in your Botox mouth and smoke it. Oh, my God, Rose is rubbing off on me.* When I extend my hand to her, she looks like she is on the verge of a fit or a seizure of some kind. I can only imagine what she would have done had he called me his wife. Crap, I would have paid every penny in my bank account to see that.

When the nurse calls my name, I gladly gather my ton of paperwork, which I'm not even halfway finished with, and turn to find that Lucian has already picked up my purse and seems determined to go back with me. I would rather see the doctor alone, but I don't want to leave him out here with Botox Barbie. From the speed he's rushing me through the doorway, he must feel the same way. He holds my clipboard while the nurse ushers me to the scales and takes my weight. He is smart enough to turn away until the nurse is finished. I don't know many women who would gladly have a man know her weight, regardless of the number. Some things in life just need to remain a mystery.

When we reach the exam room, the nurse motions for me to step up onto the table and says the doctor will be in soon. Lucian sets my stuff on the countertop next to the sink before walking over to me. He raises a brow at the stirrups on either side of my legs. "This table has a lot of possibilities. I wonder if they sell to individuals."

"You're sick," I giggle, feeling lighter than I have in days. Even meeting his perfect ex hasn't shaken me...too much. Well, it does make me wonder why his taste in women has changed so dramatically. I'm nothing at all like the stick-thin, haughty woman I just met.

Since he is so relaxed, I decide to put the question before him. "So...Laurie, huh?"

Instead of looking uncomfortable, he actually smirks. "Yeah, sorry to put you through that. We both got off pretty easy, though."

I smile in return. "I think it was the whole 'girlfriend' thing that had her so tongue-tied. I couldn't decide if she was going to faint or throw up."

"I'd have paid good money to see the first one," Lucian admits. "I've only seen her rattled a few times."

I shake my head saying, "Let me guess, the last time before today was when you broke up with her?"

He cringes dramatically. "That was just ugly. When she figured out that she wasn't going to be able to talk me out of it, she threw a fucking vase at my head."

I begin laughing, unable to imagine the woman in the waiting room doing something so...normal, at least for a teenager. "No! Did she hit her target?"

"Hell no," he says, looking offended. "I move a little faster than that, and she throws like a girl."

We are both laughing over his comment when the door opens and someone I presume is the doctor steps in. She appears to be in her fifties, with shoulder-length brown hair, heavily

tinged with gray. I like her immediately
when she puts her hands on her hips and
looks at Lucian with a resigned huff.
"What are you doing in here with my
patient, Lucian Quinn?"

He grins in return, looking a tad
sheepish. "We're together," he says,
taking my hand. "I'm Lia's boyfriend."

She takes his sleeve and starts
ushering him toward the door. "I don't
care if you're her God, you'll have to go
back to the waiting area. I have to adhere
to all of these privacy policies they have
floating around now." I almost laugh
when I see him holding onto the
doorframe, clearly torn about leaving. Dr.
Kay gives him a reassuring pat on the
shoulder, saying, "I'll take care of her,
Luc." He reluctantly walks out into the
hallway and she shuts the door behind
him. She turns back to me, shaking her
head. "I swear that boy is just as
stubborn today as he was when he was a
child."

I smile in answer, feeling myself relax.
I'm secretly glad she made Lucian leave
the room, although I hope Laurie has
already gone. "So, you knew the boy
before the man?" I ask, dying of curiosity.
I wonder if she knew Lucian's parents
before they passed away.

She walks to the sink to wash her hands, looking back over her shoulder as she says, "Oh, yes, his mother and I were childhood friends. I still miss her," she adds quietly, seeming lost in thought for a moment. As she dries her hands, she looks me over before sitting on a stool next to the exam table. "Luc told me what happened to you when he called to make your appointment. I'm very sorry that you had to endure something like that, Lia."

I feel my eyes well up at her kindness. I feel the crazy urge to lay my head on her shoulder and soak up all the comfort I know I would find there. My emotions, it seems, are still all over the place. Instead, I manage to get out a shaky, "Thank you."

She reaches over to pat my hand before opening a file. "Luc had a copy of your chart sent to me from the hospital." She digs a pair of glasses from her jacket pocket and glances through the papers the folder contains. "I know I need to use that fancy iPad for all of this, but I still love to flip through pages." Raising her brow, she whispers, "Plus, I've already broken one of the things by dropping it a dozen times." I laugh in response, relieved that I've recovered from the threatened crying jag of a few moments ago. "All right, Lia, let's look at your nose first."

Gently, she removes the bandages and the splint from my nasal area, throwing them into the trashcan behind her. She gently probes my nose, causing me to wince, as the area is still tender. When she pulls back, I look up and ask, "Has it healed?"

She nods, saying, "It looks good. There is some remaining swelling, and as you noticed, it's still tender. You may end up with a small bump on the ridge of it, but it's too early to tell. Just let me know if you have any issues with severe congestion. As for your wrist and fingers, you're a few weeks away from removing the cast. I'll have the girls out front schedule another appointment for that."

"Okay," I say disappointed. I had hoped to get rid of it all today, but at least my nose is free now.

She drops back on her stool and studies me for a moment. "How are the contusions on your body healing?"

"They're mostly fading now." I hope she won't press me on seeing for herself. That's still not something I want others looking at, even if the evidence is almost gone now.

She nods, seeming satisfied with my answer. She looks in my folder again, asking, "Are you having any headaches, even minor?"

"Just a bit the first few days I was home but nothing since then."

She makes a note in my chart. "Good. I'll want to schedule one more CT scan just to make sure all of the swelling in your brain has subsided. According to your chart, it was almost normal when the hospital released you. Are you still taking the pain pills you were prescribed?"

"No," I wrinkle my nose, thinking about how bad the pills made me feel. "I really haven't needed anything, even Tylenol, in days."

"And the only medication you're currently taking is birth control pills?"

"Yes," I say automatically before I freeze. My breath wheezes from my lungs, and I feel dizzy with shock. "No! Oh, dear Lord, I haven't taken them since..." I'm in complete panic mode now, unable to believe that something I've done for so long has completely slipped my mind for not just days, but weeks.

"Lia." She pats my knee reassuringly. "It's perfectly understandable that you would forget that with everything that has happened. Have you had sexual relations since you left the hospital?"

I squeeze my eyes shut, unable to believe this is happening. "Yes, daily...for four or five days," I admit haltingly.

Sometimes more than once a day, but I don't add that part. Why, oh why couldn't we have waited to have sex until I had seen the doctor?

She still looks calm, even in the face of my obvious distress. "Do you know where you are in your cycle?"

"I have no idea," I say, wracking my brain. "I don't have a period very often since I went on the birth control pills, so I haven't been keeping up with it. I've never had a reason to." She probably assumes I said that because I've always been careful when in reality, other than once, I never had sex before I met Lucian. "I'll take one as soon as I get home."

"No, don't start them again yet. It's probably fine, Lia, and I don't want to scare you, but on the outside chance that you've conceived, you don't need to take them until we know for sure. I...there is another option if you are interested. There is a prescription for a morning-after pill called Ella, which is actually effective up to five days after intercourse. This is completely up to you, Lia."

I feel a wave of relief roll through me at her words. But before I can say yes, I'm filled with uncertainty. I know it's my body, but isn't this something I should discuss with Lucian? I can't hide something like this from him, can I?

"Do...I mean...is there time to talk to Luc first?" A part of me can't believe I'm even asking her this. There is no choice to be made here is there? Lucian and I aren't ready to be parents. I have a stepfather who tried to rape me somewhere out in the world and Lucian is mired in a past which still haunts him. What decision is to be made here? Shit, I still can't do this without him knowing. I'll tell him and then we'll both just be relieved that we found out in time.

"I think it's a very good idea to speak with your partner...or Luc, in this case. Just call my office tomorrow morning after you've talked it over and let me know what you decide. You'd need to take the pill at some point tomorrow, though, to ensure its effectiveness."

We talk for a few more minutes before she ushers me to the door. Lucian is standing against the opposite wall, thumbing through his smartphone. For a moment, I'm afraid he overheard our conversation, but the easy smile on his face says differently. "Okay, baby?" he asks as he walks over to look at my newly uncovered nose.

Dr. Kay clucks her tongue at him. "Just couldn't go to the waiting room as you were told, could you?"

He gives her his best innocent look. "I was staying close in case Lia needed me." He gives me a wink, and we both know it's because he wanted to avoid another possible run-in with Laurie. We say goodbye to the doctor and he peels off some bills to pay for the visit despite my protests. I make another appointment to have my cast removed and a follow-up CT scan. Lucian guides me through the Laurie-free waiting room and to the car idling at the curb. We say a few words to Sam before settling onto the leather seats. He picks up my hand, kissing my fingers before asking, "Did you like Dr. Kay?"

"She's wonderful," I murmur, still reeling from the conversation she and I had had. *Should I tell him now? No, if I do, he more than likely won't go to the office and he needs this today.* He already seems more relaxed than he has in days. We'll talk tonight when he comes home. I'll make him dinner and wear something other than my usual home attire of yoga pants. "She sure knows how to handle you," I tease, trying to lighten the mood. I want his happy mood to continue, and he's far too perceptive where I'm concerned.

My mouth drops open as he reaches down to palm his cock through the pants he's wearing. "Well, she's seen this many times through the years. It didn't start out this big, you know." I don't know who's choking on laughter more, Sam or me. The other man might not be able to see where Lucian's hand is, but I'm certain by the way his shoulders are shaking that Sam knows what Lucian's referring to.

"So, she's holding that secret over your head?" I manage to choke out. He gives me a naughty look at my use of the word 'head' and I smack his leg. "Stop, Luc, or I'll never be able to look the woman in the eyes again." He removes his hand from his crotch, still teasing me playfully.

When we reach his office, he asks me if I want to come in. Even though I'm tempted, I decide to go back to the apartment to regroup. I also need to check my online grades from my final exams and make sure I have the classes I need before my last semester begins. In other words, I need to do normal things today to try to find my routine again and so does he. "Call me when you get home, baby," he says. When I just nod, he adds sternly, "I mean it, Lia. I'm not trying to smother you, but at least for a while, I need to know that you're okay."

I cup his face in my hand, stroking his smooth, shaven cheek. "I know, Luc, and I promise I will." He kisses my lips briefly and starts to exit the car before coming back and kissing me more leisurely. We are both breathing heavily when he finally pulls away. "Something to remember me by today," he whispers as he steps out and shuts the door behind him. The ache between my legs after his expert kisses assures me that I will indeed think of him all day.

Lucian

Cindy looks up from her desk in surprise when I stride off the elevator in front of her. "Luc! I wasn't expecting you in today. How's Lia doing?" She looks around behind me, as if expecting her to be there. If I had my way, she would be chained to my side right now and not going back home alone.

"Good morning, Cindy. No, Lia is on her way home. She had a doctor's appointment this morning. I decided to come in for the rest of the day afterwards."

Cindy crooks a brow at me and finally calls bullshit. "She kicked you out, huh?"

I grin as I say, "Something like that. Has Aidan had any problems while I've been away?" I know without a doubt that Cindy knows exactly what's been going on at Quinn Software, so she's my first stop before calling Aidan in for a status update.

"Things have been running smoothly, Luc. Aidan met with Kenson yesterday and said it went well." Kenson is a software company I'm interested in acquiring. They are one of Quinn's partners and would prosper under better management. Their current owners are too busy bickering amongst themselves to realize what a goldmine they're sitting on. It's a good time to buy while they hate each other and are ready to walk away.

"That sounds good. Can you have him come to my office, please? And Lia is doing well. It's been tough for her, but she is starting to get back on her feet again."

"I'm glad, Luc," she says softly. "I've been praying for you both."

I incline my head before walking into my office. It still looks exactly the same as when I left it in a panic to go find Lia weeks ago. I walk behind my desk and settle in my chair. Damn, I never knew how much I missed this normalcy until now. Before my unusual sentimental thoughts can continue, Aidan knocks once before walking in. His face looks drawn and tired, and I feel a stab of guilt at dumping so much on him so suddenly. "Luc! Good to see you back here, man. I wasn't expecting that for at least another week." I stand as he gives me a brief bro-hug before settling into one of the chairs in front of my desk. "So, I take it that Lia is doing well if you're here?"

"She is doing better. She had a check-up this morning and was able to remove the splint from her nose." Her usual pert nose was still swollen and now has a small bump on the ridge of it.

"That's great, I'm glad to hear it. How is she doing...with the other stuff?"

I recline back in my chair, thumbing a pen on my knee. "It's been hard for her. She's dealing with a lot, but I think she's turned a corner. Lia is much stronger than people imagine; she's had to be. She caught me doing a line a few days ago," I admit, needing someone to talk to about it.

His eyes are huge as he processes my words. "Shit! I thought you were trying to quit?"

"I was...I am," I say as I run my hands through my hair. "After we made it home, some shit happened, and it just fucked with my resolve. Even though it makes me sick that she knows, maybe it's better.

I have to stop, no matter what it takes, and it was getting hard to hide. She deserves better than that."

"So do you," Aidan adds softly, ever the loyal friend. I think back to Lia staring at me in shock as I prepared to snort a line, and I want to be whole again for the first time in eight years. And not just for her. Finally, I want it for myself. I want to be a man Lia is proud to have by her side...always. There is no way her childhood Prince Charming used coke. I refuse to be another person in her life who has disappointed her, and that is exactly what I felt like. Even though she handled it better than I would have imagined, it was still a humiliating moment that I don't want to relive. Aidan grimaces. "Does this mean you're going to continue your new chain-smoking hobby?"

I shake my head, wanting to cringe at the thought. "Hell, no. I'm not sure why that offends you so much since you smoke."

"I'm just a social smoker," he grins. "Well, maybe a stress one, as well. Plus, the chicks dig it."

"You fucking liar," I deadpan. "In my brief time of smoking, I saw more female noses turning up as I walked by than I care to admit. My aunt may actually be relieved it's not my vice of choice."

Aidan almost falls out of his chair as he leans forward. "You're not seriously going to tell Aunt Fae you're doing cocaine?"

"I am," I say calmly, although inside I'm just as nervous as he is. I love my aunt, but she's probably going to kick my ass. I need her help, though. I don't want to enter a treatment facility, but I know it's going to be too hard to stop on my own and possibly even dangerous. I need her medical expertise.

"Dude," Aidan shifts looking nervous, "please don't rat me out. I haven't done any of that in ages." I give him a look that lets him know his life is his own. He knows I'd never betray his trust just as I know he wouldn't betray mine. "So, you mentioned some stuff going on since Lia's been home?"

I realize in that moment that Aidan and I haven't had a chance to really talk in the last few weeks, which is unusual. He has been my confidant since we were boys, and there is very little of importance that goes on in my life that he doesn't know. "Well, I know who Lia's father is."

He looks thoughtful for a moment before saying, "And this isn't good news?"

Aidan, of course, isn't surprised that I would look into Lia's background. He doesn't know that, unlike other women I've been involved with, it was almost an afterthought. I don't think there could have been anything which would have kept me away from her. I was too far gone from the moment I met her. "You've heard of Lee Jacks?"

"Of course," he answers before his mouth falls open. I seem to be surprising Aidan a lot today, which is hard to do. "You aren't saying..." When I incline my head, he whistles. "Holy shit! How in the hell did that happen?" Before I can make a sarcastic comment, he waves me off. "I know *how,* smartass. I mean, how did Lia's mother end up with Jacks? From what I've gathered, they wouldn't exactly run in the same circles."

"I believe that their circumstances were more similar at one time than they are now. It was just a brief thing, and he never knew about Lia. Actually, if I hadn't tipped him off by checking into his personal life after finding out about the association with Lia's mother, he would probably never have known."

"Wow," Aidan muses still looking shell-shocked. "Jacks is somewhat of a mystery man. But there are rumors and plenty of them. Does she know?"

"No," I admit, "but I don't know how long I can keep it from her. He's pushing hard to tell her, but I think she needs some time to recover from everything she's been through first. This will be a huge shock to her."

"No kidding. If the guy has a single ounce of humanity in his body, then he's got to be choking on guilt for all that Lia has endured."

"Unless he's a good actor, he's feeling it. I don't know if it's driven by mere curiosity or something more, but he seems very drawn to her. Enough to crash our dinner last week to meet her."

"This is like Jerry Springer shit," Aidan marvels. "They write books about this kind of messed-up stuff. Wait; did he have anything to do with her mother turning herself in out of the blue?"

I had mentioned her mother's arrest to Aidan over the phone but hadn't gone into any details. "Yeah, and he's looking for her stepfather."

"Prison's too good for that bastard," Aidan snarls, echoing my sentiments exactly. It's something Lee and I don't see eye-to-eye on, but what am I supposed to do? Recommend he kill the sick fuck instead, or better yet, help me find him so I can have the pleasure? "Man, no wonder you're stressed. That's a lot to deal with."

"It is what it is," I say simply. I look him over, noticing again how tired he looks. "What's going on with you? You look like shit." Aidan and I are nothing if not blunt with each other.

"Thanks," he says dryly as he runs a hand along his jaw. "I'm just not sleeping that well. You know I have problems with that at the best of times." Aidan has always been somewhat of an insomniac, but it looks as if things have been worse than usual lately.

"I appreciate you stepping in and running things here while I was with Lia. I apologize for dumping that on you; I know it was a lot to ask."

"You know I've always got your back. And that's not the cause of my stress," he adds quietly. Fuck, I know what's coming, and I don't want to hear it, but it's so clear that he needs to talk right now. There is only one thing, or one person that can brings him this low.

"It's Cassie," I say as more of a statement than a question. Where Aidan is concerned, no matter how many women he screws, it's always her. He has spent most of his adult life trying to fuck her out of his heart and his head.

"Luc, it's finally happening. She's coming out of it." I look at his hopeful face and don't know what to say. I don't know how many times I've heard this from him through the years and nothing ever changes. When she said his nickname a few weeks ago, it gave him hope. I admit that it's something new, but there have been other things which seemed to indicate she had some awareness of her surroundings and nothing's ever come of it. No matter how I feel about Cassie, it kills me to see him go through this kind of torture.

"Aidan...you shouldn't read too much into her saying your name. She—"

"It's more than that," he interrupts me, looking almost excited now. "Her doctor says she's been interacting some with her nurses and the other patients."

"Interacting how exactly?" I ask, feeling a ripple of unease running through me.

"Saying thank you and answering questions from fellow patients."

My ripple of unease is more like a fucking tidal wave now. Aidan is right; this is a new development. Cassie has spoken through the years, but generally words that have no place in the conversation at hand. The doctors have always believed she was talking to herself and not responding to whoever is present at the time. She also has a gut-wrenching habit of rubbing her stomach and humming as if she were still pregnant and singing to her unborn child...my fucking child. I can't be around her and risk seeing it. I told her doctor to stop sending me reports after the last one, which included that bit of information. It's a completely messed-up state of affairs that I'm her legal guardian and pay for her care, even though she killed my baby and tried to kill me. It's pure fucking guilt on my part. I long ago instructed the facility to send their reports to Aidan and Max; I simply couldn't handle it. "Aidan," I say, trying to get back on track, but still reeling from his news. "She has spoken at times through the years."

"But her doctors say this is the first time her words are in the right context. Luc, the new medication regimen they are trying with her is doing something. She's starting to come back, I can feel it." Fuck, the only thing I feel at his words is nauseous. I love Aidan like a brother, but his dreams are my nightmares. I don't want a world that involves Cassie, and I wonder if he even knows what he's hoping for. She's killing him little by little without ever laying a hand on him.

I give him the usual song and dance about not getting his hopes up, but I'm only going through the motions. I'm too rattled to put much into it. Finally, I change the subject, and we go through the list he's made of items that need my attention. When Cindy buzzes my phone to tell me I have a call, I'm grateful. I'm afraid he'll start talking about Cassie again, and I know that regardless of how much I want to support my friend, this is one subject we'll never agree on again.

Lia

I'm in the kitchen finishing a simple meal of tacos and Spanish rice. I still haven't had much of an appetite, so when I was actually craving Mexican food, I decided to seize the opportunity. Luckily, Lucian's cabinets are fully stocked with most of my favorites from the grocery service we use. I hear the front door open and tense before Lucian's voice rings through the apartment. "Lia, where are you?"

"I'm in the kitchen," I call back as I sit a glass of sweet tea in front of my plate and a Corona with a lime wedge in front of his.

"What's all of this?" he asks, looking surprised as he takes in the plates of food I have on the bar. He closes his arms around me, pulling my back into his front. He runs his nose down my neck, smelling my scent as he does so often before dropping a soft kiss there.

I relax into his big body, loving how safe I feel. "I thought I would make dinner for us tonight. I'm getting kind of tired of restaurant food, and I figured you were, as well."

When I feel him tug on my ponytail, I smile as I wait for him to explore my new ponytail holder. "Is this...? I see him look over to the trashcan in the corner, which I had pulled out to empty after dinner. The yellow tie hanging from one side is a perfect match for the one I have tied into a bow in my hair. He gives a dramatic sigh. "Thank God, it's not my underwear this time." He spins me around until I'm facing him and takes my mouth immediately. I keep my mouth shut to tease him, and then yelp in surprise when he bites my lower lip before licking the sting with his tongue. Lucian's kiss as usual takes no prisoners. He is a master, knowing exactly how to stroke, suck, and explore. I move against his kiss restlessly, immediately wanting those heavy lips to move lower...much lower, but he cuts me off just as I'm on the verge of begging.

"I'm starving, how about you?" He gives me a devilish grin as I stand pouting up at him. The ass knows exactly what kind of fire he's started within me. I know that it would only take a few well-placed strokes to change his mind, and I'm seriously debating my next course of action when it hits me. We can't have sex again until we talk about birth control, or rather the lack of it recently. I had managed to put it out of my mind for the last hour while cooking, but now the fear has reared its head once again. He seems disappointed when I pull away and take my seat at the bar. I feel certain that guilt is written all over my face even though I haven't put us in this position on purpose. I feel as though there is very little likelihood that we've conceived, since I've been on birth control for quite a while, but we can't take any more chances.

"So, how was your day?" I ask when he sits next to me and takes a long sip of his beer. We sound so domesticated in that moment that I find myself trying to swallow a smile. Has there ever been another woman in Lucian's life who had this with him? I feel a pang as I think of Cassie. Lucian said that no other woman has been in this apartment, but Cassie was obviously a big part of his past. He has promised to tell me about her soon, and I feel as if this will be the last key to understanding who he really is and what he's been through because I know it's something horrible from his nightmares.

"It was good…busy. Aidan's done a great job of keeping things running, so there weren't many problems to deal with. How about you?"

"It was fine," I say brightly…going just a tad overboard on the enthusiasm. Between obsessing over my birth control oversight and jumping at every single sound, it has been an exhausting day. I'm wiped out, even though I did nothing physically taxing…well, other than in the shower this morning.

Lucian puts his hand over mine, squeezing it. "I'm proud of you," he says quietly. I feel my eyes well up, and I'm so grateful when he starts eating without adding anything further. Kindness has been so rare in my life that I still have a hard time processing it when it happens.

When we finish dinner, Lucian insists on cleaning up and orders me to the couch to rest for a while. I fidget nervously, waiting for him to join me. I know the time has arrived for me to talk to him about my doctor's appointment this morning, but I'd rather have a tooth pulled than have this conversation.

I've worked myself into a jittery mess by the time he sits down next to me.

When he picks up the television remote, I put my hand over his, stopping him from turning it on. "I...need to talk to you about something," I begin. He immediately sets the remote back down and turns to give me his full attention. Shit, it's even worse now. Maybe I should have emailed or texted him instead.

When I don't say anything else, he finally prompts, "Lia? What is it, baby?"

I normally love his tendency to call me 'baby,' but at this moment, I find myself wincing at his choice of endearment. He is beginning to look worried as I sit here floundering, so I close my eyes briefly and fight for composure before speaking. "I...when I saw Dr. Kay this morning, she asked me some questions, and one of them was concerning birth control." I feel his hand twitch beneath mine and his expression looks frozen.

"Are you pregnant, Lia?" he asks, sounding panicked. His eyes are locked on mine, as if searching for the answer.

"No!" He relaxes minutely before I add, "I mean, I don't think so."

He drops my hand, jumping to his feet. "What the hell do you mean, 'you don't think so'?' You either are or you aren't," he says in a voice just under a shout. Suddenly, it feels as if he and I have switched places and I'm the calm one and he's off the deep end. It's crazy, but the shift has helped to center me. I can't focus on my own emotions when I'm worried about him.

"Luc," I say soothingly. "Calm down and just listen for a moment. There is no need to freak out." He snorts at my statement, and I feel the urge to do something Rose-like and flip him off, but that wouldn't go over well in his present mood. "When Dr. Kay was reviewing my medical records this morning she noticed that I'm on birth control pills. It hit me when she mentioned it that I hadn't taken the pills while I was in the hospital."

"We weren't exactly having sex in the hospital, Lia," he says condescendingly. My foot twitches as I hold myself back from throwing something at him. He is always so gentle and considerate with me that I find it hard to believe the person vibrating with tension mere steps away is my Lucian. Quite obviously, pregnancy is a trigger for him...a big one.

"I know that," I snap back, unable to hold my temper. I bluntly finish what I had been trying to say when he rudely interrupted me. "We have had sex for four days, and I haven't taken my birth control pills since the day of my attack." I watch him in alarm as he turns completely white, weaving on his feet unsteadily. I rush to add, "Dr. Kay said she can give me a prescription for a morning-after pill which is actually effective for up to five days. It would keep a pregnancy from happening."

If I thought my words would comfort him, then I'm dead wrong. "What!" he roars. "You want to terminate the pregnancy?"

I jump to my feet, placing my hands on his heaving chest. "Luc, there is no pregnancy yet, and it's quite possible there wouldn't be even without the pill. I'm sorry that I didn't realize I'd missed my pills, and I promise you that it was an accident." I don't know why I feel the need to assure him of that, but he's so upset that I'm just trying to calm him down.

He steps back, causing my hands to drop to my sides. "I've got to get out of here for a while," he says over his shoulder as he walks toward the door at a fast clip. My jaw drops in shock as he leaves the apartment as if the hounds of Hell are nipping at his heels. I sag weakly to the couch, trying to figure out what just happened. I knew he would probably be upset, but this was more than that; he went all to pieces. *Oh, God, what if he has an accident?* I get back to my feet and start pacing the floor. I run to the entryway table and grab my cellphone from my purse. I call his number, but it goes to voicemail after a few rings. My texts to him go unanswered, as well. Another few minutes pass before I look through my contacts and click on Sam's name. He's the only person I know other than Aidan who might be able to help me.

CHAPTER ELEVEN

Lucian

"Fuck!" I growl, as I realize I slammed out of the apartment without the keys to any of my vehicles. I can't go back in and see Lia yet, though; I just can't. With no other choice, I set off on foot and walk a couple of blocks until I come to the sports bar at the end of the block. Apparently, it's ladies' night, so there is a crowd of hopeful women and horny men hanging all over them. I find a quiet spot in the corner of the bar.

The bartender, an attractive woman about Lia's age wearing a T-shirt pulled tight across her big tits, puts a napkin down in front of me and gives an appreciative smack of her red lips. She's not hiding the fact that she likes what she sees, but I couldn't give a good fuck.

"Hey, sugar, what can I do for you tonight?" I don't miss the double entendre in her voice, but I ignore it.

"Bourbon, neat and make it a double. Actually, just bring me the bottle and a glass." Fuck trying to wait on her to come back once she gets busy.

She smirks, shaking her head. "Sugar, that's expensive. How about we just go glass by glass for now?" I wordlessly pull out my wallet and throw my black American Express Card on the bar. Her eyes widen as she picks it up. She's obviously been around enough to know that a black credit card usually means money and a lot of it. "You got it, sugar," she says, turning away with an extra sway in her hips to get the bottle. Her tiny shorts display an award-winning ass, but I'm not interested. She sets the bottle and the glass down before pouring a generous measure. "What else can I get you?" she asks, leaning against the bar. I can plainly see her skimpy bra as the V-neck of her T-shirt gapes open. I'm sure she's an expert at that move and I look away, not even vaguely tempted to take her up on her silent offer. Finally, she gets the message and moves away, thank fuck.

I'm three glasses in when I feel a hand on my shoulder. I jerk around in surprise to see Sam standing there. He doesn't seem surprised to see me at all, so I know this isn't an accidental meeting. He points to the bottle in front of me, asking, "Think you can get me another glass?" Instead of shouting for the eager bartender, I stretch across the bar and manage to hook a glass from under the cabinet. "Impressive," Sam smirks as he pours a small amount into his glass.

"Why are you here?" I ask bluntly. I'm in no mood for company and just wish he'd leave.

"Lia called me. She was worried about you. She had already checked to see if you took your car keys so I knew you were on foot." Pointing toward the front of the bar, he adds, "Since there are nothing but restaurants and stores here, I took a wild guess you'd be in the first bar you happened along."

I'm surprised Lia called him but as I think back, I realize she and I have never really had a fight. We've had disagreements, like most people, but I can't recall either of us slamming out of the apartment. Even as upset as I am, I feel guilty. She's been through so much, and I know she doesn't need this added stress on top of everything else. While there are plenty of men who might panic at the thought of an unplanned pregnancy, she has no idea that it's my biggest trigger. I take another drink of my bourbon before saying, "I'm fine, Sam. You can go on home. I won't be here much longer."

I can literally see him settling onto his barstool. "I don't have anywhere else to be, so I'll just keep you company." At least ten minutes pass as I continue to drink and brood while he pretends to watch the football game on the bar television.

I surprise myself when I blurt out, "Lia might be pregnant." I see him freeze in the act of lifting his glass just for a split second before he resumes the movement.

"I see." He doesn't say anything else as if waiting for me to continue.

"She hasn't been taking her pills since her attack. She didn't realize it until Dr. Kay mentioned it this morning."

Sam nods, looking far calmer than I feel. "That's perfectly understandable, Luc. She has been dealing with a lot."

I nervously shred a napkin with my fingers as I stare into my drink. "I know that, and I'm not blaming her. It just...threw me. I shouldn't have been so damn careless. I mean, how many times do I need to learn that lesson?"

"Lia isn't Cassie, and you don't even know that she *is* pregnant, do you?"

I find myself glaring at one of the few people in my life who I love. I'm not in the mood to be soothed; I want to drink and forget. "Don't you think that I, of all people, know the difference between Lia and Cassie?"

"Do you?" he throws back immediately, causing me to surge to my feet unsteadily. "Sit down!" he snaps, and I'm so surprised by the command in his tone that I obey instantly. He turns sideways on his bench to face me fully. "Luc, you're like a son to me and I love you. You're a rich, successful man with more drive and ambition than anyone I've ever known. You've bottled up every ounce of rage inside you and used it to succeed beyond anyone's wildest dreams. You keep women in a neat corner of your life and never allow yourself to feel anything for them."

"There's a woman living with me right now, Sam, and she doesn't fit into any 'neat corner of my life,' trust me on that." I say, hoping he'll stop talking. He's forcing me to think, and that's the last thing I want to do tonight.

"She may not fit in a neat corner, but she fits with you perfectly. She loves you, Luc, and not just for what you can give her. That girl has been to Hell and back just as you have. Unlike Cassie, it has only made her stronger. She is your match in every way, and I think you know that."

My gut clenches as I say the truth, which haunts me. "I can't lose anyone else I love. I won't survive it."

"Something can happen to any of us at any time. There are no guarantees in life, son. I wish there were. What I *do* know is that Lia loves you and you love her, as well. You can deny it to yourself all you want, but it's been plain to everyone else almost from the beginning. You've never let another woman this close to you, even Cassie, if we're being honest."

"After all that has happened to Lia, the thought of her being pregnant fucking terrifies me," I tell him. "It caused something inside of Cassie to snap. What if the same thing happens to Lia? You know they come from similar pasts."

"Maybe they do," Sam admits, "but that's all they have in common. Cassie was always different. I've never seen someone's mood alter as fast as hers could, and she thrived on causing conflict between you and Aidan. Cassie wasn't happy unless someone around her was unhappy, which was usually Aidan."

I'm completely surprised by his words. I mean, I knew Aidan was pissed off a lot of the time because he loved Cassie and wanted her to return his feelings. We were all friends, though, and I never noticed her trying to start trouble between us. On the contrary, most of her attention seemed to be centered on controlling me through a mixture of threats, blackmail, and whatever mind game she could dream up that day. "I think you're mistaken about that," I try to tell Sam. "Cassie loved the attention we both gave her too much to want to push Aidan away."

Sam gives me a sad smile before saying, "She didn't want Aidan to leave her, and she wanted him to turn against you. She wanted to be the sole focus of you both, and that happened more when you were at odds with your friend. That way you both turned to her, and she was number one within your group." When I start to protest, he adds, "It's always easier for someone on the outside to see things that people close to the situation miss. I spent even more time around you back then than I do now. I knew that something would happen between you all eventually. I just...couldn't have guessed what she would do. I'm sorry, Luc; maybe we should have talked about this years ago."

I mull over his words, knowing he's right. Cassie was constantly saying negative things about Aidan to me back then, and if what Sam says is true, then she was probably doing the same to him. Our friendship was severely strained in high school and college, and our worst arguments usually occurred when one of us had spent time alone with Cassie. I always put it down to competitive jealousy, but maybe that was not the case. It was so long ago that I'm not sure it even matters anymore other than to add a new element to what is already a tragic story between friends. I put my hand on Sam's arm. "There is nothing you could have said back then that would have mattered." Giving him a tired grin, I add, "We knew it all, remember?" If I'd have seen Cassie for who she really was that first day we met, I'd have fucking run and never looked back.

Sam laughs softly, nodding his head. "You certainly did. Now, why don't you let me be the know-it-all tonight and tell you to crawl out of that bottle of bourbon while you can still walk and go home. Things are different for you now, Luc. If Lia *is* pregnant, that will be different, as well. Your past only defines you if you let it."

I reluctantly push my glass aside, knowing he's right. I can't keep making Lia pay for Cassie's sins; she has already paid far too much in her life for other people's mistakes. I signal for the bill from my still-overly-friendly bartender and turn back to Sam. "Thanks for the talk and for wasting your evening in a bar with me."

"It's fine. Cindy's doing something with her church group tonight, so I had nothing but time on my hands. I might have possibly been doing a final drive-by of your apartment when Lia called, so I was in the area."

I knew Sam was keeping an eye out for Lia so that doesn't surprise me, but his casual referral to Cindy does. Of course, I know there was something going on between them; I'm not blind. However, neither has ever come out and admitted it as he just has. "So, you and Cindy, huh...?"

He doesn't look the slightest bit uncomfortable as he says easily, "Of course. Don't even try to act surprised; it's not as if it's exactly a secret. Cindy just didn't want to advertise the fact at the office. Personally, I couldn't care less. Life's too short to spend time pretending. I'd marry that woman tomorrow if she'd only say yes."

Now I'm floored. I didn't know things were quite that serious between them. I'm not sure I'm ready for a world in which I might walk in on Sam and Cindy getting hot and heavy. Cindy thrives on being professional, even more so than is warranted most of the time, so surely she would never subject me to that. "I'm happy for you," I say honestly. "Cindy is a hell of a woman, and I know I don't have to threaten you to treat her right."

Before he can answer, the bartender arrives with my check. "Here ya go, sugar." She leans closer to me, rubbing a tit against my hand. I see Sam smirking from the corner of my eye. He's enjoying this far too much. Most of the women he's seen throw themselves at me over the years are horny socialites; the eager bartender is something a bit new. "I get off at midnight. Why don't I meet you somewhere?"

I sign the check as quickly as I can, leaving her a hefty tip. Hell, I'd double it just to get her to leave me alone. "Er...I don't think so." When she still doesn't look discouraged I throw out, "I've got a girlfriend."

She leans closer, running a hand over my chest. "Doesn't matter to me, sugar. I have a boyfriend, too. We have an open relationship, so it's all good. If your girlfriend looks anything like you do, then bring her along. I'm not shy, and I have no problem sharing." I push abruptly back from the bar, causing her hand to fall away. Holy fuck, she's staring at my crotch now as if trying to imagine the size of my cock. *Yeah, baby, keep looking because I have no interest whatsoever in what you've got to offer.*

I grab Sam's arm and usher him toward the door, weaving slightly on my feet. The alcohol I've consumed is hitting me hard, but I'm ready to get the hell out of here. "Fuck," I roar as we make it to the sidewalk. "That bitch was crazy!"

"Oh, come on," Sam laughs, looking like the whole incident was hilarious. "I seem to recall you and Aidan having some interesting...gatherings over the years. That girl was probably tame compared to what you two have done."

I find myself doing something that happens rarely: feeling embarrassed. Sam has been my driver forever, so of course he's picked me up on some of my drunken evenings. I've been far from a monk over the years and one-night stands were always my preferred way to fuck. Aidan and I had on occasion shared a woman...or several. It's not something I did on a regular basis, but it happened; more so in the immediate years after Cassie than in the last several. I finally settled more into exclusive fucking such as with Laurie. One woman for a few months at a time. As I gained money and power, it became more beneficial to have a woman by my side at social gatherings. It kept the Moniques of the world at bay and provided the added benefit of the illusion of stability to those in the business world. Although a lot of them fuck around, they still tend to look down on those who present themselves as nothing but playboys.

"Leave me alone," I say as I start to walk away. I can hear him laughing behind me and know he'll follow me all the way back to the apartment. After walking in silence for a few minutes he says, "You're pretty drunk, aren't you?"

I whirl around, which is a big mistake with this much booze sloshing around in my stomach, and almost fall off the sidewalk. Sam quickly grabs my arm, halting my progress. "Thanks for stating the obvious," I slur. I don't know what happened, but I didn't feel nearly this drunk when I was throwing them back in the bar. It's as if the fresh air has caused the bourbon to go straight to my head. Hell, if Sam weren't here, I would probably be in a ditch somewhere or worse yet...at Bartender Girl's mercy. "Why am I so fucking drunk?" I ask myself, but Sam answers anyway.

"I believe because you drank a large amount of liquor in a small amount of time. Just a guess..."

"You know, I hate you sometimes," I snap as I turn to wobble on. Where in the hell is my apartment? I feel like I've been walking around for hours. As I turn another corner, Sam pulls my arm in a different direction.

"We've already walked in this circle three times. Wouldn't you like to actually go home now?" he asks dryly.

"Are you fucking kidding me?" I try to stare him down but keep blinking as my eyes blur. "Why didn't you stop me? I'm dying here, if you haven't noticed."

"I was doing it for Lia," he says from behind me. "I thought the air might help sober you up some, but I don't think it's working. We need to move on to just letting you pass out in the bed."

I feel a wave of emotion hit me at the mention of Lia's name. *What if she's pregnant? Wasn't she telling me before I stomped out that she could still get rid of the baby?* I try to recall our exact conversation, but the words are fuzzy and truthfully, after her first few words, I heard nothing in my head but *pregnant.* "I have to talk to her; I have to see her...now." I pick up my pace, finally recognizing my building in the distance.

Behind me, I hear Sam say, "Slow down, you're going to bust your..." Just as I trip over a fucking flowerpot in front of the building and go sprawling on my ass. "Dammit, Luc, I told you." He huffs to a stop next to me with his hands on his hips. He shakes his head in resignation and extends a hand down to me. "You're not hurt, are you?"

"Only my pride," I mumble as I get to my feet. In truth, the jarring and unexpected tumble hurt like hell. I'm too old to be falling down drunk; that much is perfectly clear to me. Thankfully, Sam has my door and elevator codes, so I let him handle it. I feel the slight urge to puke as the elevator rises to the top floor. I bolt from the small space as it stops. Sam opens the front door and motions me in.

"Do you need anything else tonight, Luc?" he asks, still looking far too amused at my expense. Maybe I would have been better off in a ditch somewhere, after all. At least then, I wouldn't know the person laughing at me.

"No, thanks for the help," I say as I close the door. Fucking good riddance. I can't remember the last time I've seen so many of Sam's teeth. I've never hated a smile that much.

I walk slowly toward the bedroom, wondering what I'll say to Lia, when I notice the light on in the living room. I turn that way and find her huddled in the corner of the couch, sound asleep. She's curled up tight, as if cold...or upset. She looks impossibly young and beautiful in simple yoga pants and a T-shirt. Lia is a natural beauty. She looks gorgeous makeup-free with her hair in a simple ponytail. She needs no artificial enhancers.

My heart almost pounds out of my chest as I think of her carrying my child. I'm fucking terrified at the idea but also oddly fascinated. I spent most of the time Cassie was pregnant trying to talk her off one ledge or another. She freaked out when she found out she was pregnant and immediately wanted an abortion. One of the reasons I proposed to her was to try to settle her down. She was so convinced the baby was a mistake and it would ruin her life. In hindsight, maybe she knew more than I did. I couldn't stand the thought of her aborting my child, so I did my best each day to assure her that I loved her and everything would be wonderful once the baby was born. She just had to hold on for nine months and then I would do everything for her and the baby.

Her doctor had taken her off the bipolar medication that she'd been taking for years. That was tricky for a month, but she seemed to return to her normal self, which while not pleasant was at least predictable. I should have known when her usual threats stopped and she instead seemed almost blissfully peaceful that something was wrong. Maybe it lulled me into a false sense of security, and I wasn't as observant as I should have been.

Lia stirs, her eyes blinking open. She gasps as she sees me standing there, looking panicked for a moment before seeming to recognize me. "I'm sorry for frightening you, baby," I say as I move to her and drop to my knees on the floor in front of the couch. We stare at each other for a long moment. When her nose wrinkles slightly, I can tell she smells the alcohol on me.

"Are you all right?" she asks quietly.

Instead of answering her question, I lean closer to her body and place my head gently on her flat stomach. I feel her breath catch as she freezes. Finally, she relaxes under me and her hand goes to my head, digging into my hair. I moan as she strokes my scalp, giving me comfort even though I've been an ass to her tonight. "I'm sorry," I say, giving her the apology she deserves. I don't want her to feel as if she needs to keep things from me because I'll freak out; she doesn't deserve that from me.

Her hand tightens in my hair, and I wince at the sting but remain silent. "When you left tonight, I was surprised by your reaction. I mean, I know neither of us is ready for a baby, but I wasn't expecting you to be that upset. I'll be honest and say that none of this has really seemed real to me until you slammed out the door."

"Lia..." I begin, wanting to comfort her.

"No, Luc, let me finish please." I remain quiet while she gathers her thoughts. "We're probably needlessly upsetting ourselves about something that will not even happen, but it made me think." Her hand begins moving in my hair once again, as if trying to soothe me as she says, "Luc, I can't take that pill. This might sound crazy, but all I keep thinking is if I do, then how am I any better than my mother is? According to what I read on the internet, it's not terminating a pregnancy because one doesn't even exist at that point. It's just stopping it from happening." I grasp her leg, feeling my hand shaking as I listen to her emotional plea for me to understand. She has no idea that I not only understand her turmoil but I feel, it as well. "But...what if they're wrong? I...I just can't take that chance, Luc," she says on a sob. "I'm sorry, I'm so sorry because I know you don't want this."

"Baby, stop," I say, pulling her from the couch and into my arms. She is crying into my chest, and it wouldn't take much more for me to join her. She doesn't need that now, though. She needs to hear that I understand and agree with her decision. Actually, I'm so fucking grateful that she feels the same as I do that I'm almost weak with relief. "Lia, sweetheart, listen..." I say as I pull back enough to see her face. "Baby, look at me." She shakes her head, seeming terrified of what I'm going to say. Apparently, my earlier anger is still fresh in her mind. "Please, baby." Tears run down her cheeks as she finally allows me to tilt her head upwards. "I understand and I agree," I say softly as I use my thumb to wipe her tears away to no avail.

"You...you do?" She stares up at me as if she can't believe she's heard me correctly.

"Yes, I do. Lia...Cassie and I were going to have a baby eight years ago and she..." Fuck, why can't I get the words out? Lia needs to know why I lost it earlier, but I just can't tell her the full truth, not tonight. I'm too raw. "She ended his life." Lia looks at me in something akin to horror. Her tears have stopped as she struggles to understand what I'm saying to her. There is no way she can come up with the true picture, even with the mother she had.

"Oh, Luc," she whispers, looking as devastated as I feel. "She had an abortion without your consent?" I can't just completely lie to her, so I pull her close without answering. In a way, that is exactly what Cassie did, only in a much more horrific manner. I don't know why I find it so difficult to tell Lia the entire story. Maybe because I don't want to see the pity in her eyes or even worse, I'm afraid she will see that my life is too ugly for her. Giving her pieces of my past is the coward's way out, but right now, it's all I'm capable of. She is carrying too much of her own baggage to assume the weight of mine, as well. We both need to be stronger before that happens.

We lay there for a while longer before we go to bed. We don't make love, but instead we hold on to each other as if by some unspoken truth, we both know there's a storm coming and tonight is merely the calm before it hits.

CHAPTER TWELVE

Lia

"I need you to have Max come get me out of jail." I turn sideways on my barstool to look at Lucian. We are having breakfast before he leaves for work. As if sensing my eyes on him, he looks up from his perusal of the morning stock report and arches a brow at me in question.

I hold up my finger, telling him to give me a minute as I ask Rose, "What have you done?" I have a bad feeling she has been continuing her crusade to make Jake pay for screwing around on her. I knew things had been entirely too quiet on that front for the last few days.

"Well..." She lowers her voice before continuing, "I might have used my key to go into his apartment while he wasn't there and put Bengay in his shampoo and body wash. I might also have replaced all of the water in his refrigerator with white vinegar and I maybe used his iPad while I was there and sent an email to his entire contact list asking for advice on the best sexual positions for men with small penises. I even found a small pecker picture on the internet to attach so people could see the scope of the problem. Oh, and I sewed the pants legs closed on all of his jeans. I would have done more, but his roommate interrupted me...and ratted me out."

"Oh, my God," I sputter, causing Lucian too look at me warily. "Rose, have you lost your mind? You just got out of jail, and out of curiosity, how in the world did you sew his pants legs closed?"

"I took my portable sewing machine with me. I was going to sew the holes closed on everything the bastard owned, but I got caught."

I have no idea why, but the whole thing strikes me as hilarious. I start laughing, falling against the bar and almost upending my plate in my lap. When Lucian moves it out of my reach, I laugh even harder. Picturing my Martha Stewart/Lorena Bobbitt friend going to do evil things to her cheating ex with a tube of Bengay in one hand and a sewing machine in the other is just too much. Only Rose would be threading a needle shortly after breaking and entering. When I finally manage to catch my breath, I ask, "So, um, why do you need Max? Aren't your parents back in town now?"

"Yeah," she sighs, "they are, but I don't want to call them. Daddy will be so disappointed in me." I'm a little puzzled by her statement since she assured me the last time that her daddy would be proud of her for her violence against Jake's car.

"I thought you said he would be okay with you getting into trouble if you were doing your whole payback thing?"

"He was fine the last time," she says, "but he wouldn't be happy with how I went about continuing my revenge. Daddy believes in meeting your problems and solving them head-on. He would think me weak and silly for doing the stuff I did."

I give Lucian a WTF shrug of confusion as I say slowly, "So, if you had busted up his apartment with a shovel, he would be proud? But since you didn't resort to violence, he would...not be?" I grimace knowing how crazy this conversation must sound to the man sitting next to me.

"That's right. I wasn't raised to play around with people. That doesn't earn respect."

"Good grief, Rose, who is your father, Hitler?" I ask, only half-joking. He sounds completely insane. Apparently, the man had drilled the whole 'eye for an eye' mantra in his daughter from an early age, and he meant it, literally. I bet Jake will seriously rue the day he ever met her before this is over.

"It's just the way we are," she says, not seeming to understand my amazement at the whole thing. "So listen, Deputy what's-his-face over here is telling me my time is up. Can you please call Max and send him down here? He's not taking my calls."

"Wait...what? Maybe he's just busy this morning."

"He hasn't been taking my calls since we got hot and heavy in his car. He's trying to take the moral high ground even though he's dying to fuck me." I hear someone in the background, choking out, 'time's up.' "I gotta go. Please have Lucian call him." The line goes dead and I pull my cellphone away, staring at it as if it holds the answers I desperately need. Has the world gone completely mad? My best friend sure has.

Lucian plucks the phone from my hand and sits patiently, waiting for an explanation. "So...do you think you could ask Max to go to the police station and help Rose out this morning?"

After taking a long sip of his coffee, he says, "Of course. And what shall I tell Max is the problem this time?" His face is a cross between amused and resigned as I drop my head in my hands before repeating what Rose just told me. When I'm finished, he deadpans, "Your friend and her family are fucking nuts."

"Luc!" I protest, although I know it's weak at best. "She's just going through a tough time right now." It's all I've got in the way of defense for her. After her comment about Max, I'm beginning to wonder whether she's on a mission for revenge on Jake or to get Max Decker's attention. Whichever it is, I hope she stops before she ends up behind bars for more than a few hours.

Lucian grabs his own phone and places a call to Max. I hear the other man yelling from where I'm sitting. Finally, Luc seems to have heard enough and snaps, "If you don't want to do it, send one of the junior lawyers." Max says something else I don't catch. "All right then, take care of it."

"Is someone going to help her?" I ask tentatively when he continues to scan the stock reports as if nothing has happened.

"Max is on his way to the police department now. I'm sure he'll be able to get her out."

"Max is going himself?" I ask for clarification. After all of the yelling, I can't imagine him going if he could send someone else.

Lucian puts his iPad aside as he pulls me from my chair and onto his lap. "Yep, apparently he can't stand to be around her but doesn't want anyone else to be either. Go figure." Before I can reply, he lowers his mouth to mine, nipping at my lower lip before slipping his tongue inside my mouth when I gasp. His tongue plunges over and over, reminding me of how he fucks. I wasn't sure how he would act this morning after everything that happened between us last night, but he has been relaxed and almost loving. That seems to have changed, though, in the last few moments. Now he's like a barely-leashed stallion, just on the edge of breaking free.

As his mouth continues to devour mine, he pushes a hand up my thin T-shirt, finding my bare, erect nipple. I moan into his mouth as he pulls on the sensitive peak, causing it to throb and

beg for his attention. My core floods with
moisture as he continues to work my body
into a frenzy. I rub my bottom against his
rapidly hardening cock, frustrated by the
clothing separating us. "Luc, please," I
cry, as he drops his hand to the needy
spot between my legs. "I need you now," I
groan. He has just touched my wet slit
when there is a knock at the door. His
hand pauses and I almost scream in
frustration. "No! They'll go away," I
whisper against him as I lick his neck. I
feel him shudder. His hand begins to
move against my clit again before another
knock sounds.

"Ah, fuck." He sounds as desperate as I
feel. "It's Sam, baby. I've got a meeting in
half an hour, and he's here to pick me
up."

"No, no," I moan as I throw my arms
around his neck. "Stay with me today."

He chuckles softly as he pries my
hands loose. "You have no idea how much
I'd like that, sweetheart. Sam's not going
away, though, and as much as I hate it,
I've got to go." He gives me another kiss
before putting me down on my feet. We
both look at his prominently displayed
cock, which is pushing against the zipper
of his pants as if fighting to get out. I
hand him his suit jacket off the back of
the chair.

"You might want to cover that before someone gets hurt," I joke, perversely glad to see he is suffering as much as I am. I walk him to the door where he calls to Sam that he'll be out in a minute.

I jump in shock when he suddenly palms my core, resting his hand between my legs. "No touching this today, no matter how much you want to. This belongs to me, and I'll have it tonight." When I only laugh in reply, he pushes me back against the wall, growling in my ear. "Who owns your pussy, baby?"

I wonder briefly why his show of dominance after all I've been through doesn't scare me. I think it's because I want nothing more than to belong to this man and no matter how much he likes to dominate me in bed, I know he would never raise a hand to physically hurt me. Even knowing what he does, he doesn't treat me as if I'm fragile. He lets me know how much he wants me with every look and every touch. I lower my hand to cover his, until we are both pressing against my damp heat. "You own it, Luc. You and only you."

Our joined hands are rubbing my aching clit when an amused voice calls through the door. "Come on, kids; Luc needs to go to work now." We both burst out laughing, feeling like teenagers caught making out. I give him a quick kiss and push him out the door before Sam can see my bedraggled appearance. I'm certain he knows what we were up to, though.

The desire to finish what we started is pounding through me, but I resist. An idea is forming as I walk back toward the kitchen to clean up our breakfast dishes. I have a few hours left to shower and call Debra to catch up before I head downtown to deliver a surprise lunch to Lucian: me.

Lucian

I'm frustrated as I finish my call with Peter Jacks. Peter told me Lee is out of town on business and should be back by the end of the week. I had asked the other man point-blank if his brother had security on Lia. The extra security I have in place at the apartment has noticed a couple of guys who appeared to be doing some type of surveillance. Peter hadn't wanted to admit anything at first, but when I threatened to have the men arrested the next time, he admitted they were employed by his brother. Truthfully,

I'm relieved. Even though I don't think Jim Dawson could get past my security, I'm still glad to have a few extra sets of eyes on the building.

If not for Lia's stepfather still being somewhere out there, I'd be happy not to hear from Lee Jacks for a while. He is a ticking time bomb, which I don't have the time or the energy to deal with right now. Lia and I are in a good place despite the drama of last night. I think we are both at peace with our decision to leave any consequences that arise from our unprotected sex to fate. We will of course use condoms until we know for sure one way or the other, but there is nothing to do now but wait.

I had actually been shocked to discover that Lia felt as I did about not taking the morning-after pill. Even though it would have been hard, I would have supported any decision she made.

When Cassie had found out she was pregnant, she had been determined to have an abortion. I had been in no way ready to be a father, but after losing my parents in an accident, which I had had no control over, I just couldn't stand the thought of voluntarily ending a life. I had promised Cassie the world if she would go through with the pregnancy.

Even with medication, her mental and emotional health had always been shaky at best. She would be on top of the world one minute and staring at the walls without speaking the next. As close as Aidan and I were to her, she had gone weeks at a time without speaking to us. Then suddenly, out of the blue, she would be back to normal as if nothing had happened. There was never any rhyme or reason to these drastic mood swings, at least that we were aware of. I suspected that much of her troubles centered on her home life, but she never actually came out and admitted that. For all of the years I was friends and then more with her, I find when I think back that I never really knew her.

Cassie was a girl and then a woman of secrets. I met her father on a few occasions through the years and he seemed perfectly normal, although Cassie always seemed almost afraid of him. Her mother had passed away when she was a baby, or at least that was Cassie's version of the story. Her father was the manager at a local lumber mill and worked long hours. Cassie seemed to have the freedom to come and go as she pleased, which I used to envy when Aunt Fae was keeping tighter reins on me. I've often wondered in the last eight years if my feelings of unease about her father were totally off. Could it have been Cassie who was the problem all along, and her father just another victim of her sickness? Maybe he was as powerless as I was to help someone who continued to spiral out of control. He took off shortly after Cassie and I were engaged. I have no idea where he is now. I do know he was contacted when she was hospitalized, but he never showed up. Regardless of what she had done, the burden of caring for her ultimately fell on my shoulders, especially since I refused to press charges against her. What was the fucking point? She was completely out of it and would have been institutionalized anyway, and again, the guilt I felt for my part in her ultimate undoing was also a big factor.

I jerk in surprise as my cell phone rings. I see Max's name on the ID and brace myself to hear him raging over Lia's friend, Rose. I have no idea what is going on there, and I don't really want to know. I suspect from Max's reaction to her that he has either fucked her or is damn close. "Quinn," I answer, resigned to hearing the tirade I know is coming.

"Luc...I need to see you today." Just wonderful. Apparently, it's bad enough that he wants some face time to rant. Maybe fucking Rose is exactly what he needs; they both appear to be wound entirely too tight. Of course, she's likely to sew his balls to his leg when it's over, but everyone has problems.

"Max," I sigh, as I twirl my pen between my fingers. "She's Lia's friend. I know she's crazy, but just do this…"

"It's not that," he says in a tone, which sounds dead serious. "I'm probably going to be a couple more hours between getting Rose released and dropping off some papers at the courthouse. Are you going to be in the office all afternoon?"

He has my attention now. Max isn't one to cry wolf without a reason. "Yeah, I'll be in. Stop by when you arrive." I'm uneasy when the call ends, wondering what's going on. I ponder calling him back and demanding an explanation, but if he wants to meet in person, then there's a reason. Instead of dwelling on it, I grab some workout clothes and decide to burn off some adrenaline before I have Cindy pick up my lunch.

I've just rounded the five-mile mark on the treadmill as sweat trickles down my chest when I hear a noise behind me. I glance over, expecting to see Cindy, but instead the sight that greets me damn near causes me to break my fucking neck. Lia is standing there with a hungry expression as her eyes devour me, and she's completely...naked. Not a stitch of clothing in sight. I stumble, precariously close to going down as she runs over and unplugs the treadmill. I manage to hold it together until the belt stops.

"OH, MY GOD! I'm so sorry." She puts a hand over her chest as if trying to calm herself. "I wanted to surprise you, but I never thought about it making you fall." She looks at me in alarm as I exit the machine, my legs jelly-like and wobbly. She takes my arm as if bracing me. "Are you okay?" Actually, now that the shock has worn off and I've made it to steady ground without crashing, I'm just horny...completely turned-on by the woman clutching me.

I use the arm she's not holding to grab my water bottle and swallow half of it. I wipe the excess off with the back of my hand before answering. "No, I seem to have a problem...a big one." At my words, her eyes run up and down my body, scanning for injuries and finding none. She looks adorably confused and concerned. I decide to take mercy on her and help her out. Taking her hand from my arm, I lower it until she is holding my hard cock in her palm. "That's what I need help with, baby." I thrust against her hold and chuckle as her eyes go big as saucers. She seems so surprised that it makes me wonder what she'd been expecting when she walked in here naked. She has to know by now that I only have to see her to get hard. I am a fucking walking erection since I met her. The fact that she doesn't seem to know it makes me want her more.

She licks her lips, and I almost lose it. "You're not wearing a shirt," she says on something similar to a moan. I grin wolfishly as my hands slide over her silky flesh. Her eyes are glazed, and I know without touching her that she's wet for me. I begin pulling her closer when she suddenly drops through my hands and onto her knees. Okay, I'll admit, I didn't see that coming, but I'm more than ready to see where she's going with this. My cock is hoping it'll involve those plump, pink lips. When she looks up at me and starts tugging my shorts down, I fight the urge to fist pump. Her nails drag across my thighs as she lowers my shorts, causing shivers to race through my body. My dick literally leaps free from the waistband and I hiss as the cool air hits the hot flesh. She is sitting back on her heels now, staring at it, as if mesmerized.

"Suck it, baby," I urge as I take the length in my hand and shake it lightly in her face. When her tongue reaches out and delicately licks the bead of moisture off the tip, I almost blow my load all over her. I plant my legs firmly and brace myself as she begins licking me as if I'm the best ice cream she's ever had. Her hand nudges mine away from the base of my cock as she encircles my girth and starts pumping upwards to meet her lips. Watching her mouth take me is one of the hottest things I've ever seen in my life. Fuck, who am I kidding? It's the hottest hands-down. I'm too big for her to take all the way, but she gives it her best shot. I feel myself sliding halfway down her throat as she struggles to control her gag reflex. When I start to pull back, she holds on, refusing to let me stop. "Ah, fuck, that feels so good," I moan as I run my hand through her hair, guiding her mouth.

I try to draw back when I feel my balls tighten, and I know I'm seconds from blowing. "Baby, I'm coming," I warn, trying to give her a chance to release me. Instead, she sucks harder, her mouth forming a vacuum that I'm helpless to resist. I feel my spine tingle as the first spurt shoots from my cock and into her hot mouth. It seems to go on forever, and I wonder how she's keeping up without choking. She swallows everything I give her and licks my cock as if asking for more.

I slump back against the wall behind me, feeling faint as she finally releases me. When she raises her hand to wipe a trickle of cum from the corner of her mouth and then licks her finger, I almost declare my love on the spot. However, having me profess my undying devotion seconds after she sucked my cock might not exactly be the romantic gesture she's been dreaming of, so I wisely keep my mouth shut. "Was it...good?" she asks shyly. I wonder how she could possibly doubt that it was mind-blowing; everyone on this floor probably heard me yelling out my pleasure.

"It was phenomenal," I assure her as I finally find the strength to move. I pick her up before lowering her to the treadmill. I flip her onto her stomach then fall to my knees behind her. She moves her legs apart instinctively and I groan when I see the moisture glistening between her thighs. Even in this position, it's impossible to miss how wet and swollen she is. She is past ready to be fucked.

"I...I brought some condoms," she manages to say, as I trail a finger over her slit. I see her pointing to a box on the floor beside her purse. It's not the brand I've always purchased so I know she bought these herself. As I study the box, she stutters, "I...um...had Sam stop on the way. I...didn't know if you had any." I smile in reply, not wanting to burst her bubble by telling her that every man over the age of fifteen has a condom on hand. I didn't want her to think for even a moment that I kept them for anyone else.

"And did you tell Sam what you were buying?" I pick up the box and feel like a stud when I see she's bought the large size. It just so happens that she knows that part of my body well, and the rubber is a perfect fit. After I sheath myself, I return my attention to her sopping pussy.

"I...er...no," she moans as I push one finger inside her snug passage.

"What reason did you give him then?" I bite off a chuckle as she gives me a snort of impatience. Her hips push back against my hand, trying to force me deeper. She is clearly tired of my idle conversation and my teasing finger, which hasn't fully penetrated her yet. "Answer the question," I say, smacking her ass to get her attention.

"Ouch!" she yells, but I hear her breathing catch as fresh moisture flows onto my hand. "I didn't tell him what I needed!" she snaps. "I know he could tell I was embarrassed, so he probably assumed it was for...personal products."

"Good girl." I praise her patience as I remove my finger. She is in the middle of protesting when I line my cock up with her opening and bury myself to the hilt inside her, my balls slapping against her ass. I work my body over hers, holding my full weight from her on my arms. My chest rests against her back and my groin is on top of her ass. The position is gritty, erotic, and dominant—all of the things I love.

"Luc!" she shudders, as her body struggles to accommodate me. I still for a moment, buried deep inside her as she adjusts. When her hips start to circle, I pull out almost completely before surging back in. She's so tight and wet her body makes a sucking noise as if trying to hold me inside as I thrust repeatedly. "Luc…Oh, God, yes!" she moans. It sends me over the edge when she says my name in that high, breathy way. I've joked before that she only calls me Luc when she's coming, and that's exactly what she's doing now. Her body is beginning to spasm, and I'm lost. She wrings my cock dry as I explode inside her. In that moment, I hate the fucking condom that keeps me from bathing her pussy in my cum. It's the basest of needs to stake my claim, even though no one but me would know.

I wrap one arm around her waist and roll us both off the treadmill and to the side. I sit her aside for a moment to dispose of the condom in my bathroom trashcan before returning to the floor. I put my back against the wall and she sits in my lap, my cock now at half-mast against her hip. She feels boneless against me as our hearts race in tandem before slowing. "You okay?" I ask as I slowly stroke my hand up and down her arm. I smile against the top of her head as goose bumps cover the skin I touch. No matter how many times we're together, our reaction to each other never lessens. After coming twice, I could be ready to go again with just a look or touch from her.

"I'm great," she answers, snuggling further into my chest. I've never been much of a cuddler, but I love holding her. In moments such as this, I can almost believe that nothing will ever come between us. While she's relaxed and content, I decide to dig deeper. I'm worried about how she's dealing with everything that's happened to her. She seems to have turned a corner almost overnight, and truthfully, even though I'm happy, it also unsettles me to think that maybe she's trying to bury what happened to her instead of confronting it. I know that it's completely fucked-up on my part to try to push her to deal with her trauma when I've done nothing for eight years but run from mine. I just can't stand for her to let it all fester, though, and end up eating away at her day-by-day as mine has. "Are you really okay?" She freezes against me and know she understands my question has nothing to do with where she is in this moment.

"I...I'm fine, Lucian," she laughs, but it's devoid of humor. "How could I not be after that?" she asks, trying to deflect the question.

"I'm just worried about you. You were so depressed after we came home from the hospital, but the last few days you've been almost your usual self again. I don't want you to feel as if you have to pretend with me. I'm here for you. Anything you need, baby, I've got you."

She pulls away both physically and emotionally, and I let her. What right do I have to force her to open herself up to me when I haven't done the same with her? She is almost out of my lap when suddenly she stops. I sit quietly, waiting to see what she's going to do. I continue to stay quiet when she drops back into my lap. My arms automatically come back around her. "You know when I told you how I hated hearing people at the hospital tell me I was so lucky I survived and wasn't raped?"

My gut clenches, but I keep my voice level as I say, "I remember."

"The thing is, this last attack was more unexpected and violent, which was harder for me to get over, but...this is my normal, Lucian. It wasn't the first time he put his hands on me. That he touched me that way. As sick as it is, I'm not as messed-up as I should be because I long ago learned that it was something I had to lock away in order to live my life. If I didn't, the shame and humiliation would kill me. I'd crawl into myself and never come back out. Therefore, as much as I never wanted to tell you this or admit it to you, I'm okay because I long ago accepted that I had to be. Otherwise, he wins every time, and that is something I cannot live with, even now. I hate him. I fucking hate that he gets to breathe the same air I do. But even though he's brought me down time and again, he hasn't kept me down. I'll never let him have the satisfaction of doing that to me. Maybe that makes me a coward for accepting what I've never been able to change, but it's how I'm still here."

"Oh, baby." I pull her closer, once again feeling awed at her strength and destroyed at what she's gone through.

"Don't ever think of yourself as a coward.
There isn't a weak bone in your body. You
are an amazing woman, and I…"

"Luc, are you in there?" We both gasp
when a voice rings out in the next room.
"Max is here to see you. Should I send
him in?" Lia squeals in horror, jumping to
her feet and grabbing frantically for her
clothes.

I can't help it; the whole thing is
comical to me. Lia is shooting daggers at
me as she hops around with one foot in
her pants, trying to balance while she
finds the other opening. "Lucian! What
are you laughing at? For God's sake, put
some clothes on and tell Cindy to wait!
She wasn't at her desk when I came in.
Sam brought me up and then left for
lunch. He was supposed to pick me up in
an hour."

I finally pull myself to my feet and
stroll naked out of the room and into my
office. I'm far from a prude, but the last
thing Max probably wants to see today is
my cock. I push the button to answer
Cindy's page. "Give me just a minute;
I'm…finishing up something here." I see
Lia in the doorway of the workout room
with her pants now on. She is attempting
to snap her front closure bra and
fumbling because of the cast on one hand.

My dick is watching her tits bounce in rapt attention.

She sees my hardening length and holds up a hand as if to ward me off. "No, oh, no! Put that thing away now." I know it's evil, but I can't help but tease her first. I palm my cock, stroking it as I stare at her. Her hands stop as she watches me mesmerized. I walk slowly, continuing my movements until I'm directly in front of her. "I...I..."

I chuckle as she continues to stammer out words that make no sense. I know with certainty that if I touched her now, she'd let me go balls-deep again without protesting. We are both slaves to our desire for each other. I point to her tits, tossing her earlier words back at her. "Put those away before someone comes in." I help her with the snap before I move to find my own clothes. Having a little fun at her expense probably wasn't the best idea. I wince as I stuff my hard cock back into my boxers and then my slacks. I gingerly pull the zipper up and shift my dick to a more comfortable location. After running and having sex, I could desperately use a shower, but there is no time now.

By the time I finish dressing, Lia is fully clothed and waiting in my office. I put my arm around her, pulling her into me for a brief kiss. I have my hand on the doorknob, turning it to see her out, when she looks back over her shoulder and says, "I love you," before pulling the door open. I melt inside, now starting to crave those words from her instead of dreading them. I wonder if she has any idea that those same words had been on the tip of my tongue when Cindy interrupted us.

There is no more time to think as Max walks toward us, looking nervous while Cindy and Sam are smiling as if Christmas has just come early. What in the hell is wrong with everyone today? "I'll call you later, baby," I say to Lia as Max walks into my office. "Sam, make sure Lia gets into the apartment before you leave." As I shut the doors to my office, I see Cindy beaming at Lia. Yeah, she's the golden child here now, and I wouldn't have it any other way.

I'm in a mellow, relaxed mood after my lunch encounter when I settle behind my desk and wait for Max to begin his rant on Lia's friend. Maybe she mauled him in his car again. I am in no way expecting the words that finally come from his lips. "Jim Dawson is dead. Carly called me a few hours ago and told me his body had been pulled from the French Broad River last night."

"Son of a bitch," I hiss. That's the last thing I was expecting to hear. "He drowned?"

Max shakes his head, looking somber. "No, cause of death was a gunshot wound to the head. They estimate he'd been in the water about eight hours before he was caught on a tree branch and someone walking by saw him." My mind goes to Lee Jacks' absence, and I can't help but wonder. The man in me who's Hell-bent on retribution for Lia wants to fucking shout for joy. Regardless of Lee's need to make Jim Dawson suffer for his crimes against Lia, we both knew she would never really be free while he was still alive.

I give my lawyer and friend a blank look, saying, "If you're looking for some sign that I give a damn the bastard is dead, then you'll be sorely disappointed. Good fucking riddance to another piece of trash the world doesn't want nor need." I think it's the kindest statement I can make about someone I loathe so much.

Max exhales and leans back in his chair. "Personally, Luc, I agree with every word you just said. Professionally, I'd advise you to keep those sentiments to yourself. I don't expect it to be anything other than a formality, but the police want to question both you and Lia."

"You're kidding!" I look at Max incredulously. "Why in the world would we be questioned because that bastard is dead? No one's heard from him since he attacked Lia."

"I know, Luc, but you're both the most likely people to have had a grudge against him. I can tell you now, though, that the police are just going through the motions with this one. There's not going to be anyone on the sidelines jumping up and down, demanding justice. It'll be a quick few questions about your whereabouts and whether you've had any contact with him."

My anger spikes as I imagine Lia having to go through something else involving her stepfather. She is doing so much better that I hate to bring the memories crashing down on her. "Listen, I'll talk to them. They can ask me whatever the hell they want, but I don't want them talking to Lia."

Max runs a hand through his hair, looking tired but resigned. "I'm sorry, but neither of you have a choice. Carly will be dropping by your apartment this evening to talk to both of you. You need to go ahead and tell Lia what's happened so she'll be prepared. I'll be there, too, if you need me."

"Fuck!" I snarl, slamming my hand on my desk. Even dead, this bastard just won't go away.

"Luc, in the scope of things, this is good news for Lia, I would think. She can live her life now without looking over her shoulder and other than being questioned tonight, this ends the police investigation. When her mother turned herself in, she confessed and pleaded guilty, so the judge will decide her fate. You just have to get through this and it's over."

"You're right," I say, finally relaxing somewhat. This is more closure than Lia could have probably ever hoped for. "Do you think you need to be there tonight when we're questioned?"

"No." He shakes his head. "As I said, Carly pretty much let me know that this is strictly for paperwork. If she thought it necessary, she would have made that clear. Have you...thought anymore about telling Lia about her real father?"

I know full well what he's really doing. Both he and I know it's a little coincidental that Jim Dawson has suddenly turned up dead a short time after Lee Jacks found out he had a daughter. The lawyer in him doesn't want to ask me such a pointed question. "As soon as she's fully recovered, I'll try to find a way to approach it. I believe he's out of town right now, though."

"In Chicago visiting a new company he just acquired," Max surprises me by volunteering. "I saw it in the business section of the paper yesterday. Pretty high-profile photo-op with the mayor."

"Hmmm," I say in the way of a reply. Maybe Lee Jacks is building an alibi should he ever need one. He would have to realize that when his connection to Lia becomes known, he might be a suspect in her stepfather's death, especially with his sketchy background. I'd find it hard to believe the police would be interested in going after someone of Lee's influence, though. I imagine he's banking on that fact but is laying a safety net just in case.

"Listen, I also checked into that other matter which recently reawakened, so to speak."

My thoughts are immediately pulled from Lee and focused back on Max. "What matter would that be?" I say, curious. The last thing I need right now is another fucking problem on my plate.

"So, you didn't officially tell me to check into it, but I spoke with Cassie's care coordinator to get an update as to what's happening with her..."

"I believe I told you not to do anything right now." It's not that I'm pissed that he ignored what I said; hell, I pay him a small fortune to overthink things for me. I just don't want to be forced to think of Cassie today...or any other day, for that matter. Maybe I'm a heartless bastard, but how much can I be expected to forgive? She already owns my dreams; do I have to give her my waking hours, as well? Even after what he witnessed eight years ago, I know Aidan still wants me to forgive her, if for nothing else than old times' sake. It's never gonna fucking happen. As close as we are, there are things he doesn't know. He wants to blame what she did to me on mental illness. What he doesn't know is that she was doing her best to end me before she ever took a knife to my throat.

"It's my job to keep you advised on any changes with her. That's why you added me as a guardian along with Aidan. I was curious after our last conversation and felt I needed to know what was going on...for your sake."

"And?" I ask, not wanting to hear him confirm Aidan's assessment that Cassie is getting better.

"Her coordinator believes she is showing marked improvement for the first time." My stomach rolls and see by the look in his eyes that he understands the effect his words are having on me.

"Just how much improvement are we talking here?"

"It's hard to say without seeing her in person, but they seem quite surprised by her rapid turnaround. I believe they called it, 'communicating effectively,' whatever the hell that means." Looking as grave as I feel, he says, "Maybe you should visit her and see for yourself."

"That's never going to happen," I reply, leaving no room for argument in my voice. I don't want to see her again...ever.

"I understand," he answers, and I know he does. "I instructed her coordinator to send me weekly progress reports for now. It may not turn out to be anything, but I believe we should closely monitor the situation until we know more." If it were anyone but Cassie, it might almost seem sad to hear someone reduced to being called a 'situation.' In her case, however, it's a kindness compared to the alternatives. "One thing, though, surprised me from her report this month. I had them email it to me following our conversation." I wave my hand impatiently, wanting to be finished with this. "There has been one other visitor twice this month, besides Aidan."

He has my full attention now as I look at him in shock. I never had restrictions placed on her visitors because there was no need. To my knowledge, she had no one in her life other than her father, Aidan, and myself. "What? Who?"

When he says the name, I can only gape at him. "Why in the hell would Monique Chandler be visiting Cassie?" I know Aidan has been casually dating...fucking her, but I can't believe he would have her accompany him on his visit to the woman he's in love with. "Aidan has lost his mind." Actually, that much was apparent when he continued to see the bitch after their initial date. Once had been more than enough for me. Monique was the kind of woman who made a man want to put a hand over his cock and run in the other direction.

"That's just it." Max shakes his head in apparent confusion. "She wasn't there on the same day either time that Aidan was. She appears to have visited her on her own."

"That makes no sense whatsoever." I'm truly puzzled by this information and more than a little troubled. If Aidan has gone as far as to tell Monique about Cassie, I wouldn't be surprised that she would try to check her competition out. She's a nosy bitch, and it's something I wouldn't put past her. Maybe she was double-checking Aidan's story if he gave her one. But why the second visit?

"I can have them block her from seeing Cassie again if you would like. I have no idea what's going on, but I don't like it."

I thumb my hand on the desk for a moment before saying, "no, let's not take that step yet. I want to know if she continues to go. If the first time was out of sheer nosiness and she didn't manage to satisfy her curiosity for some reason, she might have gone back. If it happens again, then something's going on. Don't mention it to Aidan yet. I don't want him putting a stop to it or tipping Monique off that we know. Tell them that you want to be notified immediately if and when she visits again."

"Consider it done," he replies as he rises from his chair. "Lia looks good." He gives a genuine smile for the first time since entering my office.

"She is amazing." I decide not to tell him about the pregnancy scare until when and if it becomes an actual reality. Right now, it's just a lot of speculation of what could happen. We are still weeks away from knowing whether our rounds of unprotected sex have consequences. He is almost at the door when I ask, "By the way, how did things work out with Rose this morning?" If not for watching him closely, I would have missed the tightening of his shoulders and the stiffening of his spine. It appears I've hit on a sore subject.

He spins back around, looking flushed. I study him in amazement. My normally cool chief counsel only seems to lose it when Rose is involved. Interesting. We all have an Achilles' heel, and it would appear that she is his. "That woman is fucking insane! If not for Lia, I would have instructed the police to leave her there. I swear, she was completely unconcerned with her arrest. When I got there, she had two female deputies taking notes on how to make their own scented candles with common household items. I mean, in the last few weeks alone, she has taken a shovel to her ex-boyfriend's car and then done a whole laundry list of evil shit to his apartment."

I burst out laughing, unable to stop myself. The look of sheer incredulity on his face is priceless. "I believe she answers to Martha Harry," I say, remembering her and Lia laughing over it on her recent visit to the apartment. It sounds accurate. I go on to explain the reasoning behind the name to Max who nods in complete agreement.

"That sounds about right. I'm telling you, Luc, she scares the ever-living hell out of me. The shit she does, and then afterwards, instead of regretting her actions, she's on some kind of a high...a humping-my-leg one."

By the look on his face, I don't think he meant to verbalize that last part of his statement. He is shifting around uncomfortably now, looking like he's ready to bolt. No doubt, Lia will have the full story soon. I'm not sure I even want to know. I decide to take pity on him and not question him about the humping part. "Er...so, I take it you got her off?" *Oh, fucking hell,* I inwardly groan at my poor choice of words. Max turns his face into the door and collapses against it. "I meant the charges, dammit!" I say laughingly. "I don't want to know what you two did afterwards. I mean, crime doesn't pay, right?" It's evil, but I can't resist adding, "But it sure as hell makes you horny."

He wrenches the door open, not bothering to look back. "Fuck you, Quinn," he throws over his shoulder. I lose it again when I hear Cindy scolding him for his language from the reception area. "Sorry, Cindy," he grovels as he slinks off. God, that woman is amazing. She doesn't take any shit off any of us, especially if it's directed at me. I work hard to stay on her good side. I make a mental note to give her another pay raise; she deserves it for adding insult to Max's injury.

Glancing at my watch, I see I have about fifteen minutes before my next meeting. Just enough time to finish some emails so I can head home immediately after the meeting. I need to talk to Lia before she hears about Jim Dawson from someone else. If not for Lee Jacks lurking on the horizon, I would believe that this is the final key to setting her free from her past.

CHAPTER THIRTEEN

Lia

"Honey, I'm telling you I had two orgasms before that fella finished patting me down. If I had known you had all of that going on here, I would have been visiting daily."

I can't help but giggle as Debra tells me in detail about her encounter with the security guys in the lobby of the apartment. I've noticed the few times I've left the building since my attack that the security here is tighter than ever, but I have never been frisked, as Debra is describing. "I can't believe they did that to you. I mean, I let them know you were coming. Maybe Lucian can speak with them about it."

"No! Don't you dare say anything. I insisted they do it. I informed that cute boy with the tattoos that I was feeling a little dangerous today and needed to be fully checked for my own good. He didn't want to, but I told him I wouldn't go away until he did."

"Oh, my God." I fall against the cushions laughing. Only Debra—or maybe Rose—would do something like that. Was that why all my friends were insisting on visiting more than usual? Just to be felt up?

I hear the front door slam, and I can't help the small jump of fear that goes through me. What I told Lucian was the truth; I am better, but I still look over my shoulder...a lot. I don't know if that will ever go away. When you truly face how vulnerable you are every day, it does something to you. I thought I was stripped of my innocence long ago, but I don't think that really happened until I was pulled into the storage room of a busy apartment building without anyone seeing it happen.

I relax when Lucian walks into sight, thumbing through the mail he must have collected on the way up. He looks surprised to see Debra sitting next to me on the couch but not annoyed. Even though he's such a private person, he never seems to mind having my few friends visit me here at his home...or ours, as he likes to point out. He walks directly to my side, dropping a kiss on my upturned mouth. "Hey, baby," he says before turning to Debra. I'm further surprised and just a little charmed when he drops a brief kiss onto my friend's cheek. "It's good to see you again, Debra. Is Martin with you?" My tough friend looks like she's on the verge of swooning at Lucian's friendly gesture.

"Oh...um...no, he couldn't get away. The man works entirely too much, but that's the way it goes when you own a retail business."

"I'm sorry to hear that," he says sincerely. "Maybe you and Lia can work out a day and time for us to have dinner together. I know she misses you." Well, now it's official: both Debra and I are putty in his oh-so-thoughtful hands. It makes me realize how much I've come to take his kindness for granted. He has arranged so much of his life to conform to mine almost from the start. Swallowing back tears, I acknowledge how lucky I am to have him. He has secrets and a past, which has shattered, but not broken, him. I have had so few people in my life that I could trust and depend on, and two of them are with me now. I don't know where I would be now without Debra, and I don't know how I survived for so long without the man looking down at me now with a soft smile that still manages to be full of possessive hunger. I love him so much my heart hurts when he's near. A part of me knows he feels the same way, but I wonder if he'll ever be able to tell me.

Cassie scared him. Now I know that they were going to have a baby until she terminated it. I had long suspected that the relationship between her and Lucian was a romantic one; his words have now confirmed it. What I don't understand is all the secrecy which seems to shroud anything concerning her. Sam and Lucian's aunt acts just as shuttered as he does when any mention of Cassie arises. I would think her dead if not for being told she doesn't live here anymore. I'm beginning to grow impatient for the rest of her story. I'm certain now more than ever that the key to unlocking Lucian's nightmares is to understand what happened with her. The fear that I've given my love to someone who can never fully accept or return it is beginning to consume me.

When I feel an elbow in my side, followed by an amused chuckle, I jerk out of the trance I had apparently fallen in. "Girl, you've got it bad, don't you?" My face heats when I realize I've been staring at Lucian, even though I wasn't really seeing him. He raises a brow in question, to which I give a weak smile of reassurance in answer. I'm sure what I was thinking must be written all over my face, so I'm more than happy for Debra, and hopefully Lucian, to assume I was just ogling him.

"Mmm, yeah," I say, playing along, "sorry about that." Lucian doesn't look like he's buying it but lets it go without comment.

As Debra stands, saying something about needing to get going, Lucian walks to the coffee table in front of us and sits down. "Debra, do you have some extra time? I have some news for Lia that I would like you to hear, as well." Debra relaxes back in her seat looking just as curious as I feel. When he leans forward to take one of my hands, I become nervous. *What's left in my life to upset me?* It's unlikely he'd want Debra for a witness just to break up with me.

Suddenly, I grip his hand in fear as a thought occurs to me. "Oh, my God, has something happened to Rose?" He looks nonplussed for a moment before squeezing my hand in return.

"No, baby. I'm sorry you thought that. Rose is fine and driving Max out of his mind probably as we speak." The deep breath he takes doesn't do anything to dispel my anxiety.

I want to clap when Debra says, "Well, come on, son. Your girl's about to have a heart attack if you haven't noticed."

"All right, I didn't mean to cause any panic. I just didn't know how to begin, so here goes. Detective Michaels called Max this morning..."

"They caught him," I whisper hopefully. *Please let him be behind bars now where he has always belonged.*

He hesitates and my spirits plummet thinking he's still out there. Still waiting to catch me unaware again. "Lia, he's dead." I hear Debra hiss beside me, but I can't seem to process his words. Who is he talking about? It can't be my stepfather. I asked God to punish him for years, but it never happened, and I can't comprehend that it would now.

"No...not him...never him," I say in a daze. I can't get my hopes up, because I'll never be free of him. Hasn't he assured me of that repeatedly? Lucian comes closer until my legs are wedged between his. He takes my face between his big hands, forcing me to look at him. "He's never letting me go," I say to him as Debra chokes on what sounds like a sob beside us.

"Baby, listen to me. Jim Dawson is dead. They found him earlier this morning in the French Broad River. He's gone...for good."

I give Lucian a dejected look as I say, "He knows how to swim. He was on his high school swim team so he would never have drowned." I know my words must sound crazy to him. Most people would assume that my refusal to accept that my stepfather is dead stems from not wanting to lose him. It's not that at all...I just can't let myself believe it because I'll break completely apart when we find out he is alive, well, and coming after me. It's been literally beat into me over and over all my life to never wish for anything. There may be a fine line between love and hate, but the line between dreams and nightmares is even thinner, almost transparent at times.

When his lips suddenly lock on mine, all thoughts are driven from my head. The daze of a few moments ago is gone, and I feel nothing but him. His familiar smell and taste surround me as I lose myself to the stroke of his tongue. When he refuses to deepen the kiss, I raise my hands and dig them into his hair, trying to pull him closer. When Debra drawls, "Whew, have mercy," it's like a bucket of cold water over my head.

I was seconds away from crawling into Lucian's lap and wrapping myself around him. Just one touch from him and I'd completely forgotten her presence and...his words. "He's really dead?" I gasp out, finally allowing it to penetrate the protective shell I had been in. The reason for Lucian's sudden kiss is clear to me now. He was attempting to break down my walls and get me to really hear him.

"He is," Lucian agrees gently, rubbing my arms.

"Do the police know what happened?" Debra asks as she begins to visibly relax.

Once again, Lucian hesitates before saying, "It was a gunshot wound. He was probably dumped in the river after the fact." My hands start to shake as everything sinks in. "He's gone, baby...he is really gone," Lucian adds before pulling me into his arms.

Lucian and I both startle as Debra jumps from the couch and starts throwing her arms in the air. "Hell, yes! Ding dong, the devil is dead!" Then she does something that looks suspiciously like an attempt at moonwalking mixed with some sort of break dancing. I know both of our mouths are hanging open as she continues to act as if she just won the lottery. "Hey, I'm happy as a pig in shit! If that makes me a bad person, then so fucking be it. My baby girl is finally free."

Unbelievably, as Debra celebrates, I cry...and I mean ugly cry. I know Lucian and Debra must think I've gone insane. How can I possibly be crying right now? The odd thing is that my tears have nothing to do with sadness and everything to do with a twisted kind of loss. Like someone suffering from a type of reverse Stockholm syndrome, I don't know how to react now that the evil which has defined me for years is gone.

For as long as I can remember, my life has been about survival. First with my mother, then with the monster she brought into our lives, and finally trying to make it on my own. Who am I now that I'm no longer that girl? Can I even adjust to being a person with the normal hopes and fears of a woman my age? With him gone, I comprehend that I've been his puppet on a string even when I thought I had won my freedom the day I left home. I was only ever as free as he allowed me to be. His very existence still controlled every aspect of my world.

The realization snaps something inside me. I wrench myself from Lucian's arms and completely lose it. My anger bubbles like molten lava flowing through my veins as I begin throwing everything in

my path. I'm like a whirlwind of
destruction as I smash a glass vase
against the wall. The lack of clutter in
Lucian's apartment means there isn't
much readily available on tabletops, so I
move on to the bar area and start
grabbing the crystal glasses and
decanters there. I see Debra, out of the
corner of my eye, starting to approach me
before Lucian pulls her back. "She needs
this; just let her go."

You're fucking right I need it, I think to
myself as I continue to destroy the bar
area. I'm vaguely aware of Debra leaving
before I lose all meaning of time and
place. My throat begins to throb and I
wonder idly why when I realize I'm
screaming and my voice has gone
unusually husky. *Have I been doing that
this entire time?* My movements slow
almost as if having to think about
something so mundane has brought me
back to the present. I look down in
surprise at the bottle of whiskey I'm
holding. As I move to sit it on the bar
behind me, something crunches beneath
my feet. I glance down in disbelief to see
broken glass everywhere. The room looks
like it has been ransacked. A wave of
relief washes over me when I notice
Lucian standing off to the side, almost as
if waiting for my next move. "Luc?" I ask

uncertainly. "I...oh, my God, I did this!" The words tumble from my lips as I stare at him in horror.

He reaches me just as I would have fallen to my knees in the jagged glass graveyard below my feet. He doesn't say anything as he effortlessly swings me into his arms and leaves the carnage behind. He carries me straight to the bathroom before setting me on my feet. His eyes move over my face as if searching for something as he strips my clothing from my body. I stand, waiting obediently as he makes quick work of his own before dropping his hands to my hips. He leads me into the steaming shower and under the hot spray of water.

He washes me thoroughly and then himself. When I turn to step out, he pulls me back, enfolding me in his arms. He joins our lips in a kiss that is devoid of anything other than comfort. He is connecting with me in the fastest way he knows. This kiss is all about helping me find my center, grounding me with him in the moment, and I need it. I put my arms tightly around his neck, and he hoists me up so I can wrap my legs around his waist. He rocks from side to side, comforting me like a child. "Are you okay?" he asks against my lips as he rains soft kisses across my exposed skin.

"I'm sorry about what I did," I say, ashamed to have lost control and wrecked his beautiful apartment. "I'll clean it all up right now." I begin unwrapping my legs from around him, but he stops my downward descent by refusing to release my ass. He carries me from the shower before putting me back on my feet.

"The cleaning service is on their way over now, so please stay away from all of the glass in the living room. They'll have it taken care of in no time." He continues to ignore my objections while we dry ourselves off. I am walking toward the closet to dress when he captures my hand before dropping to the bed and pulling me into his lap. He is wearing a pair of form-fitting, black boxer briefs and I'm in a light blue bra and panty set. "I need to tell you something else, but first I need to know that you're okay. I'd pour you a drink first, but we seem to be fresh out of glasses."

Maybe we both have a sick sense of humor, but the laugh that his joke brings forth from both of us is a much-needed tension-breaker. "I don't know what happened to me. First, I couldn't accept that he was actually dead after tormenting me all of these years, then I got so angry at myself and at him when I realized that I've still continued to let him run my life. Almost every decision I've made since that monster came into my life has been influenced by him." I find myself choking up again, as I admit, "I never got away. Don't you see? I was living on borrowed time and deep down I knew it. I just didn't want to accept it. He was always going to come for me, just as he said."

I take his face in my hands, looking into the eyes of the man who has put his own pain on the back burner to help me deal with mine. "Loving you is the first real thing I've done just for me. Everything else has just been out of necessity. You are a dream I never dared to dream because my mother, then my stepfather, took that ability from me. That was another reason why I was so angry. He took everything from me, and I didn't even understand that until today."

Lucian wipes the tears, which are once again falling from my face with his thumbs, before kissing first my mouth, then my nose and finally my forehead. "No matter what he took, he never broke you. You are the wonderfully talented, intelligent, driven, and loving woman you are *despite* him, not because of him. I'm in no way worthy of you, but I lay my heart at your feet because you own me, baby." My heart skips a beat at his words. He is saying he loves me. Maybe not in the standard way, but there is no mistaking his meaning. If my life thus far was what I had to endure to find this man, then I would go through Hell again and again just to end up where I am now...in his arms.

"I love you, too," I say softly, wanting him to know I recognize and return the feelings he is trying to express. We kiss again, both getting lost in the moment before he pulls back with a frown.

"I almost forgot what I needed to talk to you about...That seems to happen a lot when we're together." He looks nervous, which in turn makes me anxious. "The police want to question both you and me this evening about your stepfather's death."

I jump to my feet and immediately begin pacing. Can he not just be gone? "What? Why? I don't want to relive what happened to me with them again!"

He comes to his feet, taking my shoulders between his hands. "Honey, it's not that. It's just that you're the only remaining family, other than your mother, and I'm your boyfriend. According to Max, it's just a formality and the police need to go through the motions for their paperwork. You don't have to worry; I won't let them upset you."

What is wrong with me today? I seem to be going off the deep- end over everything. It *is* a lot to take in, though, and I had mistakenly assumed that his death meant everything to do with him was over. Apparently, not quite yet. I need to get a grip and calm down. If Lucian isn't worried, and he doesn't appear to be, then it's fine. After it's all over tonight, I can regroup and truly move forward for the first time in my life. "Oh, my God," I gasp, "poor Debra! I need to call her. She is probably completely beside herself over my earlier freak-out."

"That's a good idea," Lucian agrees wryly. "I think she was in shock when she left here. I guess she's never seen you on a rampage before?"

My face flushes as I quickly walk toward the closet and pull on jeans and a sweater. Lucian is dressing when I step into the living area to find my phone. My jaw drops in shock as I take in the sight before me. Dear Lord, he wasn't kidding when he said we were out of glasses. I can hardly believe that I've completely wrecked the bar. He comes up behind me, plucking me effortlessly off my feet. "What're you doing?" I ask in surprise as he carries me through the wrecked room and into the kitchen before setting me on the countertop.

He tweaks one of my toes and shakes his head. "You don't have any shoes on, Lia."

"Oh, yeah, I didn't think about that," I admit as I look at my bare feet. "So, when is Detective Michaels going to be here?" I try to act as if I'm not nervous, but I know he sees it.

"I'm going to go grab a pair of your shoes for you and then I'm calling Max to see if we can meet them somewhere else." Before I can ask why, thinking I'd much rather do this at home, he adds, "I doubt the living room will be cleaned before the police arrive, and right now it looks and smells like a scene from a bar brawl. They'd probably lock my ass up because there is no way they would believe you did all of that."

I look at him in amazement, unable to believe he's actually laughing at his assessment of the wreck in the other room. I am completely appalled to have done something like that to his home. He should be kicking me out, not shaking in laughter. Despite myself, I am unable to stop the grin from fully forming on my mouth. "It's not funny," I attempt to scold both him and myself. "It's going to cost a lot of money to clean and replace everything I've broken." He just continues to laugh until I add, "I mean it; I'm paying you back. I'm all healed except for my wrist and fingers, so I can start cleaning again." His laugh morphs into a scowl before I can complete my sentence.

"Don't even start that with me, baby. You aren't my housekeeper, and you're not going to be." When I start to protest, he suddenly looks serious. "Please don't worry about paying for some broken glassware. What you bring to me just by being in my life is priceless. Hell, baby, I owe *you* if anything. I should be *your* housekeeper because I'll never be able to repay you for what you've given me."

"No, no, no," I whisper as my eyes water. He lifts a brow, looking bemused by my reaction to his sweet declaration. "Um...sorry, I just don't want to cry again. It seems like that's all I do anymore. You're just so sweet to me."

He looks slightly offended and then just downright ...wicked when he steps between my parted thighs and presses his quickly hardening cock against my core. "I've got your sweet right here..."

I drop my head onto his shoulder, shaking with laughter. "You did *not* just say that. Hello, Lucian Quinn, some horny high school boy called and wants that line back."

"Oh, really," he purrs against my throat as he thrusts tighter against me.

"How many 'boys' have that?" I'm helpless to contain the moan which works its way from my throat. He turns his head and bites my ear, causing a jolt of pleasure to shoot straight to my core.

"Don't start anything we can't finish," I warn him as I wrap my legs around his waist to pull him even closer. My panties are flooded as I rub myself against his hard length, completely lost in the moment.

In the blink of an eye, he pulls back, causing my legs to drop. "You're right; we don't have time for this now. Lock and load 'em, baby," he says as he walks out of the room, leaving me stunned and not just a little frustrated.

"WHAT. THE. HELL?" I say to myself as I continue to gape after him, thinking he's going to suddenly turn and come back to put me out of my horny misery. What a perfect end to a messed-up day. I wreck Lucian's apartment, cry more than a newborn baby, and finally leave crotch drool all over his granite countertops. Okay, maybe the last part is a little bit exaggerated, but if not for my layers of clothing, it would be true. Now, dammit, I can't get down. Couldn't he have set me next to one of the stools? Well, I could jump, but I'm afraid of jarring the cast on my wrists or my fingers if I land wrong.

I'm shifting onto my stomach so I can try to shimmy down when a loud smack on my ass has me squealing. Luckily, the arm now wrapped around my waist sets me gently on my feet before I can fall on my face. "Ouch," I grumble, holding my stinging butt cheek.

He looks completely unrepentant as he says, "You know you loved it." All right, so what if I did—I'm not about to admit it to him. Instead, I take the tennis shoes he is holding out to me and wedge my feet inside them without untying the laces. He just shakes his head but wisely holds his tongue. "We're going to meet Detective Michaels at Max's house. I told him our apartment was in the middle of renovations, and we needed another place."

I stick my tongue out at his continued playful jabs over my earlier tantrum. The man is truly not right; otherwise, he'd find nothing amusing about having his multi-million dollar apartment trashed by his crazy girlfriend. "So, where does Max live?" I ask, picturing something similar to Lucian's home.

"Actually he has a house a few miles from my aunt. He hates the downtown area. He never understood why I bought a place here."

I realize I know nothing about the man who is Lucian's friend, as well as his lawyer. Curious, I ask, "So, he's not married, right?" Okay, so maybe I'm interested for Rose, in the name of sisterhood and all that.

"Nope," he replies without expounding on his answer.

"Has he ever been married, or like, involved long-term with anyone?"

"Nope, and not in years." Geez, again with the vague answers. Would it be so hard for him to just tell me a little about Max without me pulling it from him?

"Why not? I mean...Oh, no! Does he actually like women? I mean, like them for you know...sex?"

"As far as I know." When I just stare at him, he huffs out, "Yes, I've seen evidence to support that fact."

I know I'm pushing my luck when I ask, "So, you know him well then? Is he seeing anyone right now? Do you think he's interested in a relationship, or is it just all casual with him?" Yikes, I think I went too far with the last line of question. Lucian is standing in front of me now, his hands on his hips and a frown on his face.

"You know, baby, I'm really trying not to read too much into the fact that you're displaying an unusual amount of interest in my lawyer. Is there something we need to talk about?" I go all gooey inside. Jealous Lucian is seriously adorable and even hotter than usual. I want to beg him to throw me back on the countertop and fuck me...hard. However, I hold it together. Partly because I know he doesn't want to be late to meet with the police, and also because I feel strange about begging for sex after my meltdown just hours earlier. Something must surely be wrong with me lately because I'm either crying or horny. There doesn't seem to be much middle ground right now. I settle for wrapping my arms around his waist and grinning innocently up at him.

"Come on, Luc; work with me here. If I'm not interested in Max for myself...which I'm not in the slightest, then why would I be asking questions about his personal life?" He absently rubs circles on my back as he ponders my question. I see the exact moment the dots all connect for him.

"No, Lia," he says sternly as he begins shaking his head at me. "We aren't meddling in Max's love life. Besides, he thinks your friend is off her rocker."

"Lucian..." I pout. "Don't you think there's something there? I mean, look at how crazy he acts where she is concerned."

"And you think acting crazy is a good thing?" He takes my hand and starts pulling me toward the front door. "I mean it, baby; we're not getting in the middle of those two." I try to hide my smirk as he closes the door behind us and we walk into the elevator.

"I promise I'll be good," I say sweetly. "I will be good; I just can't guarantee Rose will be."

Lucian

True to Max's prediction, our interview by Detectives Michaels and Haynes is brief and uniform. I get the feeling without her putting it into words that their department doesn't like expending valuable time and resources on someone like Jim Dawson. With the testimony that first Lia, and then her mother, provided the police, they have a clear picture of the type of person he was. Unless someone runs up and down the street in front of the police station yelling 'I'm guilty,' this case will be closed in short order.

I was proud of Lia. She answered each of Detective Michaels' questions clearly and concisely. When the detective was leaving, she dropped a hand on Lia's shoulder, saying, "This wasn't exactly the way I had planned to get justice for you, but..." I was sure the other woman wanted to add something like, 'the Lord works in mysterious ways,' but she refrained from it. I thanked Max for allowing us to use his home and rushed Lia out the door before she could arrange a double-date with him.

I'll admit I was a bit pissed when she started quizzing me about him earlier. She's never asked me that many questions about Aidan or even Sam. I haven't felt jealousy over a woman in many years, and even though I enjoyed the normalcy of it, I didn't want to feel that way again where Lia was concerned. She was mine and I wasn't letting her go.

She had worried me earlier when she'd first been so resistant to the news that her stepfather was dead, and then she had completely snapped when it finally hit her. People process grief in different ways, and I know that venting was her way. Her grief was not for Jim Dawson, but for the death of her innocence all of those years ago at his hands. At some point in their lives, every person carrying around rage inside eventually needs an outlet to purge it from their system. Lia had been fueled by hate for so long that the crash was inevitable.

I'm not naive enough to believe that just because he's dead everything is suddenly perfect in her world. Her childhood was ripped from her hands, and she'll never be able to fully erase the scars that were left behind. I also know that it's ironic that I'm sitting here pondering her ghosts when I haven't dealt with my own. I plan to start taking steps in that direction tomorrow, though. I've arranged to meet my aunt at the coffee shop down the street in the morning. I am going to tell her about my cocaine addiction and ask her to help me overcome it. I've long denied to myself that I'm an addict just because I don't use every day, which is bullshit. If I wasn't addicted, I would be able to walk away from it...and I can't. I have to find the strength for myself and for Lia to leave my crutch behind. It has enabled me for years to push my demons aside instead of dealing with them. To be the person she deserves, I have to be the person I once was before Cassie and I ruined each other's lives.

After I speak with my aunt tomorrow, I plan to talk to Lia about Cassie. It's time she knew the complete story there. It's not fair that I constantly preach full disclosure on her thoughts and feelings, yet I continue to avoid any of her questions about my past. What she must think I can only imagine, but sadly, I fear it's not even close to the web of lies, hate, and betrayal that consumed my last year with Cassie. For all of the hate I feel for her, I know I'm to blame, as well. It's likely that my actions were even the catalyst for her final break with reality. Some would call it survivor's guilt, and I suppose that analogy is correct in a way. Out of Cassie, our child, and myself, I'm the only one who really still lives. Cassie may be alive, but she has been so lost in her own mind for the last eight years that she may as well have been dead. I think, in the end, as evil as she had become, she couldn't deal with what she did so she retreated in the only way she knew.

"Luc...Luc...LUCIAN!" I jerk as Lia pokes me in the side. "Good grief, where did you go?" she jokes as I focus my thoughts on her. Sometimes it's rather scary how you can drive a car for miles and be so deep in thought that you don't remember the trip. I wonder if Lia was talking to me, while I've been ignoring her.

"Sorry, baby," I say lightly as I shift the Range Rover into park and cut the engine. As usual, Lia had joked that she couldn't believe I was driving and not having Sam take us in the Mercedes. I noticed Sam and Cindy leaving the office together earlier, so I didn't think he would appreciate being disturbed on his date...or whatever the hell they do together. I don't even want to go there. "I was just thinking over everything that has happened today." I want to take those words back when I see her smile dim slightly. I'm sure the last thing she wanted was to have another postmortem on her stepfather.

She sighs, letting her head fall back against the headrest. "Yeah, it's been a hell of a day, hasn't it?"

I chuckle, tweaking her nose before opening my door. "That it has," I say as I hurry around to help her out. Putting my arm around her as we walk toward the building, I lower my voice, saying, "All I want to do is get you naked and fuck you till you beg me to stop."

She stops in her tracks, blinking up at me like an owl. She licks her plump lips and surprises me by saying, "What if I never want you to stop?" Then she drops her hand, cupping the hardening bulge in my pants. "How long do you think you can keep going?" She blushes adorably at her own bold question, making me almost blow my load in my fucking pants.

Pushing her against the building, I lower my body, letting her feel how much I want her. I rim the shell of her ear with my tongue, smiling as she shivers against me. I keep my mouth there as I whisper, "Don't confuse me for a boy, Lia. After I fuck you once, you'll feel it for a week. You'll think of nothing but my cock tomorrow when you're walking around with that sweet burn between your thighs. That's all me, baby."

"Ohhhh, myyy," she moans and nearly sags to the ground when I suddenly release her.

I swagger away, calling nonchalantly over my shoulder, "Are you coming, babe?" I can't help but notice, as I look back, that she's already walking funny. Apparently, I don't even have to fuck her to cause the sweet burn I was just enticing her with. She catches up to me just before I reach the door, wrapping her arms around me from behind and snuggling into my back. We stand there for a moment just enjoying the feeling of peace, which has been so elusive lately.

"So, Max was looking good tonight, right?" she teases before releasing me and running. I'm left standing on the sidewalk with my mouth hanging open. The little minx got me back. I grin and take my time catching up with her. She probably hasn't realized that I still have the upper hand. Unless I'm mistaken, she doesn't have her purse, which means she probably doesn't have a keycard to the elevator so she's not going anywhere.

As I stroll leisurely into the lobby, she's standing at the locked doors with a look of chagrin on her beautiful face. "I saw that going so much better in my head," she whines as she kicks the steel doors.

I pinch her ass, causing her to shriek...quite loudly. The concierge glances up from her desk in the corner frowning. I suspect that she never has sex and thinks we're pigs because we obviously do. Hell, I'd almost do it right now against the marble walls of the lobby just to see how long it would take her to call the cops. Owning a penthouse here probably wouldn't save me. Of course, what she doesn't know is that I'm pinching the ass of her boss's, Lee Jacks, daughter. That might actually buy me some serious ass-kissing...or not. She appears to hate men in general. Sam is terrified of her.

We make it in the door of our home with only some light groping in the elevator. "Clothes off," I instruct Lia as I throw my keys on the entryway table. She walks toward the bedroom grumbling under her breath. Even though we've had sex against the glass windows in the living room, she still shies away from walking through this part of the apartment nude. My little Lia might talk a good game at times, but she is still modest at heart.

I'm moving to follow her when it finally hits me that everything has been cleaned up. I had completely forgotten about the service that was to arrive this evening to handle the removal of most all of my glassware. Looking around, I am impressed. I had to give them credit; they might cost a small fortune, but everything looks just as it did. Well...other than the missing pieces which would need replacing. No wonder I was getting the evil eyes from the concierge. She had to let them in and no doubt thought Lia and I had had some out-of-control party.

I walk into the bedroom just as Lia upends a duffle bag onto the bed. I'm getting ready to comment on the fact that she's still wearing clothes when I do a double-take as one item from the bag rolls out front and center. I move closer, thinking I must be imagining what I think I'm seeing until Lia hisses, "Oh, shit!" She reaches for the big, purple vibrator just as I grab it from the bed and eye it before looking at her in question.

She is blushing furiously. "Oh, my God, Luc, give that to me!"

I hold it out of her reach, shaking my head as I cluck my tongue. "My, my, Miss Adams, what do we have here?"

"It's nothing, just give it back!" she cries as she tries to reach high enough to wrestle it from my hands. "Luc!"

"Tut, tut," I say, waving it around. "It looks like a big, purple cock to me. Now, whatever have you been doing with this?" Taking in the length and girth in my hand, I'm secretly relieved to know I still have the biggest dick in this house, but it's damn close.

"I can't believe Rose did this to me! She was only supposed to bring my underwear." She's now given up trying to get her plastic friend back, and she's standing there with a hand over her eyes, looking mortified. I want to tell her that this is tame compared to some of the things I've seen women use in the name of pleasure, but I don't think she'd appreciate that right now...or ever.

Shaking the vibrator, I say, "Well, obviously Rose thought you might need your purple friend here. Come on...tell me, have you missed using it?" She shakes her head, still refusing to look at me. "Ah, come on," I continue to tease, "you're not going to hurt my feelings by admitting it." Okay, maybe that's bullshit, because it probably would wound me a bit to know she was pining for a battery-operated boyfriend while sleeping beside the real thing.

She falls face-down on the bed, lying across the pile she had just tossed out of the bag. I barely make out her muffled voice saying, "This is so humiliating."

I hate to admit to myself that I'm suddenly even more turned on imagining what I could do to her with the toy I'm holding. Yeah, I've used all manner of things with women before, but not with Lia. I want…no, I *have* to see her take this purple dick deep into her pussy. I only hope she'll agree. For a moment, I wonder if tonight is the best time to be thinking of kinky sex with all that has happened today, but maybe we both need the stress reliever. It's sad, really, to think of the reasons why, but Lia bounces back amazingly swift from the blows life throws at her. I know it's because she conditioned herself to do just that years ago.

I drop the vibrator onto the bed and lower my body slowly over hers. I hold the brunt of my weight off her slim frame, allowing my cock to nestle against her backside. I nip the outer shell of her ear with my teeth and smile as she shudders.

Pushing my denim-covered cock into the cleft of her ass, I purr, "Feel how hard I am. That's all you, baby. Just thinking about watching you pleasure yourself is driving me out of my mind. I'll make you good and wet, and then I want you to take over. Can you do that for me?"

I hear her groaning into the bed, and I have no idea if it's in embarrassment or desire. I wait with bated breath to see what she'll do. I half-expect her to hit me over the head with the big vibrator and run, so I'm pleasantly shocked when I hear a muffled, "Um...okay."

Holy hell, my cock is on the verge of busting through my zipper at her reply. It takes all the strength I have to keep from jerking both of our pants down and plunging into her from behind. There is no way I can miss this, though, regardless of the discomfort in my pants. I roll to the side and let her turn to her back. Her face is bright red, but her nipples are hard and pressing against her shirt, and her knees are shifting together, which I know is a sure sign of her arousal.

I don't want to ruin the mood by teasing her any further, so instead I take charge. "Stand and take your clothes off," I instruct her. She barely hesitates before sitting up to kick her shoes off and then rising gracefully to her feet. She makes

eye contact with me and never looks away
as she pulls off first her shirt and then
her bra, dropping them to the floor. This
isn't a slow, erotic striptease; she wants
the clothing off because she's completely
turned on. "That's good, baby," I praise
her as she unsnaps her jeans and
shimmies them down her hips, taking her
underwear with them. She has learned to
work around her cast and is proficient
now in dressing...and undressing with it.

In what seems like record time, she is
standing before me naked and almost
defiant. I have a hard time containing my
grin. She is telling me without words that
she won't back down. She knows well that
I never thought she would go through
with this. My baby picks odd times to let
her competitive nature come out; I
fucking love it. "Lie on the bed and put a
pillow under your ass." She follows my
orders perfectly, taking only seconds to
get into position. I sit up on the bed,
unable to do anything but look at her.
God, she is so beautiful she steals the
breath from my body.

I almost choke on my tongue when she
says in a bored tone, "Are we doing this or
not?" Instead of laughing, as I want to, I
decide on a little payback.

"Stay where you are. I'll let you know
when I'm ready." With those words, I

stand and walk into the bathroom, closing
the door behind me before leaning against
the wall and laughing my ass off. How
many other women could step so far out
of their comfort zone and then neatly turn
the tables? I know her well enough to
understand that lying there exposed like
that is probably killing her, but she won't
back down. I'm betting right about now
she's cursing me under her breath and
trying to talk herself out of covering up
with the comforter.

Unfortunately for her, I have a big
problem to take care of before I go back.
Yeah, if you've ever wondered if it's true
about men jacking off before a big date,
then let me answer that question: abso-
fucking-lutely. I know I'll give in and fuck
her too soon if I don't relieve some
pressure. Therefore, I kick off my shoes
and lower my pants and boxers. I'm so
hard that no extra foreplay is needed. I go
straight for the long, rough strokes, and
within an embarrassingly short amount
of time, I'm shooting into my hand. My
moans of satisfaction have probably
alerted Lia as to what's going on. I'm
betting she wants to kill me right about
now. I take my time washing my hands
and pulling off my shirt before walking
back into the bedroom. I feel somewhat
better, but I'm still hard, and looking at

Lia lying with her legs open isn't doing anything to help that.

She's glaring daggers at me as I smirk at her. "Should I have been taking care of things on my end, as well?" she asks in a snide voice.

I manage to keep my expression impassive, but it's a struggle. "Oh, no, baby, you don't take care of anything until I'm here to watch." I sit on the side of the bed, near her hip, and idly stroke my hand down her leg, stopping just short of the juncture of her thighs. The smell of her arousal is causing my head to spin, and I know I'm only killing myself by torturing her. My control seems to have left the building. She gasps out as I drop my hand between her legs and circle her clit. She had obviously been expecting me to continue to deny her my intimate touch. I push a finger into her experimentally, finding her wet and swollen. She moans as I add another digit, sliding them easily in and out. "I think you're wet enough to take that big, purple friend of yours without my help. Is thinking of that what's got you this hot?" I'm not sure if I want to know the answer to that question. I don't think I'm ready to share her, even if the other cock is plastic.

"Mmm, no," she moans.

"Then what has you this wet?" I ask as I add a third finger, stretching her tight channel.

Her hands drop to her breasts, taking her nipples between her fingers and tugging on them. Shit, I'm feeling lightheaded. "You...watching me," she finally replies. Well, hell. I pull my fingers from her pussy before I lose it. I stick them in my mouth, sucking each one clean of her spicy essence before slowly backing away. I need some distance between us now.

"All right, baby, show me how you fuck yourself," I say as I settle in the chair at the foot of the bed, close enough to see perfectly and far enough away to keep myself from touching her. I hold off giving her further instructions because I want to watch her take charge of her own pleasure.

She leans forward to grab the purple vibrator, and then relaxes back with it lying across her stomach. She pulls on a nipple with the two free fingers of her injured hand while dropping the other to her pussy. My eyes are riveted as she massages her nipple into a stiff peak while pushing one finger inside her wet heat. Shit, at this rate, I'll never make it until she uses the vibrator. I'm on the verge of yelling mercy when she finally picks up the big cock and lowers it to her slit. She moves it up and down, coating the tip in her juices before settling the tip against her entrance. "Luc," she whimpers as she pushes the head inside.

Fuck me; I don't know if I've ever seen anything hotter than her taking that plastic cock while moaning out my name. Did she do that when she was alone in her apartment? Did she imagine the vibrator was my cock as she fucked herself with it? "Take all of me, baby," I shudder as she pushes it in to the hilt.

I take my cock in my hands, pumping up and down as I watch her plunge the purple dick in and out of her pussy. She continues to moan my name as she grinds against the plastic base. I hear the hum as she flips it onto vibrate, and I see her body tense before jerking with her release. Fuck, I can't take it anymore. I cross to her in two large strides and fall onto her like a hungry animal. She opens her eyes as I pluck the vibrator from within her body and throw it to the floor. I take a second to sheath myself in the condom she had thrown on the bed at some point. "Luc, please!" she cries as I take her ankles in my hands. I push her legs forward, completely exposing her ass and cunt, and I bury myself to the hilt. She takes me easily, still slick from her earlier orgasm. "Oh, God," she shudders as I hold her legs close to her head and pump deep.

I bottom out on each thrust, feeling my balls tighten as my release comes roaring to a head. I pull back slightly to pinch her clit, hoping to hell she is close because I can't hold off much longer. When she screams and her body clenches, I blow. I shoot load after load of cum into the condom as I come...hard. Her body milks everything I have. I drop her legs and then collapse over her thighs. I wince as my cock slides halfway out of her. I know I need to withdraw completely and dispose of the condom, but I can't resist pushing back inside as I relax over her body. We stay connected as I lean down to slide my tongue in her mouth, kissing her languidly. "Holy hell," I rasp against her now-smiling lips.

"I can't believe I did that," she says shyly. "I've never...I mean..."

"I know, baby." I smile tenderly, dropping soft kisses on her neck. "Don't ever feel embarrassed about anything we do in the bedroom or anywhere else. There isn't a part of you I don't adore."

"Ditto," she says as she reaches up to cup my cheek, rubbing her hand lightly over my stubble. Wiggling her brows, she asks, "Did you really masturbate in the bathroom earlier or were you teasing me?"

I start laughing and pull out of her snug body. I raise her leg up enough so I can pop her ass lightly before moving from the bed. "You just want the details, my little pervert. If you're nice to me in the shower, I might do a little reenactment for you..." She jumps from the bed and runs after me. Yeah, I did hit the replay button for her.

CHAPTER FOURTEEN

Lia

It's been a week since I found out my stepfather was dead. A blissfully, uneventful, stress-free week. I have a meeting this morning with my financial advisor at school to see where my finances are for my last semester. I still have the money Lucian put in my bank account shortly after we met, but I don't want to use it. I'm hopeful my scholarships are enough to cover most of my expenses. Then I'm meeting Rose to see her new apartment.

After my attack in the basement of our old place, neither of us could bear to live there anymore. She would love for me to move back in with her, but she is okay financially without a roommate. She comes from money and only had roommates because she enjoyed the company. I plan to talk with Lucian about our living arrangements. Even though I've been staying at his apartment for months, I don't want to just assume that he wants me there permanently. I think it's important that we both know where things stand between us. He knows I love him, and even though I feel that he loves me as well, he hasn't said the words yet.

I walk into the kitchen to one of my favorite parts of the day: Lucian in his suit, sans the jacket, sitting at the bar watching the morning stock report. He looks so delicious that I want to wrap myself around him and never let him go. He has a cup of coffee sitting next to a multi-grain bagel with blueberry cream cheese. I smile knowing he's made a trip down the street to the bakery on the corner. He looks up as if sensing my presence and smiles. "Hey, baby. I was getting ready to come find you. Your coffee is getting cold." He turns on the stool, opening his arms and legs for me to step between them. He kisses me thoroughly and I lick at his lips. He tastes of coffee and hazelnut creamer.

"Mmm," I hum when he finally releases me. I flush when he catches me sniffing him before I pull away.

He winks as if to say, 'caught ya.' "So, what time do I need to have Sam return to pick you up this morning? If you're going early, I can just drive myself to the office."

I shake my head as I take a bite of my bagel. "Um, no. I don't need Sam today. I'm driving myself."

He reaches a fingertip out, wiping some of the cream cheese from my lip and sticking it in his mouth. *Dear Lord, that was hot.* "Your car is a death trap. I need to have a mechanic check it over. Or better yet, I'll just get you a new car."

"Lucian Quinn," I snap around the bite of food in my mouth. I swallow and add, "You will do no such thing. My car is just fine. I don't need to be dropped off like some snotty rich girl today."

He chuckles, tweaking my nose. "God forbid you be mistaken for that. Nevertheless, if you would please take the Range Rover just to put my mind at ease. I'll have Sam check your car out." When I open my mouth to protest he says, "It's been sitting for weeks without being driven. It's the responsible thing to do, baby."

I grudgingly agree that he has a valid point. I think things are going well, until he pulls his wallet out and hands me his black credit card. "What's this for?" I ask, looking at him in confusion.

"For your tuition and any books or supplies you may need."

I drop the card in front of his plate. "I have a scholarship for that."

He sighs, not picking up the card. "Lia, you don't need to depend on aid. I'll pay for your schooling. Let someone else who needs the help have it. I want to take care of you."

I can't decide if I'm mad at him for trying to take over my life or touched he would care enough to want to. Maybe a little of both, which is why I'm not screaming right now. "Lucian, I need to do this on my own. I worked hard to get that scholarship, and dammit, I deserve it. I know you want to help me, and I love you for it, but don't ask me to stop being who I am. I want to be the woman in your life who you respect, not another obligation."

He closes his eyes for a moment, processing my words. "This is important to you," he says.

I know it was more of a statement on his part than a question, but I answer anyway. "Yes, it is. I need to see this through myself."

"Okay, baby," he says softly as he wraps a hand around my neck, pulling my forehead to his. As is also the normal morning routine, the doorbell rings, and we both know it's Sam. Lucian drops a kiss on my lips, and then stands to pull on his jacket. "Be careful today, and please call and let me know how it goes?"

"I will," I promise as I follow him to the door. Sam and I say hello and Lucian drops another kiss on my lips before leaving. I feel like I've won a small victory…he took his credit card with him. Maybe there's hope to tame my alpha male after all.

Lia

I park Lucian's Range Rover in the parking lot of the financial aid offices. Ms. Gaston is waiting for me when I reach her office. The campus is still quiet since classes don't start back for a few more weeks. "Lia, come in. I was just going through your records." I have a seat in front of her desk and watch as she slips her glasses back on before studying the monitor in front of her. "You kept an A average in all of your classes last semester which is above the requirement level, so you're fine grade-wise. Your scholarships are available." Then looking confused, she adds, "I'm just not sure why you scheduled this meeting to process the paperwork."

Now I'm even more confused than she looks. "Er...why wouldn't I? Classes start soon, and I need to begin buying my books and supplies. I'll need the money from the scholarships to do that."

"Lia...you don't need a scholarship when your tuition has already been paid in full. You also have a more than sufficient overpay to take care of anything else you might need for your classes. I mean, were you confused about the amount of money you would need? If so, I can assure you that you're more than covered."

My head is spinning, and I feel sick to my stomach. How could Lucian do this without discussing it with me first? Why hadn't he told me he had already paid for my schooling when we talked about it earlier? How dare he let me find out this way! I'm literally shaking with anger and Ms. Gaston is starting to shift uneasily in her seat at the expression on my face. Somehow, I manage to keep my voice level and below a scream as I ask, "Could you please print out something, a receipt, or anything showing when and how the money was paid for my records."

She looks surprised by my request then grateful to have something to do other than deal with my anger. "Sure, dear. I can do that." It takes her just a minute to click a few buttons, then hand me a piece of paper off her printer. She gets to her feet, ushering me toward the door. "Now, just let me know if you have any other questions." I don't bother to reply as I stalk out into the hallway. When I reach Lucian's car, I get behind the wheel and slump back. Out of curiosity, I smooth the wrinkled paper out, checking to see what date he paid my tuition. It's dated ten days earlier. I'm just folding the paper when something catches my eye. Under the notes section of the receipt, it says, 'PAID VIA CREDIT CARD. LEE JACKS, FALCO CORP.'

I stare at the piece of paper, trying to make sense of what I'm seeing. Lee Jacks? The name sounds so familiar, but I can't place where I know it from. Suddenly it hits me, and I feel completely foolish. This is obviously a mistake. They must have applied this payment to my account in error. If I hadn't caught this, Lee Jacks would certainly be angry when he found out his daughter or son's tuition was unpaid.

I'm just opening my door to go back to Ms. Gaston's office when I see her shutting the door to her tan sedan a few spaces down. Before I can get out of my car to stop her, she's pulling out of the parking lot and onto the road. "Shit," I mutter under my breath. Today is the last day the financial aid office was open until next week. I have no doubt this mistake cost someone a lot of money, and they need to know so they can have it corrected. Then it should clear the way for me to access my scholarships.

I take my phone from my purse and Google Falco Corp, looking for their phone number. I'm thrilled to see that their headquarters is just across town, not far from Quinn Software. I'll just go explain the mix-up in person and have it taken care of today. I plug their address into the Rover's GPS system because it's easy to miss a turn in the downtown area and it's far too hectic to backtrack.

As I'm driving toward Falco, I feel rather like a bitch for assuming the worst about Lucian. Thank God, I had the fortitude to ask for the receipt before I went to his office to tear into him. I was so pissed off; I doubt I would have believed any denial on his part. It's always been hard for me to trust people, for obvious reasons, but I need to try harder to listen first and react later. I can't hold him accountable for my screwed-up childhood.

When I reach the offices of Falco, I inwardly groan. The building is a huge, glass and metal tower. I have to drive past it and park in a public lot three blocks away. Maybe I should have just called after all. I'm breathing hard when I finally make it into the lobby. I really need to start exercising more.

Wow, I thought the security in Lucian's building was excessive. I'm waved toward a metal detector by one of four security guards as I move a few steps away from the door. They take my purse and run it through another scanner while I go through the full-body scan. I feel a tad violated when I'm finally handed my purse and pointed toward a reception desk. "Paranoid much?" I murmur under my breath as I approach the chic woman looking disdainfully at me. I straighten my shoulders, refusing to be intimidated. "I need to see Lee Jacks, please," I say with all the confidence I can muster.

"And you are?" she asks in a condescending voice which matches her expression perfectly.

"Lia Adams." She begins typing on the keyboard, probably to see if I have an appointment, which of course I don't. I pull the tuition receipt from my purse, ready to plead my case when she looks up at me with something akin to shock on her face.

"Oh, yes, Miss Adams. You're clear to go on up. Let me have Craig escort you." I'm still frozen in place when she motions to the closest security guard and tells him, "Please accompany Miss Adams to Mr. Jacks' floor. I will let reception know she's on the way." Turning back to me with an expression completely devoid of its earlier sneer, she smiles sweetly. "It's been a pleasure. Have a wonderful day." I feel like muttering one of Lucian's favorite sayings, 'what the fuck?' Instead, I give her what I hope passes for a smile and follow the guard toward an elevator in the corner. He says nothing as he waits for me to step inside before following me. He inserts a plastic keycard in a slot and the doors close. I'm dying to make some kind of joke to break the silence, but he doesn't seem like the type to laugh at all.

Another well-dressed woman who appears to be in her thirties is waiting when I step off the elevator. Unlike the frosty one earlier, this one is wearing a smile that actually looks genuine. Craig stays inside, I assume to return to the lobby. "Miss Adams, welcome to Falco. Can I get you anything at all? We have coffee, a variety of teas, sodas, and of course, bottled water." She seems so eager, I almost hate to say no, but this isn't a social call. I can't help but be impressed by how friendly everyone suddenly seems to be to a stranger. Well, except Craig.

"Oh, no, thank you. I...er just wanted to see Mr. Jacks for a moment. Would that be possible? I promise it won't take long at all."

"Well, of course, Ms. Adams. Mr. Jacks is just finishing a call, and then he'll be right with you." She is leading me toward a plush waiting area when a tall, blond-haired man, who looks somehow familiar steps out of the double doors behind what I assume is the receptionist desk. "Oh, Peter," the woman says fondly, "I was just showing Miss Adams to a chair until Lee is free."

The man stares at me with a stunned expression for several long moments before the woman between us clears her throat. "Yes, thank you, Liza," he says to the receptionist before extending a hand to me. "I'm Peter Jacks, Lee's brother."

I take his hand hesitantly, keeping the contact as brief as I can. The way he is looking at me makes me uncomfortable, although not in a threatening manner. It's more the strange feeling that we know each other, and he seems to feel the same way. "I'm Lia Adams; I just needed to discuss something with Lee. I could come back later if he's busy." I'm on the verge of making some excuse to leave when the double doors open once again and a man looking very similar to the one standing next to me appears in the doorway.

"Oh, Lee is free," Liza ushers me forward and past the man staring at me just as his brother had been. Lee Jacks and his brother Peter enter behind me and shut the door.

Lee Jacks walks behind his desk and almost appears to slump into his chair. What is going on here? I'm terribly uncomfortable by this point, and ready to run for the door. I must have interrupted something. God, why hadn't I called instead? Maybe something happened and I stepped right into the middle of it. Why in the world did the receptionist say it was okay for me to come up when clearly it isn't? "Um...Mr. Jacks, I'm sorry to just drop in...I could come back later..."

Like his brother, Lee Jacks is blond, tall, and muscular. He is a striking man, but somehow intimidating. He rubs his temple, as if trying to soothe a headache, and says, "So, Quinn has finally told you.

I was beginning to think I would have to take that decision from his hands."

What is he talking about? Then it hits me. I know why his name seemed so familiar. "I met you while Lucian and I were having dinner. We talked for a while." My mind is whirling wondering what this new information could possibly mean.

He inclines his head, giving me a brief smile. "That is correct. I really enjoyed our conversation that night. You're a very intelligent woman. I wanted to tell you then, but Quinn thought you had been through too much to handle another shock, and I reluctantly agreed with him."

I still have no idea what he is talking about. Tell me what? Had he paid for my schooling as some type of charity and Lucian didn't want me to know? Trying to make sense of this strange conversation, I say, "It wasn't a mistake that you paid my tuition, was it?"

He looks puzzled by my question. "Of course it wasn't. It's my right and obligation as your father to take care of your expenses. I'll have a credit card issued to you for anything else you might need."

My father? My ears are roaring and the room is spinning as I sit deathly still, trying to process the insane words he has just uttered. My hand is shaking as I again pull the receipt with his name on it from my purse. "I...no. I just came to bring this to you. They made a mistake." I get unsteadily to my feet and put the piece of paper on his desk. "I have to leave...I can't stay here..."

I hear a curse from behind me as Peter gently takes my arm. "Lee, she doesn't know. Shit, she has no idea who you are." Bile rises up my throat and I know I'm seconds away from being sick. I put my hand over my mouth and look around frantically. Peter, as if sensing what's happening, leads me a few feet to a door and pushes it open. I find myself in a pristine bathroom, with marble floors and countertops. I don't have time to appreciate it, because my stomach has other plans. I fall to my knees and purge everything from my system. I don't know how long I remained on the floor until there was a knock at the door.

"Miss Adams, it's Liza. Honey, I'm coming in to help you get cleaned up." The door opens slowly and the once-smiling receptionist is now frowning in concern. She takes a cloth from the cabinet under the sink and wets it before squatting to gently wipe my face. "Can you stand?" When I nod, she helps me to my feet and hands me a glass of water. Within a few moments, I feel more human as I brush my teeth with the new toothbrush from the cabinet. It's certainly a well-stocked bathroom. "Are you all right? Pete and Lee are really worried about you."

"I...I'm okay. I just think maybe I misunderstood something they said."

She pats my arm with a smile, saying, "That's probably it, honey. I'm sure they'll straighten it out for you." She ushers me back into Lee's office where both he and his brother halt their pacing to stare at me in concern. Liza walks quietly out of the office, shutting the door behind her. I fight the urge to beg her to stay.

Lee steps forward, giving me a wary look. "Lia, I apologize. I assumed Lucian had talked with you, thus prompting your visit here."

I'm still no closer to having the answers I need and before I can chicken out and run, I ask, "What's going on? You obviously think I know something that I don't. I came here because I found out that you paid my college expenses and I thought there was some mistake. I didn't want your son or daughter to show up for school and have problems because of it."

"Maybe you should go home and talk with Quinn," Peter says, shooting a quick look at his brother.

Even though I already know the answer to my question, I ask anyway, "Does Lucian know what you're talking about?"

"Yes," Lee answers when his brother remains quiet.

I sit down in the chair I so recently vacated and cross my arms trying to look stronger than I'm feeling inside. "Then you need to tell me because Lucian has not. If this concerns me, then I have a right to know."

"You do," Lee agrees before looking at his brother. "Pete, could you give us some privacy please?"

"Lee...I don't think—"

"Pete, leave!" Lee snaps and Peter shakes his head before walking out the door. Instead of going back to his chair behind his desk, he surprises me by taking the one adjacent to mine. My heart is pounding out of my chest. I know with everything inside of me that what this man is going to tell me will turn my life upside down. A part of me wants to tell him to stop, that I don't want to know after all, but I sit silently, waiting for the blow I know is coming. "Lia...twenty-four years ago, I had a relationship that spanned several months with Maria Adams."

"No," I say in a voice barely above a whisper. If he hears me, he gives no indication.

"Business eventually took me away from North Carolina and from Maria. Even though I considered it at the time, it wouldn't have been safe for her to accompany me. I ended things between us, and that's the last time I saw her. She never tried to contact me to let me know she was pregnant or that I had a daughter. I had no idea at all, until recently."

"How did you find out?" I ask as I stare at the man who says he is my father. I feel a sucker punch to the gut when it finally hits me. He looks so familiar to me because I see him every time I look in the mirror. There is no denying the fact that I look like him. Was this why I had been so comfortable with him in the restaurant when we first met? A feeling of kinship?

"Lucian was checking into your past, I assume looking for information on your mother and stepfather. He found the connection between Maria and me, which prompted him to look a little harder at me. Naturally, that alerted me to his interest, and I started doing a little research, as well. It appears that we both met somewhere in the middle with the same realization: I'm your father."

"You can't know that," I protest weakly, but I know there is no way I would be here now unless he was positive. Lee Jacks doesn't seem like the type of man to jump to conclusions, especially one of this magnitude.

"I can assure you that I do know it for certain. I don't make mistakes, Lia."

His self-assured statement drags me from the daze I had fallen in. Now I'm just angry and I lash out, wanting to hurt him the way I've been hurt. "Really?" My voice sounds shrill, even to my own ears. "So, you don't consider it a mistake that you lived this fucking charmed life while you left me in Hell? Do you have any idea what my life has been like?" His face has gone stark-white at my words, but I don't care. I need him to feel a piece of the pain that I've been forced to endure just because he screwed my mother and walked away.

"Lia...believe me, if I had known, that would have never happened—"

"But it did!" I cry, jumping to my feet. He stands as well, seemingly at a loss as to how to handle my emotional outburst. This is probably a crash course in fatherhood he wasn't expecting. He probably figured I would be so absurdly grateful that I would be kissing his expensive shoes by now. "My mother hated me because she despised you, didn't she? She took out all of that anger on me. I was nothing but her punching bag, and then when she got bored with that, she brought in my stepfather and turned him loose on me!" Before he can reply, I hear the door open behind me. I spin around and see Peter, or should I say my uncle, standing there hesitantly. What really catches my attention is the woman who steps in behind him. If I think I resemble Lee Jacks, then I'm almost a dead-ringer for this woman.

She is twisting her hands in front of her nervously while looking at me with equal parts curiosity and sympathy. Peter clears his throat before asking, "Is everything okay in here? We could hear your voices in the lobby."

I ignore his question as I continue to stare at the woman next to him. "Who are you?" I ask fearing for a moment that I have a sister whom I've never met.

She gives me a timid smile before taking a few steps closer. She is dressed in obviously expensive slacks with a silk blouse. I fight the urge to straighten my clothing, feeling frumpy compared to her. I hate that I feel so inferior to these people. She holds out a hand, which I

ignore until she finally drops it. "I'm
Kara." She points to Peter, adding,
"That's my father, and Lee is my uncle. I
also have a brother, Kyle, who's away at
college right now.

There is a crushing weight sitting on
my chest, and I desperately need to leave
before I break down. Almost in a panic, I
look around frantically until I spot my
purse lying on the floor next to my
recently- vacated chair. I grab it and am
almost at the door before a hand on my
arm stops me. I turn to find Lee standing
behind me, looking almost as bad as I
feel. I'm shaking now and am powerless
to stop it. "Lia, you don't have to be afraid
anymore," Lee says reassuringly,
mistaking my anxiety for fear. "I will
never let anyone hurt you again."

I pull my arm free, squaring my
shoulders. "Your absence from my life has
done nothing but hurt me since the day I
was born." I look briefly at Kara as I pass,
noting almost idly that she has a tear
streaking down her cheek. Maybe I have
the Jacks' genes to thank for my
penchant for crying at the drop of a
hat...especially lately. I hear whom I
assume is Lee calling my name as I walk
toward the elevator at a fast clip. I sag
weakly against the wall when the door

closes, extremely grateful that no one followed me.

All I can think of is going home and feeling Lucian's arms around me, until suddenly the reality of what just happened slams into me. He knew. Lucian knew Lee was my father and didn't tell me. How could he have kept something like this from me? I have a whole family I didn't know existed. I have a father, and Luc has apparently known it for some time. I walked into that mess today completely unprepared because he kept it from me. His betrayal of my trust guts me more than the revelation of my long-lost father ever could.

CHAPTER FIFTEEN

Lucian

I rush into the apartment in a blind panic. I had been in the middle of a meeting at the office when Lee called and dropped a bomb on me: Lia knew he was her father. Through one big, clusterfucking chain of events, she ended up at his office after she'd found out he paid her tuition. He said she hadn't taken the news well at all, and was upset when she left. He had one of his men follow her back to the apartment, where she was now.

I stand listening until I hear movement in the bedroom. I am terrified when I push open the partially- closed door to find her cramming clothing into her duffle bag. "What are you doing, baby?" She makes another trip to the closet, returning with more clothes before turning to face me. Her eyes are red-rimmed, and I can tell she's been crying. I want nothing more than to take her in my arms, but her posture is so closed –off, that I know to keep my distance.

"I'm going to stay with Rose for a while. I need time to process everything that's happened today."

Feeling fear rise to choke me, I walk over to push the duffle bag away, as if it will stop her from leaving me. "You can do that here. I'll help you."

"Just like you helped me by telling me about my father?" I flinch at her words, hearing the hint of betrayal behind them. "I see you're not surprised that I know. I guess you and dear old Daddy talked about me as soon as I left."

"Baby...it's not like that. I didn't think you could handle anything else right after the attack. I was trying to protect you."

She picks up the damn duffle bag again and continues to put clothes inside it. "Well, it was certainly better the way it happened today. It's so much easier to be blindsided than to have someone you love be honest with you, right?" Her calm statements are completely unnerving me. I'd feel better if she were screaming and throwing things. I don't know quite how to deal with this quiet, disappointed tone she's using instead.

I hiss audibly, knowing I don't have a leg to stand on here. Maybe I did it for all the right reasons, but she's right; I kept something potentially life-altering from her. This isn't the way I wanted to do this, but I can't let her leave here without telling her how I feel. My voice sounds rusty when I say the words I haven't uttered to a woman in so many years. "Lia, I love you. Please don't leave."

She freezes in mid-motion. The shirt she had in her hands to pack is suspended in mid-air. She whirls around looking unbelievably beautiful...and furious. Not exactly the reaction I was looking for after my profession of love. "Don't you dare say that to me now when I'm leaving! I've longed to hear those words from you but not when you're under duress!" Her movements are jerky now as if she can barely control her anger. "I have let you keep your secrets, Lucian, because they're a part of who you are. I didn't freak out and run for the door when I found you snorting cocaine in the middle of the night because, in some screwed-up way, I understood the need to escape, no matter what the means. She looks so fucking sad that I prefer the anger of a few minutes ago.

"We've hit a roadblock now. Your secrets are tearing us apart." She picks up her bag, along with her purse, and walks toward me. "If you really do love me, as you say, and want to save this relationship, then I need to know it all. No more walls, Lucian, and no more lies. Please, don't contact me until you're ready to do that." She goes up on her toes and drops what feels like a final kiss on my lips before leaving the room and our home quietly.

I have no idea how long I stand frozen in place before I move forward and sink to the bed. I drop my head in my hands. I'm at a crossroads in my life, and I'm terrified. One path leads to Lia and my possible redemption and the other leads to a continued life of self-loathing hatred. Of the two paths, the first is somehow the most daunting because my love for her has given her complete control over my destiny.

Then another staggering thought rocks me. God, she might be pregnant. Has either of us given thought to what that could mean? We haven't really discussed it since the night she told me about her doctor's appointment. I don't know if we're in complete denial, or maybe some part of us doesn't want to get our hopes up and have them dashed when it doesn't happen. She has a follow-up appointment next week, and there is no way in Hell I'll let her go alone.

I get to my feet and walk to the door with complete resolve. It's past time for Lia to know everything I've been keeping from her. I can only hope that afterwards she'll still love me. Because without her, my heart is fractured beyond repair.

Coming Spring of 2015, the 3rd book in the Lucian & Lia Trilogy, **Mended.**

ABOUT THE AUTHOR

Sydney Landon lives in Greenville, South Carolina and previously worked in accounting before writing her first book. Sydney met her own prince charming in 2000 and received the most romantic proposal on a pier in Myrtle Beach, South Carolina, thus creating her eternal love for the city. The fact that her future husband was a fellow computer geek completely sealed the deal for her. She credits him with keeping her calm and rational while also understanding her need for a new pair of shoes every other week. They have two children who keep life interesting and borderline insane, but never boring.

The idea of the Danvers' Series popped into her head and refused to go away. She started writing the first story never imagining that it would ever be finished. Three months later it turned into her first book, Weekends Required. Within a few months, it had quickly made the best-seller list on Amazon, and went on to make the New York Times Best Seller List. Barely taking a breath between books, Sydney followed up with the second book in the series, Not Planning on You. Within the first month, this book also became a best-seller. The third book in the series, Fall For Me, was released in February 2013 and became a New York Times Best Seller. The fourth book in the series, Fighting For You, released in paperback in February 2014. Sydney is currently working on the sixth book in the Danvers' Series and the third book in the Lucian and Lia Trilogy. When she isn't writing, Sydney enjoys reading, swimming, and being a mini-van driving soccer mom.

Please enjoy this special preview of

No Denying You

A Danvers novel
By Sydney Landon

~Now Available~

CHAPTER ONE

"Honey, have you given any more thought to getting some bigger tits?"

Emma rolled her eyes and dropped her head onto her desk. Why couldn't her mother bake cookies, knit sweaters or do any of that other Betty Crocker shit? No-o-o, she couldn't be that lucky. Katrina Davis—or Kat, as she liked to be called—had always wanted to be the cool mom on the block. Heck, most of Emma's childhood friends still called her mother for advice. The woman didn't pull any punches. "God, Mom, can we please not talk about my tits today? Or lack of them?"

"Em, it's for your own good. You're too attractive to sit at home all the time. Men are visual creatures so maybe a new rack is exactly what you need. Your father can't keep his hands off mine. And you're not getting any younger. You don't want to wake up one day and have them fall out of bed before you do."

"Gross, Mom. This whole conversation is really gross. I don't want to hear anything about your sex life with Daddy. Ever. I'd like to be able to look him in the eyes just once without the constant stream of images in my head of the things you feel the need to confide to me. Maybe you should just go Catholic—then you could confess to someone with a more professional opinion."

"Oh, Em, get over it. I'm just trying to help. You know what? I'll even pay if I can pick them out. I'll e-mail you some information and you can let me know what you think."

"Mom, for the last time, I like my tits just fine!" As soon as she shouted that last bit, Emma froze at the sound of a throat clearing behind her. *Please tell me that the asswipe isn't behind me, ple-e-ease.* As she swiveled slowly in her chair, she groaned. Fate definitely wasn't on her side. Her boss, Brant Stone, stood behind her with his usual condescending smirk. She quickly said her good-byes to her mother although she could hear her still speaking as she gingerly placed the receiver back in the cradle. Determined not to give him the satisfaction of seeing her rattled, she raised a brow, asking as politely as she could manage, "Did you need something?"

"Apparently not as badly as you do, Emma."

Oh great, here it comes, another jab at my work performance. I wonder how much jail time I would get if I choked him with the paisley tie he's wearing? Turning her back to nonchalantly pick up her coffee cup, she said, "Pardon?"

"I am positively riveted by your plight," he replied.

More obscure code to unravel. She spent half of her time trying to figure out what in the hell he was talking about. She knew he did it on purpose, the sneaky bastard. "I bet you are considering you cause most of my misery." She knew it was unprofessional as well as career suicide to talk to her boss this way, but she kept hoping he would have her transferred to another department so that he could find someone more suitable for his assistant. So far, that hadn't happened. She had even started dropping hints, but, like every suggestion she made, he seemed to completely ignore it.

"That's flattering, Emma, but I don't

think I can accept responsibility for your . . . shortcomings."

Her coffee cup fell from her suddenly limp fingers and crashed to the floor. Then she plowed into him as she jumped back to avoid the hot liquid. "Shit!" The carnage continued as they both fell backward like dominoes. When she managed to get her bearings, she was horrified to realize that Brant was laid out on the floor underneath her, and her butt was nestled firmly near his crotch. Coffee stains were splattered all over his perfectly creased slacks, and it took her a moment to realize why her legs seemed so bare as they lay tangled with his. Her short skirt had blown up during their fall and was now resting well above the level considered legal in most states. Was that . . . ? No, it couldn't be. . . .

Without thinking, she wiggled around experimentally. *No way!* Her boss, the spawn from hell, was not growing hard against her bottom. *Oh my God, he was!*

"I didn't realize that ruining my clothing also came with a lap dance." When she froze, he chuckled. "Oh, by all means, don't stop now. Even someone with small tits is a turn-on when she's grinding against your lap."

A special preview of the new book
Barred
by Paisley Walker

PROLOGUE

Kimberly climbs behind the wheel of her Ford Explorer as she sends Sarah a text.

Kimberly: Heading that way now, see you in a bit. She puts the phone down in the drink holder as she cranks the car. The little light comes on notifying her that she received a text back.

Sarah: Okay be careful, but hurry. I think something is wrong. Immediately, Kimberly throws the car in reverse, sliding the phone back into the cup holder without turning it off like normal. Sarah normally doesn't act like something is wrong, so when things like this come up, it scares her. A month ago, Sarah found a lump on her breast but kept it a secret, afraid of what would happen if she brought it to light. She finally confided in her sister and Kimberly made her go to the doctor to have it checked. Today was the day for that, and wouldn't you know it would be storming. Kimberly made sure to have Barb cover the daycare today while she went with Sarah.

She was running about twenty minutes late because the storm knocked her power out. She had her music playing lowly through the car as she was coming to curve in the road about two miles from the hospital. Her phone lit up, and thinking it could have been Sarah, she reached for it.

Sarah: Doctor wants to remove it for biopsy, pretty sure it's cancerous.

The words she never wanted to hear from her sister were there on that screen. Just when she was about to type a response, a horn honked making Kimberly jerk her head up just in time to see a car coming head on. She jerked her wheel to the right, hitting the curb and stomping the gas instead of the brake. The last thing she remembered before her mind went blank, was the sign of the One Stop Shop as she crashed into the corner of the building.

CHAPTER ONE

Looking up at the immaculate building of Phillips & Stanley, Kimberly immediately begins to shake in her heels. She'd heard of the amazing things that Jonathon Phillips and Emerson Stanley could do with cases like hers. She was released from jail two nights ago after she totaled her car in an accident involving her cell phone. She takes a deep breath as she walks up the stone building leading into the dens of hell. When she walks through the sliding glass doors at the top of the stairs, her eyes find an incredibly attractive blonde woman sitting behind a white and black marble desk. The desk matches the tiles on the ground to a tee. Immediately, Kimberly looks down at her attire and back to the woman who is now staring at her.

"May I help you, ma'am?" The woman with Nicole on her name tag asks. Kimberly looks around the lobby of the building. Her eyes land on a black couch with two white plush recliners sitting across from it. A black coffee table sits between them on a red rug, the only contrast in the room other than the white vase holding the dozen red roses. Kimberly's eyes finally rest upon the woman with the grey dress behind the counter.

"Yes ma'am. I'm so sorry. I have an appointment with Mr. Phillips and Mr. Stanley at one o'clock."

"Your name?"

"My name is Kimberly Weston." She responds as she looks down at the only pair of decent heels she has. They are nude pumps that she bought on sale a few months back. They went well with the black lace-open-back shirt she had tucked into a grey high-waist pencil skirt.

"I will let them know you are here Ms. Weston. Please have a seat and I'll call when they are ready for you." Nicole says as she ushers Kimberly to the chairs. "Would you like some coffee or water?"

"Water would be great please."

"Yes ma'am."

With that, Kimberly is left alone to wait for the two men that may or may not be able to help her. Two weeks ago her entire life changed. She is lost in thought when Nicole hands her the bottle of water. Kimberly's right leg shakes as it's crossed over the left.

"Thank you." Kimberly replies as she looks up to see the person who gives her the water. Only it isn't Nicole, and her breath is instantly pushed from her lungs. Her eyes rake over the man standing in front of her. He has to be at least six-foot-five and has broad shoulders in a sleek gray suit. She starts at his black polished shoes and trails her eyes up to his pants. Which look as if they were made just for him, which could probably be if he is one of the main associates. She can see his cock in his pants, which must mean the man is packing, considering it's not hard. As she trails up his defined stomach, up to his brood shoulders to his defined jawline with a five o'clock shadow, to the crooked nose he sports, she can't help but blush. His green eyes sparkling with mischief as if he knows she is ogling him.

"Ms. Weston, I presume?"

"Um... Yes sir." She replies as a blush creeps up her neck to her face.

"Hello, I am Emerson Stanley. Jonathon is assisting another client at the moment but I would be glad to go over your case with you." He straightens his cuff link before adding. "If you'll follow me." He gestures with his hand for her to

stand. He walks across the marble
flooring towards the steel elevators to the
right of the desk. He pushes the button as
he places his hand on the small of her
back. A smile crosses his face, showing a
set of dimples as Kimberly gasps at the
contact his hand makes to her skin. It
feels as if there is a flame setting her on
fire. As the elevator closes, Emerson
pushes the button for the sixth floor. The
silence is deafening but the electricity
flowing through them is piercing.
Emerson can't help but steal a glance at
the beautiful woman standing beside him.
The way the light hits her wavy hair,
looks as if she could be an angel. He turns
his attention back to the steel doors as
the elevator carries them to his office.
Once it stops, he smiles as he watches her
nervously straighten her blouse. "Right
this way Ms. Weston." He walks out of
the elevator and as she follows behind
him, she can't help but stare at how
amazing his ass looks in those slacks.

"Please come in. Have a seat."
Emerson says as he pushes the heavy
door open, leading Kimberly into a light,
sky-blue office, with two brown leather
chairs, and sitting in front of an
enormous mahogany desk. Behind the
desk, there are two plants in either corner
of the office as well as floor-to-ceiling

windows overlooking the Mississippi River. As she sits down into one of the plush leather chairs, Emerson walks by her, sliding his suit jacket off his shoulders and placing it on the back of his massive leather chair, behind his desk. As he sets it down, his muscles flex under the light blue of his shirt. She can't help but stare at the Adonis in front of her. He lights up the room, and if the dampness of her panties has anything to do with it, he seems to ignite her libido as well.

"Mr. Stanley, I hear you are the best in the state of Louisiana. I need the best."

"Is that so?" He sits behind his desk, hands resting in front of him as he listens to her.

"Yes, I was involved in an accident. Luckily, no one else was hurt, but I ran into a building and damaged enough to be in trouble."

"What type of accident?"

"I was sending a quick text message to my sister."

"So texting and driving? That's against the law Ms. Weston. If caught doing so, you could potentially spend up to five years in prison."

"Yes, I'm aware. That's why I'm here to see you."

"No need to get catty Ms. Weston. I am only trying to give you the facts."

"I'm not being catty Mr. Stanley. I'm only saying that's why I'm with the best. Now, can you tell me what the expenses will be like?"

"Right down to business. I like that in a woman." As he speaks the words, she realizes the innuendo in the man's words. She squeezes her legs tighter and shifts in the chair as she opens the forgotten water bottle in her hands to help calm her frazzled nerves. "It depends on the case and how long it will take. For something like this, I would say it would be around fifty-thousand dollars."

She looks at him as if he's lost his mind. "Fif... fifty thousand?"

"Did I stutter? You want the best, you have to pay for the best." He stands with a knowing smile before turning to look out at the sights of downtown Baton Rouge.

"I... I don't have that type of money." She finally lets out deflated. The feeling that overcomes Emerson is not one that he is used to. Sympathy. Why does he feel sympathetic to this woman? It was not him who was texting while driving.

"Well, I suppose this meeting is adjourned. I am sure you can see yourself out Kimberly."

As he says her first name, she catches the dismissal. To her surprise, the dismissal stuns her and knocks her pride down a notch. "Well... thank you for your time." She stands, staring at his back. All she can think of is how arrogant the man standing in front of her is. Also wishing he was staring at her, instead of that damn view from the window. Emerson nods his head in acknowledgment that he has heard her as she turns to walk out of the door.

Kimberly hangs her head as she walks to the elevator. Pushing the button, she senses another presence behind her. She turns and is captivated by the most stunning pair of crystal-blue eyes. She takes in the features of the man standing before her. He looks to be around six-foot-two and of an athletic build. He is wearing a white, button-down shirt with the top two buttons undone. The sleeves are pushed up right below his elbows and the shirt is tucked into the dark gray slacks he has on.

"Go ahead and stare. It's not rude or anything."

"Oh my God! I'm so sorry." Kimberly replies, turning a shade of crimson.

"It's quite alright. I actually like having beautiful women get flustered around me. Means I still have my game." He lets out a chuckle as the elevator dings, signaling its arrival. "I'm Jonathon and you are?"

"Kimberly."

"Coming from Stanley's office?"

"Yes, but it looks as if I won't be able to afford him." She lets out a defeated sigh.

"Well, maybe you're just going about it the wrong way. You're a beautiful woman. You'll think of something."

"Like?" She cocks her head to the side, looking at him.

"Well, had I had a beautiful woman in my office, instead of the old men over the board, I may have had her spread over my desk," he smiles a naughty smile before nodding his head and exiting the elevator.

"What the hell was that?" Kimberly asks more to herself than anyone else as she exits the building and makes her way to her rental car.